A TIME TO DIE

A TIME TO DIE

BARBARA NADEL

Allison & Busby Limited
11 Wardour Mews
London W1F 8AN
allisonandbusby.com

First published in Great Britain by Allison & Busby in 2020.

A CIP catalogue record for this book is available from
the British Library.

First Edition

ISBN 978-0-7490-2461-1

Typeset in 12/17 pt Sabon LT Pro by
Allison & Busby Ltd.

The paper used for this Allison & Busby publication
has been produced from trees that have been legally sourced
from well-managed and credibly certified forests.

Printed and bound by
CPI Group (UK) Ltd, Croydon, CR0 4YY

To every kid who ever walked
through the Woolwich Foot Tunnel

PROLOGUE

Where was the little shit-bag? Brenda lit one cigarette off the butt of her last smoke and breathed out shakily. John was ten and so he should be able to get himself from Silvertown, through the foot tunnel to Woolwich with no bother. But this was John . . .

Why was her baby brother such a div? Was it because he'd been born so long after she had, that their parents had babied him? Hardly. Brenda couldn't remember a time when her dad wasn't mostly down the pub and her mum just sort of wafted around the flat in a tranquillised fug. Since the old man had left, to no doubt drink himself to death, John had largely been abandoned to his own devices. And maybe that was the problem. Always a dreamer, John wandered around aimlessly when he wasn't at school. With no friends to take him out of himself, the kid was like a tit in a trance.

Brenda had only offered to have the boy for the day because her mum had a hospital appointment. Devon, Brenda's husband, had no great love for the kid and so she hadn't wanted to take him, not really. She'd seen him wave at her from the northern shore of the Thames before he went into the Edwardian rotunda that marked the entrance to the tunnel under the river, so she knew he was on his way. Brenda looked at her watch. The silly sod was probably daydreaming down there, counting the tiles on the walls or something else equally as daft.

Nobody really liked walking through the old foot tunnel. It was smelly and kids mucked about down there. But it was the only way to get from North Woolwich to South Woolwich without taking the ferry. That had been out of action for a week and so it was the tunnel or nothing.

People got mugged down in the damp hideous old passage under the river, which was why Brenda had made sure John waved to her before he crossed, so that she could time him. It took about ten minutes to walk briskly through the tunnel, which was what Brenda, if she had to use it at all, made sure she always did. The place gave her the heebie-jeebies with its jaundiced lighting, musty smell and occasional alarming drip from the tiled ceiling. Her brother, with his morbid interest in anything dark, creepy and generally putrid, was probably having a bloody brilliant time down there imagining ghosts, running away from weird noises and frightening the shit out of himself. He was a strange little tyke – which would have been fine – had he not been so unlikeable.

What it was about John nobody seemed able to take to was something Brenda could never fully understand – he wasn't really a bad kid. Maybe it was the fact that he never appeared to listen to anything anyone ever said? The feeling he gave off of being away with the fairies all the time? Or was it perhaps the suspicion Brenda had that this airy-fairy thing was all an act and that underneath all of it was a calculating mind that knew exactly what it was doing.

As far as Brenda was aware, John had never bullied anyone or been cruel to animals. He didn't interact with anyone – animal or human. But he did have a lot of cuts and scars on his arms and legs and she wondered whether he was hurting himself. Maybe for attention? Not that it had succeeded. When Brenda had told her mother about John's wounds all she had said had been, 'What you talking about? I don't know of no wounds.'

Brenda looked at her watch. The silly sod had been down there for nearly twenty bloody minutes! What the fuck was he up to down there?

ONE

'Took me over forty years to find the answer to that question,' Brenda Joseph said. 'If I have . . .'

'Which is why you're here?'

'Yeah.'

Brenda Joseph was a small, dark woman in her early sixties. Twice married and mother to seven children, she was also the possessor of a strange experience, deep in her past, involving her younger brother, John. During the long, hot summer of 1976, ten-year-old John Saunders had gone down into the Edwardian foot tunnel at North Woolwich and disappeared. In spite of the best efforts of his sister, who, after half an hour waiting on the southern shore, had entered the tunnel herself to look for him, plus an extensive police investigation, nothing had been heard from or of John until he had, apparently, arrived at Brenda's house in Canning Town just before Christmas 2018.

'I've never found out how he got my address,' Brenda told private detective Mumtaz Hakim. 'I moved there back in 2008 when I married Des.'

The Arnold Private Detective Agency had been operating out of its tiny office on Green Street Upton Park since 2010. Opened initially as a one-man band by ex-policeman Lee Arnold, Mumtaz had joined the firm in 2012. A psychology graduate and mother of one, Mumtaz was the only full-time employee apart from Arnold himself who was currently out on a job in Romford.

'It's difficult for me to say whether or not this John looks like our John,' Brenda continued. 'He was ten when I last saw him.'

'What about other members of your family?'

'Mum died back in 1990 and me dad left us before John disappeared,' Brenda said. 'He's dead now. All the aunts and uncles have gone too, and none of me cousins really kept in touch. Anyway, John weren't exactly someone you'd remember. Away with the fairies most of the time. He was a strange kid.'

'Friends?'

'He didn't have any. Spent most of his time drifting about on his own. Done a lot of reading in his bedroom.' She leant forwards. 'We've had DNA tests, me and this bloke. According to them he is my brother, but . . . There's something wrong here.'

'In what sense?'

'I dunno. That's what's so horrible about all this. I should be grateful that he's come back after all these years, but I'm not. And the story he tells about what happened is just, well, it's fantastic – and not in a good way.'

'So tell me,' Mumtaz said.

* * *

12

'He says our dad was waiting for him in the tunnel,' Brenda said. 'I never saw him. I saw John wave from the other end just before he went in, but I never saw the old man and I certainly never saw John come out my end. Anyway, the way this bloke tells it, they come up the stairs and not in the lift, and then they waited until I was looking away until they come out. What do I know? But anyway, the first thing that occurred to me when this "John" was telling his tale was why?'

'Why?'

'Why did our old man, Reg, take him? He was a drinker, he didn't ever seem to me as if he liked kids and he never wanted to work. And yet John claims that Reg took him to America.'

'People can change.'

'Normally I'd say, right enough, of course they can, if I hadn't been to my old man's funeral with me mum back in 1982.'

Mumtaz leant back in her chair. She hadn't been expecting that.

'We had to go out to Wales,' Brenda continued. 'Mum identified the body and everything.'

'Do you know what he was doing in Wales?'

Brenda shrugged. 'He died of cirrhosis of the liver and so he hadn't changed his ways. Me and Mum met this nun who looked after him when he was dying. I s'pose I should've paid more attention to what she said, but I never. I was so mad at the old git, I just wanted to get the funeral over with and get back home to the kids. Now Mum's dead I don't stand a chance of knowing what the woman was on about. Although, that said, what I do know is that Dad was a tramp by that time. That was why Mum had to go and identify him. Although the nuns took him in, there was no proof on him of who he was.'

'So your father must have told the nuns his name.'

'I s'pose so.'

'And what did this John say when you told him about your father's death?'

'He thanked me. Said he hadn't known.'

'So, your father takes him to America and then . . .'

Brenda breathed in deeply. 'Well, this is where it all gets a bit mental,' she said.

Standing up beside a tea stall in the middle of Romford Market seemed to be a strange place to have a conversation about a dead marriage, but then the man Lee Arnold had come to see, Jason Pritchard, was far from being what people thought of as your typical 'Essex' man.

The wrong side of fifty and with a nose that was splattered rather than placed at the middle of his face, Jason looked and talked the part but, as his oldest mate, Dave, had told Lee right from the start, 'He's got some funny ideas.'

The top of Jason's 'funny ideas' list concerned Britain's referendum back in 2016 about whether or not to stay in or come out of the European Union. The country had voted by a narrow margin to come out, with Romford being one of the most determinedly 'Brexit' areas of the country.

'But not him,' Dave had said pointing to Jason when Lee had first met the blokes. 'Talks about it being a financial disaster. I don't know where he gets it from.'

Lee did. He too had voted to remain in the EU and could fully understand Jason's point of view.

'You hear 'em round here all the time,' Jason told Lee as Dave walked away. '"Just get us out!" they say. Tossers. Anyway, sick to buggery of Brexit, what's happening with that old slapper?'

The 'old slapper' in question was Jason's ex-wife, Lorraine. The

14

two of them had parted a year before and Jason had started divorce proceedings. But Lorraine was apparently playing rough and was claiming that her ex had left her destitute when he'd taken off with a bingo caller from Southend. She wanted more money. Jason, for his part, contended that he'd given Lorraine their house, debt-free, that he still gave her an allowance and that the only reason she was destitute was because she was addicted to Tinder, the online dating site. Officially no loans had been taken out against the considerable equity in the house, but that didn't mean they didn't exist.

'She had a handbag spree at Lakeside at the weekend,' Lee said.

The only thing that had made Lee's trip to Lakeside Shopping Centre at all pleasant had been the fact that it had been under cover. The previous Saturday had been very wet.

'How much?' Jason asked.

'Best part of two and a half grand.'

'Fuck me!'

'She's no fool,' Lee said. 'On one level.'

Lorraine Pritchard had started funding her addiction to, mainly, younger men, by taking out small loans in pawnshops against her jewellery. By Jason's own admission, Lorraine's 'jewels' were mainly Ratners specials, so she hadn't made much. This had then progressed to taking out unsecured loans with various high street loan companies, which had now, her husband suspected, progressed further to coming under the influence of actual loan sharks. As yet, Jason didn't know who they were. But if she carried on her life of luxury, it wouldn't be long before Lorraine got hurt. And, although he wanted nothing more to do with his ex, Jason didn't want her to either lose their house or get hurt.

'You know where it's coming from yet?' Jason asked.

Lee shook his head. 'Not exactly.'

'What's that mean?'

'Means that I've got some ideas but nothing concrete,' Lee said.

Lorraine was making occasional trips out to Langdon Hills in Thurrock, which didn't make a lot of sense given that all her family and friends lived in Romford. Also, she had no car and so every trip that she made out to this 'posh' part of Thurrock based around a golf club, was difficult and costly. Lee didn't know any obvious 'villains' who lived in that area, but that didn't mean they didn't exist. The house she visited was registered to a Mr and Mrs Barzan Rajput. The name rang no bells, but why was she going there? And how had she got to know these people? He'd asked Jason about any possible Langdon Hills connections before, but he'd come up empty. Lee didn't want to labour the point now.

'She been out this week?' Jason asked.

Unlike the 'old days', following people engaged in sexual relationships wasn't so easy in the twenty-first century. Back when he'd been a copper, hooky types tended to meet their 'dates' in pubs, clubs and discos. But in the modern world of 'hook-ups' this all happened online, and although Lee had 'friended' Lorraine on social media, he had noticed that she was rather reticent when it came to details about her movements. But for the skilled PI, for whom patience wasn't so much a virtue as a necessity, this was not a great problem.

'Sunday she had lunch at a pub in Havering-atte-Bower and then went back with the bloke she'd met there for two hours.'

'Some suit?'

'He wore a suit but it didn't define him,' Lee said. 'His home turned out to be of the mobile variety.'

'Slummin' it.'

'Not really, no,' Lee said. 'He was probably twenty-five, tops.

16

What he lacked in readies he more than made up for in youth.'

Jason shook his head. 'Dirty mare.'

'Dad used to work on the docks when I was a kid,' Brenda said. 'Then when everything moved down to Tilbury, he got a job on the cruise ships. But he got caught nicking stuff and so they sacked him. But, probably because he was always good for a pint or twelve, he knew everyone wherever he worked. Mainly he knew the villains. Someone must've got him and John on that ship across the Atlantic. This John man didn't talk about that much.'

Mumtaz noticed how Brenda never referred to John as her brother, in spite of the apparent DNA proof.

'All I know is they landed at New York where they were met by this couple.' She shook her head. 'It sounds mad, especially if you'd known me dad. How he found these people . . . Well anyway, they were called the Gustavssons. This John when he mentioned them started going on about them being billionaires and all that, and I thought he was full of shit, you know. My dad was a toerag, how'd he get to be with people like them? But I looked them up. Or rather I got our Kenton to look them up on Google and there they were. Etta and Michael Gustavsson of Orange County, California, one son – John. They're bloody loaded.'

Mumtaz was just thinking that she'd never heard of them when Brenda said, 'Funny people, though. All that money but you'll never see their names in the papers or nothing. This John geezer's their only heir too! And he's got no family, so he says, so it'll all come to my lot. So he says. But it don't add up.'

Mumtaz frowned.

'I mean, don't think I'm being grasping or nothing, but if you was rich and then you come back to your family after donkey's years, don't you think you'd want them to see you'd done well? Like wearing nice clothes? Driving up in a posh car?'

'He didn't?'

'Rocked up in a taxi from Plaistow, after getting the Tube, so he said. Looked like he'd slept in his clothes.'

'If he's come from America then maybe he had,' Mumtaz said. 'On the plane.'

'Yeah, but why? If you had a lot of money you'd go first class, wouldn't you? I know I would. Anyway, that's just a detail really. What I'm really interested to know is why he's here.'

'Why does he say he's here?'

'To see us.' She shook her head. 'So he says.'

'But you don't believe him?'

'I don't.'

'Why not?'

Brenda sighed. 'Look, I can understand why he don't want to stay with us. He could, I've offered, but he says he don't want to be no bother. I'm not saying the house is a tip, but . . . I got kids still at home, Des, and then there's his youngest boy, in and out as he pleases. Grandchildren . . . It's like Charing Cross Station, but if he has really come to see us why is he staying up West? And why in a Travelodge?'

Mumtaz said, 'Not all rich people want to splash their money around.'

'Oh, I get that his people are not flash. They wouldn't hide themselves away if they was. But he don't spend time with us. He says he's over here to see us but then he's always off somewhere. When he is with us, he sits in a corner and reads. And yes, I know he might be embarrassed and maybe he wants to see things after so long away but . . . This is going to sound daft, but I think he's here for some other reason. I feel we're an excuse. I don't trust him.' She moved in closer to Mumtaz and said, 'I mean, I don't know him, do I?'

'Tel.'

'Jase.'

There was no actual hostility between the two men, but Lee could see there was no love lost either.

When the older, much fatter, man had walked past he said to Jason, 'Who was that?'

Jason rolled his eyes. 'Her uncle.'

'What?'

'The missus,' he said. 'Terry Gilbert. He's the only member of her family who'll so much as pass the time of day. Not that I blame 'em. Some'd say I done wrong going off with Sandra, especially the wife's family. But living with Lorraine had been doing my head in for years. And it's not like the kids are babies . . .'

'So, could he be a possible source . . . ?'

'For Lorraine? Nah. Reason he's still civil to me is that his family can't stand the sight of him.'

'Why not?'

Jason offered Lee a fag, which he took and then they both lit up.

'They call him Tall Tel round here,' Jason said. 'And, yeah, I know he's knee-high to a short cat, but you know how it is.'

Lee nodded. Many people in Romford originated from the East End where there was a long tradition of inappropriate or strange nicknames. Lee's mother's sister, his Auntie Grace, for instance, was known to everyone as 'Polly' because she was always putting the kettle on.

'Yeah.'

'Mind you,' Jason said. 'There's truth in the Tall Tel thing because he's always telling tales.'

'What? Lies?'

'Depends how you view these things,' Jason said. 'He's always been, so he says, convinced the earth is flat. I thought he just done it for attention when I first met him, but he don't. Sods off every so often to look for the Loch Ness Monster, thinks there's a coven of witches that operate out of St Paul's Cathedral. You wanna hear him about the tunnels underneath the Thames! And, of course, now he's full of shit about George Soros taking over the world. Donald Trump's his kind of geezer, which tells you all you need to know about Terry Gilbert and part of the reason why I left his niece.'

'Lorraine tell tall stories?'

'Nah. Not really. She just never questioned nothing. Long as she got her manicures and her hair done, she never give a shit about nothing important. I got fucked off with it. I mean, I know I look like the type of bloke who drives a Range Rover and puts up UKIP posters in me front windows, but I'm not like that and neither's Sandra.'

'Which is why you fell for her.'

'Yeah.' He looked up at the cloud-filled sky and then he said, 'That and her tits.'

Shortly after Brenda Joseph left the office, Mumtaz took a trip down to North Woolwich. It was many years since she'd walked through the old foot tunnel and now, in view of Brenda's story, she felt as if she needed to reacquaint herself with it. She parked up just behind a derelict pub on Manor Way and began to walk down towards the northern embarkation point for the Woolwich

Ferry. The entrance to the foot tunnel was just in front of the slip road for vehicles queuing for the boat.

With grey and cloudy skies up above and a low, riverine landscape all around, her walk was far from cheerful. North Woolwich was one of the forgotten corners of London. Heavily bombed in World War Two, it had been redeveloped first in the 1960s when numerous poorly built tower blocks sprang up. The Tube had never come out as far as North Woolwich and so, in those days, it was only served by infrequent trains on the old overground North London Line. But then in the eighties and nineties a second wave of development hit, bringing with it, eventually, the Docklands Light Railway and very pricey flats for rich people with uninterrupted river views. But, for all that, the tower blocks still stood, as did the cheap takeaway joints, the bookies and the corner shops where, if you knew the right people, you could access cheap fags.

As ever, the queue for the free ferry across the Thames was long and those waiting to use the foot tunnel were few. Built back in 1912, Woolwich Foot Tunnel was entered via matching brick-built, copper-roofed rotundas on the northern and southern shores of the river. On the northern shore the building was plonked on its own in the middle of a tangle of roads servicing the ferry and local buses. But on the southern shore the rotunda was less easy to discern. Before she descended, Mumtaz looked across the Thames to see how quickly she could spot it. It wasn't easy. The southern rotunda was hemmed in by newer buildings. But it was possible, as Brenda Joseph had claimed, to see someone waving outside the opposite structure.

Mumtaz entered the northern rotunda. The smell that hit her, a mixture of piss and fag ash, was very familiar in this kind of environment. Although brick-built the inside of the rotunda was

21

lined with what had once been white, now grey, tiles. Similar in size and appearance to the tiles one routinely found in Victorian toilets, these were what Lee always called 'bog tiles' and they always smelt like this. Many years ago, Mumtaz remembered walking down the staircase behind the lift to the tunnel and so she pressed the button to call the elevator. As she recalled, those stairs had been spiral and dark and she'd felt as if she was descending into hell. The lift was at least quick, even if it too was dark and unsettling with its strange wooden panels scarred by unimaginative graffiti. When the automatic doors opened, she found herself looking down a deserted tile-lined tube illuminated by flickering yellow lights. On the ground, down the middle of the tunnel was a long drainage hollow. Everything about this place seemed to be designed to cause the user anxiety.

TWO

'What made you go down there on your own?' Lee asked.

Mumtaz sipped from the cup of tea he'd just put down in front of her.

'I wanted to see whether the tunnel was still as horrible as I remembered,' she said.

'And it was.'

'Of course. It's in Woolwich, the land time forgot,' she said.

'And I suppose you walked back through it?'

'Yes.'

He rolled his eyes. It had been a long day. The traffic had been bad going to and returning from Romford and Mumtaz's latest client's problem had sounded odd.

Lee sat down behind his desk. 'I'm always wary of jobs based on feelings,' he said. 'I mean if this woman and her brother have had DNA tests . . .'

'She's not disputing that he's her brother,' Mumtaz said. 'She's just wary about his motives.'

'So he's a bit weird . . .' Lee turned to his computer screen. 'Says here that the Gustavssons are major donors to Christian charities. Also says they're staunch Republicans. Maybe John Saunders has come over here to support Trump.'

American president Donald Trump was due to arrive in London for a state visit in five days' time on the 3rd June.

'Why?'

'What – why come over here to support Trump?' Lee laughed. 'Well, no one else is.'

'Yes, but why would John Saunders keep that from his sister?'

'Embarrassment?'

'Brenda Joseph doesn't strike me as the kind of woman who'd be necessarily against Trump,' Mumtaz said.

Lee shrugged. 'So what did you say to her?'

'I said I'd look into it,' she said. 'He's staying at the Travelodge in Marylebone. He arrived just before Christmas and went straight from the airport to Brenda's house in Canning Town. He says he found her through Facebook, although she'd no proof of that.'

'So he's been here six months and she's only got round to feeling strange about him now?'

Mumtaz shrugged. 'Seems so. Maybe she's had enough of him.'

'What about this DNA test?'

'My understanding is that it's one of those quick, off-the-peg jobs,' Mumtaz said.

'Which can be wrong.'

'Mmm. Brenda and her husband Des both work in low-paid jobs for the NHS. He's a porter and she's a cleaner,' Mumtaz said. 'They rent their house from the council and between them

24

they've got seven kids plus assorted grandchildren. John can't want anything from her, she hasn't got anything.'

'What does he do?'

'He's part of his adoptive parents' charity. I don't think that he does work, as such. What does it say about him on Wiki?'

'Just that he exists,' Lee said. 'Born 1966. That's it. Maybe he doesn't want anything from his sister? Maybe he just wants to know her and her family.'

'It would seem so. But his behaviour isn't what you'd call normal. He insists on seeing Brenda every day, at her house for preference. Then all he does is sit about and read.'

'Maybe he's autistic?'

'Really?' she shook her head. 'Lee, that's a bit of a jump . . .'

'Obsessive behaviour . . .'

'Autistic people don't conform to one size fits all. I think you may have watched *Rain Man* one too many times. Or maybe you're right? I have yet to see this man. And then there's the story about how he came to be in America. I mean, is it possible for someone to travel across the Atlantic on a liner, get off in New York and just become someone else?'

Lee said, 'Probably. I don't know how, but sometimes people can just get through the system. When I was a copper, we had a case of a psychiatric patient who somehow flew to Dallas, Texas. So Goodmayes Hospital to Dallas with no passport and an empty birdcage as luggage. How he even got on the plane remains a mystery. Flight attendants claimed they just took the cage from him and then let him on. No passports checks. You ask me! God knows how he did it!'

'Really?'

'Really. But if this Gustavsson pair met John and his dad in New York, was that maybe prearranged? If you're right about the dad not being much involved with the kids, then did he somehow do a deal with these people? For the kid?'

Brenda had started out cooking very English food for her brother when he came round, but now her husband was getting bored, not to mention the kids.

'Not bloody meat pie again!' her daughter Kimberly said when she saw her mother popping a steak and kidney into the oven.

John was only next door in the living room and so Brenda shushed her.

Kimberly lowered her voice. 'All right, then,' she said. 'But count me out, yeah?'

'What . . .'

'I'm meeting up with Jaqueshia later – I'll eat round hers.'

Kimberly was Brenda's youngest child, the only one of the couple's many kids who was the product of both of them. At sixteen she was in the throes of doing her GCSE exams.

'Well, I hope you've asked Jaqueshia's mother whether you can invite yourself,' Brenda said.

Kimberly sucked her teeth. 'She's always got more food than they can eat.'

Then she left the kitchen.

Brenda was all too aware of the fact that her family didn't really like this interloper who now turned up every day, plonked himself on the sofa, ate – maybe read a book – and then left. Brenda didn't like him much. Unlike a lot of Americans she saw on the telly, John wasn't brash or boastful, quite the reverse. He was what her mother had always described as a 'God botherer'. Always banging on about Jesus. His parents were famously like that. Brenda didn't really understand what kind of Christians they were, but she did know that they were against abortion because John had told her about it.

'Even a child born out of wedlock has a right to life,' he'd told her. John had very fixed views about sex outside marriage – you just didn't do it. And he wasn't married – which had to mean—

'Brenda!'

She went into the living room where he was watching the six o'clock news.

'Do you think all these people are going to go out to protest against the president?'

His voice was soft and sounded what Brenda would describe as 'educated'. She looked at pictures of people on the TV talking about Trump.

'Seems so,' she said. 'A lot of people are very angry about him coming.'

'Why?'

She shrugged. She wasn't that concerned about President Trump's visit. Brenda didn't really do politics, not like Des who could bang on about it for England. Thank God he was out at work! Just the look of Trump made him almost have a seizure.

'I know a lot of people don't like him,' John said, 'but the president is doing the Lord's work. You know he plans to stop abortion completely in the States?'

'Oh.'

'Because it is like a Holocaust in our country,' he continued. 'Millions of defenceless babies destroyed like rubbish every year by sinful women.'

Brenda didn't know what to say. She knew women who'd had abortions, but she wouldn't have described any of them as especially sinful. Poor, frightened and dumped, yes. But she held her tongue. Now that she'd engaged Mrs Hakim to find out more about John she did feel a little bit guilty. It was going to cost a pretty penny too. But she was using her own money, cash she'd salted away over many years of car-boot sales and a couple of little 'private' jobs on the side, cleaning doctors' houses. Des didn't even know about it but then Brenda had always wanted it to be that way. After her first marriage failed back in the eighties, she and her then three kids had been left destitute. And although Des was a hard worker who really loved her, Brenda had vowed that she'd never again be left potless by a bloke.

Normally she wouldn't have even dreamt about spending her nest egg, but this thing with John had come at her out of the blue and she felt that just for her own sanity, she had to know the truth. When her brother had disappeared down Woolwich Foot Tunnel all those years ago, the incident had slashed a scar of uncertainty in her life that had never healed. If people could just disappear into thin air, then how could anyone hope to trust anyone or anything again?

Two in the morning was such a wretched time to wake, especially if you weren't in your own home. Mumtaz slipped silently out of the bed and made her way down the corridor to the living room. Chronus the mynah bird made a couple of strange squawking noises from his perch beside the bookcase and then turned his back. He was used to her.

Although she didn't stay over at Lee's place often these days, it was nice for Mumtaz to stay away from home once in a while. Not so long ago, she'd spent a lot of time here – not in the spare room but in Lee's bed. But that hadn't worked out. Not because they didn't care for each other but because their lives were just too complicated by family, by finance, custom and religion. As a hijab-wearing Muslim woman whose faith was important to her, Mumtaz had found the questions she was asking herself about who she really was with Lee were impossible to answer. But that didn't mean she didn't still love him – or vice versa.

She switched on a table lamp and sat down on the sofa. Chronus grumbled softly and then closed his eyes. Although nothing had actually happened in the Woolwich Foot Tunnel that afternoon, the experience had unnerved her. According to Brenda Joseph, the last time she'd seen her brother had been when she'd watched him go into the North Woolwich rotunda. For years she had speculated about whether he'd actually gone inside at all or just legged it over to what was then North Woolwich Station and run away. He'd had, by the sound of it, little to keep him. That said, he'd only been ten. Could the story adult John told now, about being taken away by his father, possibly be true?

The notion that the father had been waiting in the tunnel for his son so that he could abduct him made Mumtaz's skill crawl. What for? Had he maybe sold the boy to the Gustavssons? How would someone like Reg Saunders get to meet such people? Unless it was from his time working on cruise ships. But then what about the official paperwork one needed to leave one country and enter another? According to Brenda, her brother was now an American citizen called John Gustavsson. If indeed this was one and the same person, then John Saunders had been obliterated.

There were so many questions, they made Mumtaz's head spin. Had John come to the UK with the blessing of his American parents? What, if anything, did he remember about his life before the US? What did he feel about his father? And, as Brenda had said, why come back after so many years away?

On the one hand, Mumtaz wanted to meet John, but on the other if she was going to observe him then that wasn't a good idea. She hadn't yet formulated a plan about how this job might work, but now she wondered whether she would need some help. The agency had a small group of casual PIs who came in as and when to help out, and also Lee himself had intimated that he may be able to assist. Some work, particularly matrimonial, had dropped off a little since the winter. Why this was, Mumtaz didn't know, although she suspected it might have something to do with the UK's imminent exit from the European Union. According to their point of view everyone was either despairing or jubilant. But even those who really wanted to leave, like Lee's mother Rose, were worried. When nobody knew what could happen from one day to the next, anxieties about personal problems could pale into insignificance. If that is, one was not Mumtaz.

An email from her stepdaughter Shazia was causing her concern. It had said *Getting active re: climate change. There's only one issue and it's saving the planet*. Mumtaz had mailed back that she agreed, but then she'd warned Shazia about the possibility of getting arrested on any protest actions she might wish to join. Shazia had mailed back the following response:

Personal issues are unimportant. If we don't save the planet we're all dead. Too many people are putting their own stuff first. Not me.

And she was right. She was right and brave and she was, so far, doing brilliantly on her criminology course at Manchester

University. But Shazia's ultimate aim was to become a police detective. In fact, Mumtaz had been obliged to bribe the girl to study for a degree before applying to Hendon Police Academy straight from school. As far as she knew, Shazia still had that ambition. But if she got a police record at a march or a sit-in that option would be closed to her.

When Brenda Joseph had talked about her father, she had told Mumtaz that he had died at a place called Holywell in Wales. A vagrant by that time, Reg Saunders had breathed his last under the care of a convent of nuns responsible for looking after pilgrims visiting the nearby shrine. Only just over an hour away from Manchester, Mumtaz wondered whether she could both follow up on Reg Saunders' last days and go and visit Shazia.

If, of course, her battered Nissan Micra could make the trip . . .

Alone without even the sound of the lift behind him re-ascending, the sound of just one of his feet moving forwards made his ears cringe. The new lighting, embedded into the ceiling, just like the old forty-watt bulbs it had replaced, worked in places. Where it was inoperative, a puddle of darkness stained the grimy floor way, its middle waste water gully stinking of piss.

People had always pissed down here. One of the kids in his class had even taken a shit on a school trip underneath the river to visit Woolwich Arsenal. The teacher had gone crazy, but all the kids had laughed. Except him. What possessed a person to take a shit in a public place? It was puzzling.

One foot down, the other proceeded it, the sound echoing off the grimy tiled walls like gunshots. He was alone and, although he'd read that these days the tunnel had panic buttons scattered along its length, who, realistically would or could come to help someone trapped down here with a madman? Or a rapist . . .

Only a few metres in he stopped to look at the grouting between the tiles. Some of the kids on that long-ago school trip had convinced him that it was only the tiles and the grouting that held back the water of the Thames. He'd looked on the occasional leaks that dribbled from the walls back in those days with horror. As the possibility of his own death had begun to dawn on him, he'd burst into tears. Everyone had laughed at him, even the teacher. But no one had taken the time to convince him that he wasn't going to die. They didn't care. No one did. He was a weirdo, 'Johnny No-Mates' and his life was worthless.

The tunnel gently dipped down to its lowest point right in the middle. Above, the Woolwich ferry plied its way backwards and forwards across the river, taking people, cars and lorries from north to south and vice versa. But it was too late for the ferry now. Unlike the tunnel it didn't operate twenty-four hours a day. Ditto the Docklands Light Railway. So, if you wanted to travel from north to south or south to north in the middle of the night it was the tunnel or swim.

Of course, some – boys wishing to impress their girls, drunks – who chose the latter option usually died. The river was tidal and included hazardous undercurrents and it was full of filth. Toilet paper, wipes, fat, tampons and plastic, plastic, plastic. So the tunnel was the only choice, however afraid one may be. Not that he was afraid.

But on the odd occasion he saw someone else, he could see the fear on that person's face. Man or woman, it made no difference. The thought that they could be attacked, that the tunnel could rupture, that life would end, followed them all like a great, black veil, dragging along the oozing floor like a curse. Separated from God, they lived lives of abject terror believing idiotic stories designed to frighten the ignorant, and if he passed any one of them on his travels he gave each one of them the evil eye. Because that was real.

THREE

'Actually, he's here,' Brenda whispered into her phone. She'd been on the toilet when Mumtaz rang and was now washing her hands with the phone tucked underneath her chin. 'He turned up for breakfast. He does sometimes.'

'I'm thinking I'd like to talk to him,' Mumtaz said. 'Get to know him a little.'

'Yeah, but aren't you following him or whatever?'

'Mr Arnold has allocated some of our freelance investigators to shadow him. I'm thinking you might be able to introduce me to him.'

Brenda frowned. 'As what?'

'As a friend from work.'

'What? A cleaner?'

'Why not?'

'Well, you speak nice and . . .'

34

'Brenda, you must have some colleagues who've been to university. This is 2019, people have to do any job they can get.'

Brenda thought for a moment. There was that Tiffany who said she'd been to university, even though she talked like some tart out of *EastEnders* and looked like a druggie. And all the Poles had degrees.

Eventually she said, 'Yeah. But we'll have to meet outside the house. My family don't know I'm doing this.'

'All right. Do you know what he's doing today?'

'No. But I'm off up to Queen's Market after breakfast.'

That was just down Green Street from the Arnold Agency's office.

'Well, that would be perfect for me,' Mumtaz said. 'Try to get him to come along with you and let me know. If you take him for a cuppa at Percy Ingle's I'll meet you "by chance" in there. I won't be wearing my hijab and my name will be Aminah.'

'Oh.' Brenda felt confused. Didn't all Muslim women wear the hijab whatever they were doing?

She heard Mumtaz laugh. 'You'd be amazed the number of people who just don't recognise me without my scarf,' she said. 'Let me know what time you'll be at the market, approximate.'

Then she cut the connection. Brenda finished washing her hands and then put her phone in her pocket. She had to trust that Mrs Hakim knew what she was doing, but she hadn't counted on her wanting to meet John. Suddenly everything felt a bit more worrying than it had. She wasn't good at lying, never had been. But now she was going to have a conversation with a non-existent workmate.

Lee poured himself a dismal plastic cupful of tea from his thermos and looked at the front of Lorraine Pritchard's house. Set a good fifty metres from the street, it was a mock Georgian affair recently painted a very fashionable shade of silver grey. Not her ex's taste, that was for sure. Jason had been horrified when she'd had it done.

'Looks like a fucking public bog in some park in Dagenham,' he'd told Lee during the course of one of their meetings. It looked a lot better than that, Lee thought, but he could see why Jason didn't like it. It was very obviously 'on trend'. Unlike his tiny flat in Forest Gate.

Even if he'd had the cash to do so, Lee was averse to change when it came to his home. As things stood, he knew where everything was and, even more importantly, he knew that he could move everything easily when it came to cleaning. Because that was part of his 'thing'.

Although nearly fifty, Lee Arnold was a handsome bloke – if you liked tall, dark, slim and a bit off his rocker. Prior to being a policeman, which he'd done before he'd become a PI, Lee had been a soldier. Sent to Iraq in 1990 to fight against Saddam Hussein's Republican Guard, he had seen and experienced things that quite rightly had scarred his mind.

For years he'd hidden in booze and painkillers, but with help from a colleague, DI Violet Collins, as well as swapping one addiction for another – drugs for cleaning – he'd become as 'well' as he was ever going to get, which wasn't saying a lot. But he could live with it. He'd lived with it better when he and Mumtaz had been an item but that was now water under the bridge – except when it wasn't.

Lorraine had only half an hour ago pushed a young guy out of her front door and now, it seemed, someone else had turned up.

Judging from the car this person drove, whoever was calling was not her usual type. The boy who'd not long left had driven an Audi sports car. This by contrast was an ancient Escort. Perhaps Lorraine was branching out. But then Lee saw that the man who got out of the vehicle was so far away from her usual type, the thought of her bedding him was laughable.

He was also, Lee noted, her uncle.

'Shazia!'

'Oh, hello, Amma . . .'

Her stepdaughter sounded odd. Uncertain about something. And although Mumtaz knew it was important she didn't come across as some interfering Asian auntie, she said, 'Is everything all right?'

'Yes . . .'

Did she maybe have a boy in her room? If she did that was her business. Shazia was not a religious young woman and Mumtaz wasn't her mother – except that she was in all but name.

She said, 'Listen, darling, I may have to come up north to work in the next week or so. Don't worry, I won't ask to stay . . .'

'Oh, you can,' Shazia said. 'Of course. But I'm actually going to be coming down this Saturday. I was going to ask if I could stay . . .'

'Of course you can.'

'Only it's the anti-Trump demo on Monday. That's when he arrives.'

'Ah, yes.'

Her emails of the previous evening had obviously been a prelude to this.

All part of her activism. Mumtaz approved. But . . .

'Amma?'

Had she heard the hesitation in her voice?

'Amma, you are all right with it, aren't you?'

'What, you coming home? Of course!'

'No, the whole Trump thing. I mean you can see he's just the worst ever president, can't you?'

'I can,' Mumtaz said. 'But . . . But look, to be honest, I just worry about you and protesting. You want to be a police officer . . .'

'Yes, I do.'

'But you won't be able to do that if you've got a criminal record. I've spoken to you before about this.'

There was a pause, then Shazia said, 'I know that.'

'Well?'

Mumtaz heard her sigh. 'Sometimes you have to do things that don't tie in with your ambitions. I mean, Trump's bigger than whatever I want to do – literally. And the fact that he's coming to our country is outrageous.'

'Yes . . .'

'We're all going down from my department,' Shazia said. 'Most of us want to work in criminal justice in some capacity, but we also feel we have to do this.'

Mumtaz sympathised but she still found herself saying, 'You do know you won't be allowed anywhere near Trump, don't you?'

'Oh yes. It's the being there that's important.'

And maybe it was. When Mumtaz put the phone down after agreeing that Shazia could come home for the weekend, she considered her own views on the subject. She didn't want Trump to come to London either, but she wasn't convinced of the value of 'just being there' to oppose him. She opposed him and people like him all the time in her mind and, when challenged about her politics, she was very openly against nationalism. But she wasn't what anyone would have considered active politically and that, she recognised, didn't sit well with her.

The phone rang again. For a moment she wondered whether it was Shazia again, after a change of heart, but then she heard Brenda Joseph say, 'Sorry, I've had to call you from the market bogs so John don't hear. We'll be in Percy Ingle's in five minutes.'

'Interesting.'

'In what sense?' Lee asked.

'Well, you know I told you that no one in her family talks to Tall Tel no more? Well, that includes her, Lorraine.'

'He's still inside the house,' Lee said. 'Nearly half an hour.'

'What's he doing there?'

'I dunno, but I thought I should tell you. I know you never wanted the house wired up, but there are advantages . . .'

'Too risky,' Jason said.

'Not really. This isn't a custody situation,' Lee said. 'All your kids being adults.'

'I know, but . . .'

'What, if anything, does Tall Tel do?' Lee asked.

'What do you think?' Jason said. 'Second-hand car dealer.'

There were a lot of those in the Romford area, including Jason.

'His business is called Tel's Wheels. Over Harold Wood,' Jason added.

'Could Lorraine be getting her uncle to sub her?'

People did mad things when they tried to live beyond their means. Borrowing from loan sharks at interest rates in the thousands, swapping sexual favours for cash, getting into weird alliances with people they didn't like.

Jason said, 'I doubt it. Trade's as flat as a witch's tit. Why I hate fucking Brexit so much. Who's gonna put proper money into a motor when no bugger knows what's going on? And don't even get me going about electric.'

'Tel not got some big gaff over Brentwood?' Lee asked. A lot of the car sales fraternity had chosen to live in that now very expensive town in the past.

'If he's still in the same place, he and his missus live down the Thamesview Estate down Barking. Council place. So no. Can't tell you no more about him except he's a bit of a space cadet.'

Lee looked across at what had been Jason's house and said, 'You know, Jase, my business partner was bending my ear about her car last night. 2001 Nissan Micra, it's coming to the end of the road, so to speak.'

'Oh, I can sort you out with something, mate. Come round any time. I'll do you a good deal.'

'Thanks,' Lee said. 'But I think that I might go and have a look round Tel's Wheels first, if you know what I mean. Get the lay of the land.'

'Oh, right. Gotcha.'

'If your missus is in touch with the family nutter there must be a reason. I wonder if it's got anything to do with her visits up to Langdon Hills?'

'Fuck knows,' Jason said. 'Always wanted to buy a place up there meself when I was younger. Handsome houses.'

Lee looked once again at the house Jason had shared with Lorraine in the not-too-shabby part of Gidea Park and said, 'You ain't done too bad for yourself.'

Then Terry Gilbert left the house.

* * *

40

John Saunders was a small man, no more than five foot four, and entirely grey except for a pair of apple-red cheeks. Like his sister he had unusually vivid green eyes but otherwise he was a rather anonymous little man.

'I didn't know you had a brother,' Mumtaz/Aminah said as she sat down opposite Brenda and John.

'I lived in the States for many years,' he said by way of explanation. He had a nice voice, quite soft, his American accent unpronounced and slightly lilting.

'Oh. That must be interesting.'

Mumtaz could see that Brenda was nervous around her, probably struggling with remembering her name. But so it seemed, was John. He judiciously avoided eye contact.

'So you have the day off from the hospital too?' John asked Mumtaz.

Brenda watched her nervously over the top of a cream bun.

'Yes,' she said. She felt he wanted her to expand on this, but she didn't feel she had to. Mumtaz turned to Brenda. 'So you're showing your brother around?'

'Not really,' she said. 'Just doing a bit of shopping.'

John slowly drank his tea, looking out of the cafe window at the Caribbean food stand opposite. Stilted didn't adequately describe their conversation.

Brenda was so obviously unnerved that Mumtaz came to the conclusion any further conversation had to come from her.

'So, John,' she said. 'Whereabouts in the States do you live?'

'California.'

'Oh, how lovely! I've never been there myself, but I've heard the weather is really lovely . . .'

'It's a godless place,' he said and then turned his deep green eyes on her face. 'Do you have Jesus in your life, Aminah?'

Brenda had told her John was religious but Mumtaz hadn't been expecting that.

'I'm a Muslim, yes.' She smiled.

He didn't.

'There's only one true religion, you know,' he said.

Brenda put a hand on his arm. 'John. Enough.'

He shrugged. Then he ignored her and said, 'Up to her. I'm not forcing anyone. But with the Rapture imminent, those who are not saved will be left behind.'

Mumtaz understood the individual words but not how they were arranged.

'Pardon?'

John's voice became slightly louder. An African woman who was sitting behind Brenda turned.

'The Rapture,' John said, 'is when the Lord will take his own into his kingdom. The righteous saved.'

The African woman smiled and murmured, 'Praise Jesus!'

'And the unrighteous?'

'Armageddon will follow on from the Rapture,' John said. 'When the Antichrist will arise and assemble the forces of Evil. But Jesus will win and then time will end. The Righteous in Heaven and the unbelievers in Hell.'

'That is so,' the African woman said. 'That is so.'

Although a religious person herself, Mumtaz was not unaware of the flaws within theology. Some Muslims she otherwise respected condemned homosexuality out of hand. She did not. To her way of thinking, if someone was gay that was just the way they were. 'Gayness' didn't make someone evil. To her way of thinking the prejudice against gay people was, however, at the very least hurtful and therefore it had to be wrong. But was challenging this man's assumptions the right thing to do given that she was only where she was in order to get some measure of the man? What would an acquaintance, which she purported to be, do?

Eventually she said, 'Oh.'

John Saunders nodded. 'Sobering thought, huh? And it's almost upon us, so if you're going to take Jesus into your life you had better be quick.' He looked at Brenda, 'And you.'

Brenda looked away.

'No good saying you'll do it soon or another time. Time's running out. If it wasn't, we wouldn't have the president that we do.'

'What do you mean?'

'Oh, Mr Trump is hungry for the Rapture,' John said. 'Look how he helps Israel, he has stated that he intends to enable the Jews to rebuild the Temple of Solomon in Jerusalem. That is the signal for the End of Days. And he's saved the innocent. Soon there'll be no baby-killing doctors in America. No abortions.'

The African woman got up to leave and as she passed their table she said to John, 'Bless you, brother.'

'Bless you.'

However mysterious his disappearance might have been, Mumtaz could understand why Brenda wanted rid of him. If he went on like this all the time it was a wonder she was still sane.

Mumtaz changed the subject. 'So are you staying with Brenda?' she asked.

'No,' he said. 'One doesn't want to be a burden.'

'I'm sure—'

'Oh no, I couldn't possibly stay . . .' He was going to say something more but stopped himself.

'Will you go out and see President Trump when he comes on Monday?'

43

'I'll support him, yeah.' He nodded.

A religious fanatic? Mumtaz sipped her tea. Or was he maybe, at heart, a political animal? His adoptive parents were very influential, if mostly silent, members of the Evangelical Christian movement in America. But was he? There was so little written about the Gustavssons it was difficult to tell who they knew and who they didn't. They were not, as far as Mumtaz had been able to see, Republican Party donors. But that didn't necessarily mean they didn't have some sort of connection to Donald Trump.

Eventually John stood up and said, 'Is there a restroom here?'

'No,' Brenda said. 'You'll have to go to those toilets in the market where I went.'

'OK.'

He left. When she couldn't see him any more, Brenda said, 'See how weird he is!'

'He's religious,' Mumtaz began. 'Unusually so . . .'

'Unusually? He's a nutter!'

'Brenda, there are a lot of people who are like him across all communities,' Mumtaz said. 'It seems to be the way things are these days. And then we know his adoptive parents are religious.'

Brenda shook her head. 'There's something wrong,' she said. 'I can feel it in me water.'

And Mumtaz knew what she meant, although she had no idea why. On the face of it, John Saunders was simply a religious American (and God knew there were a lot of those!) who had come back to the country of his birth to visit his family. But why would one who had left the UK in such strange circumstances now come back? And what did his billionaire adoptive parents make of it?

* * *

On a grey day it was easy to see Gallows Corner in Romford as somewhere evil lurked. Once the site of a gallows where criminals and more often than not 'the poor' were executed, it was now covered by two huge roads, the A127 and the A12 and one massive flyover. To the south of the A127 was the district of Harold Wood where Tel's Wheels was based, within sight of the flyover.

Terry Gilbert had driven back from Lorraine Pritchard's house straight to his business, which had been minded, by the look of it, by a lad with bleached blonde hair. Dressed in the tightest jeans known to man, the boy was the epitome of Essex Metrosexual Man.

As Lee approached the garage, the young man was saying to Tel, 'I just threw in the valet he was after. I mean, I never knew what else to do?'

Terry Gilbert had the look of a man long ago beaten into submission by life. He just shrugged. 'You got the sale, you got the sale,' he told the young man. Then he saw Lee.

'Morning sir,' he said. 'What can we do for you?'

Lee glanced at a couple of random cars before saying, 'I'm looking for a small hatchback for the wife. Automatic.'

Terry nodded. 'Petrol or diesel?'

'Petrol for preference.'

He nodded again. 'I got a couple,' he said. 'Best value's a Skoda Fabia I got round the back. I know they ain't what you'd call a fashion statement . . .'

'Don't mind about that,' Lee said. 'Just want reliable and not too thirsty.'

'Ah well, you've come to the right place,' Tel said. Then he called out to the younger man, 'Dean! Shove the kettle on!' He took Lee's arm. 'Come this way, sir.'

*   *   *

Shazia hadn't told her amma about Dexter. She hadn't been sure she'd approve. But they were both going down to London on Sunday and he was dropping her off because he was doing the driving. Mumtaz would almost certainly see him outside even if he didn't want to come in. She looked at him as he grooved along to something on his headphones while reading in bed.

Dex was also a Londoner. It was something they had bonded over when they'd first met. That and an interest in forensic psychology. And sex.

When she looked over at him, Dexter smiled. All floppy blonde hair and dimpled cheeks, Amma would get a bit of a shock if she did see him. But then would she? For months she'd openly dated Lee and had always said that love should never have boundaries. But that relationship had eventually succumbed to Amma's insecurities about where being with a non-Muslim put her in the scheme of things. Shazia knew that Mumtaz would be far more liberal in her opinions where she was concerned, but she would still be disappointed.

Shazia went back to eating her toast and reading her book. Surely standing up to people like Donald Trump, people like her and Dex were making a statement about love across racial divides? Trump, ISIS and all these fanatics strove only to divide people. And, anyway, it wasn't as if she and Dex were engaged or anything . . .

Unknown to her boyfriend, Shazia's relationship to the concept of marriage was problematic. Her birth mother had lived in an abusive marriage to her father prior to her death and then when her father remarried Mumtaz it had happened again. That was quite aside from what she'd been put through. A bully, a gambler and a child abuser was what

Ahmet Hakim had been and, although she knew that on one level she still loved her late father, it was largely in spite of herself. She loved her amma and Amma's parents who had become Shazia's family in recent years and who were all supporting her through her degree and, later on she hoped, her police career. Because being a detective was what really mattered to Shazia. More than her family, her interests, more than Dexter, more than anything. Because being a detective would allow her to take revenge.

'I've got an auto mini but it's in red,' Tel said.

Lee frowned. 'I'm not too fussed about the colour, to be honest.'

'Just they get nicked more often than other motors,' Tel said. 'Red, sticks out. Know what I mean?'

He did, sort of. But then, over tea in his office, Lee had come to the conclusion that, if anything, his client Jason Pritchard had underplayed his wife's uncle's addiction to strange and usually unprovable theories. Over tea and fags, Terry had treated Lee to his views on measles vaccinations. Apparently because he'd survived measles himself in the early fifties, the current 'belief' in vaccination was 'all about scientists making money for 'emselves'. He illustrated this point with reference to various tabloid newspapers until he got to the real bread and butter of his beliefs.

'A great conflict is coming,' he'd said to a slightly unnerved Lee. 'Trust me. Gotta be ready. One of the reasons we all need decent motors. I'll level with you, mate, the future's about tinned goods and firearms. I mean, don't quote me, but between you and me . . .'

Lee hadn't said anything but Tel had carried on.

'Bunker if you can,' he'd said. 'I got mine a long time ago. Somewhere in Essex. I know, no other bugger does. Full of every tin you can put your name to.'

Lee had said, 'That must've cost you a pretty penny.'

Tel had drawn in a thin whistly breath. 'You don't know the half, mate,' he'd said.

They looked at a Renault Clio in blue as well as the Skoda Fabia, which Tall Tel declared was a 'steal' at only nine grand. It was a 2015 model and looked to be in good nick and Lee was quite tempted to actually buy it. But then he reminded himself he hadn't come to Gallows Corner for that reason. He'd come to see what Tall Tel was like, which was just as odd as Jason had described. As well as all the weird beliefs about vaccines and Holocaust preparation, Terry Gilbert was also, Lee felt, probably a flat-earther too. Expanding on his apparent hatred for scientists, Tel had given it as his opinion that 'they're keeping the truth about how we come to be here from us'.

Eventually Lee said he'd have to go away and have a think about what he'd seen. Terry gave him his business card and Lee gave him the number of his old Nokia mobile he still kept charged up for encounters just like this.

'I've been here since 1975,' he told Lee. 'So we know what we're doing. Not that it's been easy.'

Lee asked him why.

Tel said, 'Oh, it's a wicked game, the old car game, mate. Always has been. Last few years, though . . .' He shrugged. 'Should've done Brexit right away, soon as that referendum happened. Nobody knows what's happening the way it is. People who normally changed their motors have been hanging on until they know what's happening with the prices.'

48

'And what do you think will happen with prices after Brexit?' Lee asked.

Terry shook his head. 'Well, provided we get Brexit, I think that things'll look up. I mean you gotta believe in Britain, don't you? That's why I carry on, I'll be honest. Gotta put your money where your mouth is, whatever's going on.'

FOUR

Mumtaz received the email at almost midnight, which was a surprise as she had always imagined that nuns went to bed early. Set out exactly like a letter, it said:

Dear Mrs Hakim,

Thank you so much for your communication of the above date regarding Mr Reginald Saunders. We note that he was indeed a guest of ours in November 1982. As you have indicated, Mr Saunders died while in our care. A post-mortem examination gave the cause of his death as cirrhosis of the liver.

The sister who provided care to Mr Saunders while he was with us is also now deceased. Therefore, in answer to your query, no – there is no first-hand source of information here about this man. However, one of our sisters, who was

*a novice at the time, did on occasion help Sister Marianne
with her caring duties. Our dear Sister Angela has said she
is willing to speak to you on the telephone. You may ring
her on the number printed above at between 2 and 3 p.m.
tomorrow. I do hope that this will be acceptable to you.*

It was 'signed' Sister Guadalupe, which, to Mumtaz did
not sound British. Hence the very careful and formally written
email. Her father, who had arrived in Britain from Bangladesh
back in the 1960s, wrote in just the same way.

Mumtaz composed a quick reply thanking Sister Guadalupe
and agreeing to telephone Sister Angela at 2 p.m. the next day.
Then she sat back in her chair and drank what remained of
her hot chocolate. How and why had Reg Saunders ended up
in Holywell? According to Brenda, although raised a Catholic,
he'd never been a religious man. But then the story prevalent at
the time had been that Reg had spent quite some time dossing
around the town long before he ended up in the convent. As an
alcoholic he probably had a whole raft of addiction and control
issues. Chronic substance abuse rarely manifested as a single
entity and Reg had been profligate and sometimes violent. He'd
also apparently kidnapped his own son . . .

She hadn't liked John Saunders. Religious maniacs were not
her thing. They seemed to be prominent within the ranks of
most religions now. When she'd been a child growing up in the
large Asian community on and around Brick Lane, those who
as her father put it, 'banged on' about religion all the time had
been considered a bit of a joke. But with the coming of hate
preachers like Abu Hamza, and later, the atrocities attributed to
Al Qaeda, the joke had turned extremely sour. Now it appeared
intolerance was everywhere and John Saunders was part of it.

That aside, and as his sister had stated, there was something else about John that was unsettling. Mumtaz couldn't put her finger on it. Like a lot of Americans, he approved of Donald Trump – which seemed to her like a form of insanity. And given that he wasn't actually American, what did Trump's nationalism mean to him anyway?

Very little further information about his adoptive parents had come to light since her original search. The Gustavssons it seemed endowed mainly Christian charities but in such a way as to retain their anonymity. Mostly. Sometimes word got out, although it was difficult to tell via what method. Disgruntled employees maybe? There were possible links to archaeological digs in Israel, church rebuilds in Bosnia and hints about affiliations to anti-abortion groups in the US. So far, so predictable. But still there was no, even tenuous, link to the Republican Party. The way John had gone on about Trump more than signalled he was in favour of his administration. Did he diverge from his adoptive parents politically?

According to Brenda, John hadn't married and had no children. The one photograph she had been able to find of him online – and he wasn't named – was with Etta and Michael Gustavsson. Taken on a trip to Washington back in 1985, he'd looked awkward in a stiff suit and tie and much smaller than his 'father', who was known to be well over six feet. He'd looked so miserable, it was almost possible to feel the unhappiness oozing out of him almost forty years later.

'Don't go in there!'

'What?' Lorraine yelled. You had to yell to get heard.

'Don't go to the toilet,' her friend shouted in her ear. 'It's filthy in there and some of the girls are having a fight.'

Dying for a pee, Lorraine crossed her legs and said, 'So what am I s'posed to do?'

Her friend, Suze, shrugged.

Lorraine said, 'I'll try the disabled. You go and get us another bottle of Prosecco.'

'All right.'

As she pushed past the tightly packed figures snogging, tickling, attempting to dance and having rows, Lorraine reflected on the fact that being in this hellhole was all her fault. It was always like this. As soon as she managed to get hold of money, she was spending it. First the sequinned minidress from some reality 'star's' boutique, plus matching shoes and handbag, and then on the blower to Suze to get her out on the pull. They'd come to The Starlight Club in Brentwood because it was where the movers and shakers went – or so she'd thought.

Having fought her way past three girls snorting a line of coke off a Mulberry handbag, Lorraine pushed her way into the disabled toilet. She pulled her knickers down her fake-tanned legs and sat down. God that was a relief! Only one bottle of Prosecco down so far, but she wasn't as young as she used to be. And how.

Suze was five years younger than Lorraine and she looked like everyone's granny in this place. Lorraine reckoned she had to be at least thirty years older than all of them. The blokes looked like they were either builders scrubbed up for a night out or metrosexual/gay-best-friends. Not that many of them actually fell into those categories. Not really.

The whole place reeked of a thousand competing perfumes – Poison, Molecule, that soapy old tat put out by some rapper girl. As she peed, Lorraine inspected the cellulite on her legs. Who the hell was she kidding being in a place like this? She didn't even know what that roaring music playing out there was, her hair had gone all flat and her feet hurt. But she had to carry on.

Lorraine and husband Jason had split up over sex. She still wanted it, he didn't, and he wouldn't go to the doctor to get Viagra or even buy the stuff over the counter. Made him feel 'less of a man' or some old tosh. Of course, he was already shagging that Sandra by that time. And then there was money. He liked sticking it away for a rainy day while she liked to spend. And now here she was in The Starlight Club with boring Suze looking for a shag and feeling a bit tipsy.

Once she found a juicy bloke, of course, it would all have been worth it. But did she really want a knee trembler with a twenty-something round the back of Boots the chemist? Actually, it didn't matter that much. If said twenty-something had money and was prepared to pay her to keep her mouth shut, that was good enough for Lorraine. Even better if he refused.

The Starlight Club was well known as the place where all the local reality stars met up to drink, do drugs, cop off and make tits of themselves. Those who helped them in these endeavours could, so Lorraine had heard, make a pretty penny out of either the celeb or a tabloid newspaper or magazine. And she needed a pretty penny or two the way things were . . .

What a way to make a living. Lee hated honey-trap jobs. He particularly hated them when he personally had to do them. Mumtaz knew that the agency provided this service – given the recent downturn in business, Lee was up for any work that wasn't exactly illegal. But honey traps – where an investigator 'tempted' someone whose partner suspected them of infidelity – was scraping the bottom of the barrel. The actual client was usually male, often middle-aged or older, who had married a much younger woman. Although not always. One of his casual operatives, a very smart gent in his seventies, had recently romanced a woman of a similar age. Her husband had suspected her of 'playing around' with good reason.

And now here was Lee, on the trail of a woman called Susan Dean. Fifty, married to Colin, a wide boy in banking from Hainault, who had provided him with photos of his wife as well as snippets of video. She was an attractive woman, if a bit botoxed. According to Colin, Lee was just her type – tall, dark, handsome, a bit rough round the edges. Apparently, Susan had a bit of a thing for policemen, so that's what Lee was for this job. It felt strange to be back in plod mindset again.

When he'd entered The Starlight Club, Lee hadn't been surprised by any of its 'attractions'. The much vaunted real Swarovski crystal ceiling was as tacky as it had sounded and the welter of young women wearing very little, necking Prosecco, was what he had expected. If this was 'glamorous' then he'd pass on glamour.

According to her husband, Susan Dean was very 'phone savvy'. Colin had been riffling around in her phone for months and had found nothing incriminating. He'd also not discovered any other secret phone. So, if she was messing around, it was in the form of one-night stands, no names no pack drill. Not that Colin cared. As long as he caught her out and became free to pursue his own 'interests', whatever they were, he didn't give a toss. He just needed evidence of his missus' guilt so that he could present himself as squeaky clean when it came to the divorce. The couple didn't have any children and so Colin wanted his hard-earned cash and property to stay in his own hands.

Everybody in that hot, loud, stinking place was either drinking, snogging or looking at their phone. So when Lee made his way towards the bar, phone in hand, looking at Susan Dean's picture, no one turned a hair.

'All the prayin' getting you down?'

Now that she knew her husband was awake, Brenda sat up in bed and put the light on. She looked at her husband, a large black guy tangled up in a twist of disordered sheets and blankets. Bless him, poor old Des didn't need all this agg with John, who, after all, was nothing to him.

'I don't understand him,' Brenda said. She looked down at what she was wearing. Christ! Whoever would have thought she'd have finally managed to find a man who didn't give a shit about old T-shirts in bed!

Des sat up. 'You don't know him,' he said. 'None of us do. And you have to accept he's American now. They're more religious than Brits. Bit like Jamaicans but more scary. Both my grandmas talked about Jesus all the time.'

'I can't work out why he's here,' Brenda said. 'I mean, you must think it's creepy, he just turns up here whenever he wants to.'

'So give him times when he can't come,' Des said.

'He never spends the night, either.'

'Which is a mercy.'

'Yeah, but if as he says, he come all this way just to see me . . . And when's he going back? He used to keep secrets from everyone when he was a kid.'

'Thought you said you didn't believe he was your brother?'

She shook her head. 'I do and I don't.'

'DNA says otherwise.'

'I know but . . .' She didn't want to tell her husband about her involvement with the Arnold Agency and what Mumtaz had told her about the problems that could arise with online DNA testing. 'Oh, I dunno, he just makes me nervous. I can't get it out of me head that he's up to something.'

'What?'

She shrugged.

'If anything, it's you who could be considered up to something,' Des said. 'I mean he's loaded. If you played your cards right, you could probably get your hands on a nice little windfall.'

'I don't want his money,' Brenda said. 'Do you?'

He laughed. 'If it meant I could give up work, yeah,' he said. Then he put his arm around her. 'But then I know you wouldn't be comfortable with it so, no. Let the man pray all over the house if it makes him happy, and forget about it. He'll go back to the US soon and then we can go back to all the usual problems, like me forgetting to put the bins out and the kids hassling for money.'

He kissed her and Brenda smiled. He'd be asleep within minutes. That was Des. But she was still agitated. She hoped that Mumtaz Hakim might have some news for her soon.

Well that was more like it. Lorraine ran her eyes up and down the bloke Suze was talking to and liked what she saw. Tall and sort of smouldery, he wasn't young and sadly, he wasn't a celebrity, but from the point of view of pure lust . . .

Suze had immediately accepted his offer to buy her a drink. She was so cheap. She was already touching his shoulders. By the time the night was over she'd be sucking his cock. He hadn't given Lorraine a second look, in fact when Suze had told him she was with a mate, he'd just looked away.

Lorraine heard Suze ask him, 'You on your own?'

'Yeah,' he said.

Suze giggled. 'Unusual.'

Lorraine saw him shrug. 'Depends what you like to do,' he said.

'And what do you like to do, Steve?' Suze asked.

He laughed. 'What do *you* like, Suze?'

She whispered something in his ear and the man smiled.

Lorraine looked at the time on her phone. This was hopeless. The place was not exactly heaving with reality nonentities who thought they were 'someone' but there were a few about and they weren't all twenty-three. She'd seen some psychic who'd been on a *Big Brother* spin-off where the participants had to bring their own ghosts, in one of the side rooms. Partying with a load of geriatrics by the look of it, he had to be fifty if he was a day, and he'd winked at her as she'd walked past. Lorraine told Suze she was going to the toilet again and pushed her way through the crowds. Fortunately for her, the psychic, Marlon, was going to the bar. Lorraine engineered bumping into him very neatly.

'Oh, I'm sorry,' she said.

Unlike when he'd seen her pass by his private party room, his eyes met hers with coldness. Elbowing his way past, he said, 'Silly old tart.'

Lorraine felt as if she'd just been punched.

Poor old Colin Dean's missus was like a bitch on heat. Whispering in his ear all the things she'd like to do to him. It was very flattering and everything, but he was never comfortable wearing a voice recorder and also discovering that Suze's wing-woman for the evening was another client's wife, was unsettling.

Lee doubted whether Lorraine Pritchard had even registered his presence when he was following her movements, but he couldn't be sure of that. She'd buggered off somewhere leaving him alone with Suze, who was rubbing herself up against him. She had a good figure, but her face was so surgically enhanced Lee found it difficult to look at her and not grimace. Like a lot of women, young and old these days, she'd clearly asked her plastic surgeon to make her look as much like reality star Kim Kardashian as possible. Her eyebrows were frightening.

There was a brief pause in the pounding music during which Suze said, 'Do you fancy a breath of air?'

There was a small area for smokers outside the club at the back, but Lee knew she wasn't asking him out there to share a fag. There was a gate into the car park and, it was said by those in the know, many of the cars out there would be bouncing up and down to the rhythm of sex before the night was out.

'Yeah,' he said. 'Just let me go to the bog.'

The toilet stank, but at least one of the two cubicles was free. Lee locked himself in. He'd told Suze he was a copper and so he set the alarm on his phone to go off in five minutes. That would give him time to get back to her and allow for a little more seduction before it beeped.

Once out in the sharp night air again, Lee walked over to Suze and said, 'So, you want a fag?'

She shrugged. 'Only if you do,' she said. 'I thought we might go to my car.'

'What for?'

She looked at him seductively. 'Don't tell me you don't know,' she said. She took his hand and pulled him towards the back gate. All around them men sized each other up, talked about

59

football and smoked while women whispered and laughed and smoked. Sometimes, most of the time, these two groups touched. It was a meat rack. Even if Lee had been aroused by Suze this would have killed his ardour.

They began to walk towards the back of the car park. Drunk and randy, Suze clung to Lee, her hands straying down his chest towards his crotch.

'Hey! Let's get—'

'Sorry,' she said, 'just can't wait . . .'

She pushed him up against the side of a Mini Cooper and made a grab for his flies. Luckily she was too bleary-eyed to see him properly. Instead she said, 'I can do all the things them porn stars do!' She gasped. 'I'm so wet!'

Why didn't the bloody alarm go off. He let her put her tongue in his mouth and felt her guide his hands between her legs. When he, albeit reluctantly, touched her, she groaned.

'Oh, babe.' She kissed him again.

Was this the longest five minutes of his life?

Suze pulled away from him and he breathed a sigh of relief. But it was only a brief respite as she took off her knickers and then threw them into a bush. She had to realise, surely, that he wasn't aroused.

She lifted her short dress up over her hips and said, 'All yours, Officer!'

And then his phone beeped.

She was too old for this. Abused by some nonentity who thought he was something just because he was on telly, Lorraine went outside to have a fag. Suze had staggered out there earlier with her tall, dark and handsome and so no doubt they were shagging somewhere.

None of the blokes outside interested Lorraine. Mainly young geezers, if you looked closely enough you could probably see grouting under their fingernails. But then they just glanced at her and then turned away, back to the young girls giggling around them. She was way too old for them and, even if one of them decided to 'do her', it would only be for a joke. And unlike reality stars, your bog-standard brickie didn't have much money. Well not enough.

Lorraine chewed her bottom lip. Fucking Jason! She'd only got into this sodding mess because of him! If he'd only taken that Viagra and not met that tart Sandra none of this would have happened. But she couldn't live without sex and sex with blokes you didn't know, cost. There was waxing, hair extensions, Botox, manicure and then there'd been that lipo . . . If only these treatments would last! But they didn't. Neglect your Botox jabs and suddenly there were your jowls again, ditto the lipo. One eclair too many and you could say goodbye to your washboard stomach. So eating was out, which, of course, meant doing a lot of whizz was essential.

And you didn't get any of that by being an ex with no skills. Even if you did use your house as a cash cow.

One day there would be a reckoning. Lorraine shuddered. Some lines of credit were more scary than others. But in the meantime, the sight of her friend Suze, staggering about in the car park holding her shoes and crying was enough to be going along with.

So the tall, dark and handsome had let her down or humiliated her, had he?

Men were shit.

FIVE

Shazia's placard consisted of a big photograph of Donald Trump, below which was the legend, 'American Psycho'.

'Don't think it's too subtle?' Dexter said as he watched his girlfriend look at it from across the room.

She pulled a face. 'Ha, bloody, ha. You sound like my mother.'

He laughed. His own placard, which was just words, simply said 'Trump Fuck Off'.

'Just sayin',' he continued.

Then they both laughed. Dexter put his arm around her shoulders.

Shazia said, 'You do think we're doing the right thing, don't you?'

'Course.' He lit up a spliff and offered her some, but she refused. 'But your mum has a point if we do get arrested. I mean,

I don't give a shit, it's you that wants to go into the police.'

Dexter, who came from a wealthy family, was studying criminology simply because he liked the subject. He'd never really had any sort of career in mind.

She shrugged. 'I can't just do nothing,' she said.

'You can. Trump's the American president, he's nothing to do with us.'

'Dex, you know that's not true! When we leave the EU, he'll have power of life and death over us,' she said. 'The government's gagging to do a deal with him, which means they'll sell anything, including the NHS. I mean, you should hear Rachel on it! Her dad's a consultant at the Christie and he's doing his nut.'

Deep in his heart Dexter knew that whatever the UK government did or didn't do about leaving the European Union wasn't really going to affect him personally all that much. His father, a retired judge, was incensed by the whole affair, but he also knew that the family had enough money to ride out anything that resulted from it in comfort. He had imagined that their mutual friend Rachel Haworth's family would be in the same boat. And maybe they would, but apparently her oncologist father was 'doing his nut'.

Eventually he just said, 'Yeah.'

Shazia looked around her room. Almost the entire floor space was covered in either placards, rucksacks or boots.

'Anyway,' she said. 'If we're going to get down to Pete's we'd better get a move on.'

Partly in order to give Dexter's ancient Ford Focus a rest on the way down to London and also to pick up friends from Birmingham University, Shazia and her boyfriend were breaking their journey at Selly Oak to stay on campus with

Dexter's friend Pete. There was also going to be a party.

Dexter picked up three rucksacks and his placard.

'Just thought I'd let you know that I won't be over today.'

'Oh,' Brenda said.

Her brother had called her as she was mopping out the public toilets on A & E. Christ, they were fucking dreadful this morning! Looked as if an elephant had taken part in a dirty protest in there!

Brenda said, 'So you—'

'Things to do,' John said.

'Oh, well . . .' Brenda didn't ask him what these 'things' might be. Was it because she didn't want to know or did she think he wouldn't answer?

'But I'll be over tomorrow,' John continued.

He didn't say 'if that's OK with you' or anything like a normal person. But then maybe that was how they carried on in America. Brenda had never been. Years ago, some of the kids had tried to nag her into taking them to Disney World in Florida but she'd never had enough money to do that. Not like their old neighbour Deb, back in Woolwich. She'd taken all her six kids to Orlando and done the whole Disney thing in its entirety. But then she'd not paid her rent very often and had ended up getting evicted by the council.

'All right,' she said and then she ended the call. John didn't do small talk and so that was always the best thing to do.

Unwilling to stick her hands down a toilet that looked like the entrance to hell, Brenda leant on her mop. On the one hand she couldn't disbelieve that John was her brother. He'd been such a weird kid, always wandering about on his own, often talking to himself. Then there'd been the incident with the budgie.

64

They'd had Joey a long time, they'd got him just before Brenda had left home. He'd been quite old when he died, although Brenda couldn't remember how old. She'd not been around when it happened. Her mum had told her they'd buried him in the back garden. It had also been her mum who had told her about John digging the budgie up. He'd wanted to see what happened to Joey. But he hadn't done it just once. He'd dug the poor bleeder up several times, looking, as he said, at how fast he was disintegrating. Brenda's mum had smacked him and told him that you weren't supposed to dig dead things up because they were dirty and Jesus didn't like it. That had been creepy. But then what John had said then had, considering how he was now, been even stranger.

'Jesus,' John had said, 'is just a fairy story.'

And at the time, he'd never gone willingly to Sunday school. People changed and, probably under the influence of his American family he had. But all the religious stuff didn't sit well with Brenda. Her family had never been religious, in spite of the fact her mum had insisted they both go to Sunday school. That had been more about getting the kids out of the way so she could go round her mates.

Now that Jesus was in his life, if anything John seemed to be even stranger. Brenda looked into the toilet bowl again and decided that whatever was going on with her brother, that would wait no longer.

The couple, a man and a woman in their thirties, she thought, scampered off with towels under their arms as if they were about to go onto a beach in Spain. Of course, people came to the shrine for their own reasons, and for enjoyment was as good as any in these strange, secular days. But Sister Angela didn't like it. The Church wasn't respected as it had been in the past. People with no feeling for it just came and used it as they wished, like a sort of entertainment.

Sister Angela sat beside the ancient well. The young couple were now in one of the changing tents and she could hear them giggling. Men and women weren't supposed to share a tent but what was to be done? Looking down into the green watery depths of the bathing pool, the elderly nun pondered on what Mother Claire had asked her to do. She remembered the man who had come to the Sisters to die back in 1982. She didn't remember all of them, but she remembered him. An alcoholic, his liver was falling to pieces, making his skin look yellow. A lot of them ended up like that. Not that it was the man's skin that had so impressed itself upon her.

Sister Angela bent down slowly so that she could put her hands in the healing spring water. It felt icy cold in spite of the warmth of the day. It always did. For more years than she cared to recall, the nun had been dipping her arthritic fingers into the healing water, but to no avail. The arthritis never left them and the pain continued whatever she did. Was it perhaps because she didn't exhibit enough faith? And if that was the case, did God mean to humiliate her still further by making the act of writing impossible? Sister Guadalupe had written the email she had wanted sent to the woman who had requested information about the man. Mother Claire had said they were bound to help and so what else could have been done?

When she pulled them out of the water, Sister Angela's hands were still as stiff and unmoving as they had ever been, if colder. The young couple came out of their tent and the man said to the woman, 'So how's it feel to get your kit off in the thirteenth century?'

The woman just laughed and then began to lower herself into the icy water.

'Ow!'

Now the man laughed.

A lot of people remarked on the fact that the changing cubicles looked like tents from a mediaeval joust. Sometimes Sister Angela wondered whether a lot of people just came to see those. But she was allowing her mind to drift from the point, which was that a lady was going to ring her to ask about Reginald Saunders. And that wasn't good because she honestly did not know what she might say. She wasn't a priest and so she knew that what Mr Saunders had told her all those years ago wasn't under the seal of the confessional. But he had asked for her silence and she had promised it to him. His son, he had said, was never to know and, in this world of mass communication, if his son wasn't to know then no one was.

Colin Dean shrugged. He was a big man and so whenever he moved his massive shoulders the chair he was sitting on creaked. He'd thought it better he meet Lee Arnold at the latter's office rather than his place on account of the fact that his wife was at home, albeit still in bed.

'I'm not surprised,' Colin told Lee after he'd played him his recording of Susan from the previous evening. Then he laughed. 'Dirty bitch.'

Lee knew that Colin was no longer emotionally involved with Susan and so he spared him an apology for chatting up his wife. Colin was grateful.

'You done some good work there, son,' he said as he pulled a big wad of notes out of his wallet. 'You saw the bloody state of

67

her!' He shook his head. 'Was she on her own or with a mate?'

'She called the woman with her Lorraine,' Lee said as he took the man's cash.

'Oh, that'll be Lorraine Pritchard,' Colin said. 'That's another one.'

'Another what?'

'Woman off the rails,' he said. 'Left her husband and went mad she did. Mind you, the silly sod let her stay in the house. Mind you they've got kids . . .'

'Went mad?'

Did Colin know anything of any interest about Lorraine?

'Started having plastic surgery and that,' he said. 'Getting herself up like a dog's dinner to chase after fellas. Past it, like my old tart.'

'So she's got money this—'

'Nah! Up to her knickers in debt that one and not to Barclays Bank, if you know what I mean.'

'Oh, so . . .'

'Ain't up to me to tell no tales,' Colin said. 'Let's just put it this way, I've heard she's got a line of credit with some particularly unpleasant faces. Know what I mean?'

Lee knew that Lorraine Pritchard was in hock for money with someone.

'I do,' he said.

'So I'll say no more,' Colin said. 'Anyway, what you wanna know about that old slapper for? She come on to you an' all, did she?'

Lee smiled and then said, 'Might have done.'

Colin Dean laughed. 'Fuck me,' he said. 'The fucking cheek of these old boilers!'

* * *

68

The walls, built of red brick in this part of the system, were spattered with brownish lumps, many of which were connected to wispy, white-grey fibrous veils.

Henry saw the man looking at them and said, 'Wet wipes. People just fling them down the loo without a thought.'

The man said nothing. Luckily his money spoke for him. Henry, of all people, could understand his fascination. He'd been getting into places like this for almost a decade and the buzz never decreased. But would he feel that way if he was this chap? New and really rather unprepared for it all.

Encumbered, as was Henry, by a plastic coverall, tall waders, hard hat and the essential gas detector and mask you had to have down in the sewers unless you wanted to kill yourself, the man was making heavy weather of walking through the shit, piss and God knows what else that clung to every fine Victorian surface. Henry imagined he hadn't anticipated it being so hard.

The system had been built back in the nineteenth century by the peerless engineer Joseph Bazalgette and the fact it was still functioning at all was a miracle. Modern life and old sewers didn't go well together. Henry had told the man, 'People just use too much fat these days. Pouring it down sinks and into drains. It builds up, creating things the flushers, the people who clean the sewers, call fatbergs.'

But the man hadn't been interested in fatbergs or even in sewers. He had a very specific reason for wanting to go to this particular sewer, which was its connection to one of London's lost rivers, the Tyburn – or so he'd said. Incorporated into Bazalgette's sewer system during the 1860s and '70s, the Tyburn no longer existed except as part of this sewer, which started in Hampstead, wound down through London, underneath Regent's Park and came out into the Thames by Lambeth Bridge.

It was somewhere Henry had been before. Dan, who he'd met at uni, had been all about sewers and so he'd taken him on his first foray back in 2012. Smelly, at some times reeking, the sewers were fascinating but they didn't do it for Henry in the way they did it for Dan. Henry was more of an above-ground man – old asylums, ruined mansions, wrecked pubs. The world of the urban explorer was a broad church, thank God.

As usual it was very humid. Worms, snails and the inevitable rat or sixteen scuttled about in the darkness beyond the light provided by their headlamps.

Henry looked behind him and said to the man, 'Are you all right?'

He nodded. Now they were having to bend down as the sewer shortened, where even teenagers could easily run out of steam. The man was panting a bit, which did give Henry a twinge of anxiety. What the hell would happen if he died down here? He'd suggested they go up top twenty minutes ago, but the man had urged him to press on. In about ten minutes he'd suggest it again and, well, insist really. For someone so apparently enamoured with the idea of an ancient lost river, he didn't seem to have any sort of aim in mind . . .

They trudged on. Luckily the sewer began to get bigger now and the man said, 'Do you know where we are?'

Henry stopped, took off his helmet to shake some of the sweat from his hair and said, 'Underneath Regent's Park. Don't know where exactly but—'

Did he spontaneously lose his footing, or did something make him fall?

Henry would never know.

* * *

Lee was out meeting a current client and a potential new one. Mumtaz called the convent on the dot of two and, after a brief word with Sister Guadalupe, found herself talking to Sister Angela. The nun's voice was strong and sounded young.

'Hello?'

Mumtaz explained she'd been told that Sister Angela had agreed to speak to her about Reginald Saunders.

'Oh yes,' Sister Angela said. 'Although I don't know what I can tell you about him. He was already dying when he came to us.'

'I understand so,' Mumtaz said. 'Sister, I've been told that you nursed Mr Saunders.'

'Together with my Sisters . . .'

'But you are the only one sadly, who is still alive.'

'That is true.' There was a pause and then she said, 'He died from cirrhosis of the liver. He drank.'

Was she dismissing him as a sinful drinker? Sister Angela didn't sound nervous on the phone, but she did, if anything, seem a little too brisk and workmanlike.

'Do you know why he came to the convent for help?' Mumtaz asked.

'No. He had been sleeping rough around here for a while, though, and so I suppose he must have learnt that we care for the sick.'

'What happened?'

'Sister Winifred found him outside the house, if I remember correctly. She was old then and died I think only one or two years later.'

'Had he collapsed?'

There was a pause and then she said, 'He must have. I know that it took three of us to bring him inside. We couldn't carry him, but we did have to help him into the infirmary.

Three of us were registered nurses back then. Only I remain.'

'Do you remember how long Mr Saunders was with you?' Mumtaz asked.

'Not exactly. I could look it up. Dr Roberts attended him several times. It was clear that only palliative care was appropriate.'

'So he wasn't sent to hospital?'

'He wouldn't consent to go,' she said.

'So he was conscious . . .'

There was another, this time, long pause and then the nun said, 'Yes. He was.'

'To the end?'

'Almost.'

That was unusual. With cirrhosis of the liver, Reginald Saunders must have been in pain. Usually, if nothing else, the morphine needed to control it rendered the patient unconscious.

'Sister Angela, do you remember whether Mr Saunders talked about his family when you were nursing him?' Mumtaz asked.

'He was troubled,' she said. 'That I do know.'

'I've no doubt. He was very ill and—'

'He knew he was dying.'

'So yes, troubled is probably a mild way of putting it,' Mumtaz said. 'However, Sister, what I'm trying to get at is whether Mr Saunders told you anything about his family . . .'

'No.'

The word was clipped and sharp and Mumtaz didn't trust it.

'Are you sure?'

'Yes.'

'Because you see,' Mumtaz said. 'I am investigating what happened to Mr Saunders after he left his wife and children in 1976. I am working for his son and daughter . . .'

What made her say 'son' as well as daughter, Mumtaz didn't know. She was no more working for John than she was working for his late mother.

'His son?'

Her words were followed by a sharp intake of breath. The nun was clearly shocked.

'Yes. John.'

Nothing was said. Nothing. Just the nun breathing at the other end of the line. Faint wheezing.

Eventually Mumtaz said, 'I feel you know something about John, Sister. Can you tell me what it is?'

Lee got into his car and then sat for a bit. Another sodding matrimonial! The new client, a woman this time, worried her old man was playing away. She'd given him a photograph whilst extolling her husband's many virtues. Kind, muscly, *very* attractive to women, she'd said. Lee thought that either the man didn't photograph well or his wife had lost touch with reality. The last time he'd seen cauliflower ears like that was when he'd raided a bare-knuckle fight club when he'd worked for the Met.

His old Nokia rang. He looked at the screen and saw that it was Terry Gilbert, Lorraine Pritchard's uncle.

He answered. 'Hello, Tel.'

'Mate, I've got a lovely motor, might suit your missus down to the ground,' the owner of Tel's Wheels said. 'Just come in today. Lovely little Kia Picanto automatic.'

'Oh.'

Lee hadn't made a great deal of progress in finding out who Lorraine Pritchard was in hock to, in spite of seeing her in the flesh at that fucking awful nightclub. Was her uncle really a contact who could be useful to him?

He said, 'How much?'

'It's last year's model,' Terry said. 'In lovely condition. Low mileage.'

'Only one careful lady owner?'

He heard Terry laugh. The 'one careful lady owner' trope had been around for years under the heading 'things used car dealers say to do you over'.

Terry said, 'You wouldn't believe me if it was true, would you?'

'Probably not.'

'Well, look, mate, I want eight grand for it,' he said. 'I'll bung in a service. Won't hang about long at that price. What do you say? You wanna come over and have a look?'

'Mmm.'

'What?' Terry said. 'Mmm yes or Mmm no?'

'Eight grand's a bit rich for my blood, to be honest with you,' Lee said. 'You don't do finance . . .'

'Nah, too much agg all that.'

'Know what you mean,' Lee said. 'Credit scores and all that. You know how it is? No, not for me neither – just asking, like.'

A man with poor credit who baulked at the notion of paying eight grand for an almost new car in cash was probably skint. Not the sort of person a used car dealer would want to do business with, surely? It was a punt on Lee's part. What would Terry do? According to Jason Pritchard, Lorraine's uncle was always skint. But he had to be able to buy stock . . .

'Well, look why don't you just come along and have a look, anyway?' Terry said. 'Who knows, eh?'

'All right,' Lee said.

'Any time,' Terry replied. 'We don't close till seven. I ain't going nowhere, more's the bloody pity!'

* * *

It was hard for her.

'What I was told was said in confidence,' Sister Angela said. 'I don't know whether you understand anything about the Catholic Church, Mrs Hakim, but we have something called Confession . . .'

'Yes,' Mumtaz said. She'd come across this phenomenon before. When a supplicant said something to a priest under the seal of the confession, that information could be shared with no one.

Sister Angela confirmed this and then she said, 'However, what Mr Saunders told me was meant to be private and was said on his deathbed.'

'But it wasn't, strictly, a confession,' Mumtaz said. 'Sister, the family need the truth. I can't tell you why, as they are my clients, but it is important.'

There was a pause. Then the nun said, 'He had already told me he had a son and a daughter. I didn't know where they were, their ages or who their mother might be. Mr Saunders was an alcoholic, as you know, and he was dying. Sometimes he rambled, especially near the end.

'You must understand that I have no idea whether what he told me was true. After his death, when his family were discovered, I didn't meet them, but I understood that his wife and his daughter attended his funeral. There was no mention of a son. I will be honest, I persuaded myself he probably didn't exist and that may have been the case . . .'

'But?'

'But now it appears he does exist . . .' She paused and then she said, 'Mrs Hakim, can you tell me whether this person, this son, is er, is he American?'

'Yes.'

She took a deep breath. 'Mr Saunders told me he sold his son,' she said. 'To an American couple.'

This was not of course unexpected, but to hear it like this was still shocking. Mumtaz said, 'Did he say anything else?'

'No.'

'You don't know how—'

'He was dying, Mrs Hakim, he couldn't say very much.'

'I understand.'

'All I do know is that he did it so that he could have money for, as he put it, his own selfish purposes. I did not get the impression that the family were especially poor.'

'You don't know how he found these people?'

'No.'

When she got off the phone, Mumtaz made herself a cup of tea and then wrote down what she knew so far.

What appeared to be fact was that John Saunders was who he said he was. Albeit of an off-the-shelf variety, the DNA test he had performed for Brenda proved this. It was also a safe assumption to believe that it had been the Gustavssons who had bought him. Extremely pious Christians, Mumtaz wondered how they had squared this illegal action with their consciences. But then, as she knew to her cost, some people who claimed to be religious in public were something quite different in private. Like her late husband.

The only place Mumtaz could imagine someone like Reg Saunders meeting the Gustavssons was on board one of the liners on which he used to work. He had been dismissed for stealing by whatever line had employed him, so he must have met the couple prior to becoming unemployed and destitute. How had they contacted him? If they had?

She called Brenda. When she asked her which cruise line her father had worked for, she said, 'P&O, I think. He used to go from Tilbury. It was dead posh. He used to come home with loads of little individually wrapped chocolates. He boasted he got loads of tips, not that we saw of any that.'

'Do you know any of the people he worked with?' Mumtaz asked. 'Any names?'

She heard Brenda sigh.

'Not really,' she said. 'You know what East Enders are like, no one's ever called by their real name. And it was the seventies and so a lot of the nicknames people used were a bit dodgy.'

'Like?'

'Well, everyone knew someone called Chalky,' Brenda said.

'Ah.' Mumtaz could just remember when black people being called 'Chalky' was not uncommon. There'd been some white comedian on the telly who had a stock character called Chalky.

'I think me dad called all the black geezers he worked with "Chalky",' she said. 'He certainly had a couple of them on his ship.'

'He worked on one ship?'

'I think so. I don't know, really. He was such a pain in the arse I tried to pretend he was nothing to do with me.' Then she said, 'There was Mr Patel. He come to Mum's house a couple of times to see the old man. Dad said he was some high-ranking something back in India. So why he was working on the ships I don't know.'

'Maybe he was just high caste,' Mumtaz said. 'In the Hindu caste system not all those who are at the top are necessarily rich.'

'He lived up Manor Park,' Brenda said. Memories were coming to her now, albeit dim and distant ones. 'Dunno where. Not being funny, but there must be a lot of Mr Patels in Manor Park and he was Dad's age so he could be dead by

77

now. But honestly, I can't remember no one else. John's not coming over here today.'

'Yes,' Mumtaz said. 'The investigator assigned to shadow him said he'd not left his hotel this morning.'

'What's he doing in there?' Brenda asked.

SIX

There was a lot of talk in the media about everyone using cards and online banking all the time now. But this didn't apply to all Lee Arnold's clients. In fact, quite a sizeable number of people paid the agency in cash. This was particularly the case with a lot of Mumtaz's female Asian clients as well as with 'traditional' East End slightly dodgy blokes like Colin Dean. Despite being 'in banking', Colin was, at heart, an old-time gangster who preferred to pay for most things in cash.

And so, when Lee walked into his branch of NatWest Bank on East Ham High Street, he had a considerable number of fifty-pound notes on his hip. Unfortunately for him, there were a lot of shopkeepers and market traders ahead of him in the queue for the one solitary service counter. They all had plastic bags full of coins and so it was going to be a long wait.

There were of course machines to take money to be paid

in but, as usual, no bugger wanted to use them – which Lee could understand. If you could work out how to use them they usually fucked up or wouldn't give you a receipt or something. Anyway, most of the tradespeople in front of him were old and therefore deeply suspicious of something that didn't have a soul taking their money.

Lee took his phones out of his pocket and riffled through them for messages, missed calls etc. There were several messages from Mumtaz who was apparently going out to Manor Park regarding the John Saunders case. She didn't say why. There was only one voicemail message, which was from Jason Pritchard, chasing up any progress on his wife Lorraine. He'd have to let him know he'd seen her at The Starlight Club with Susan Dean. He wouldn't be either interested or surprised but, at the moment, Lee felt he didn't want to tell him any more. Lorraine's Uncle Terry was someone he was going to get to know better, he hoped, later on that day. As Jason himself had told Lee, Terry – like his niece – did look to be skint on paper. And yet they were both getting money from somewhere and although he'd only seen them together that once, Lee was finding it hard to shake the idea that they were maybe drinking from the same bowl – as it were.

White English people didn't really understand the idea of 'aunties' in Mumtaz's experience. Only the old could really grasp it, especially the notion that to be an auntie one didn't necessarily have to have either children of one's own or even nephews or nieces. Basically, aunties were a Greek chorus. Most of them were older ladies brought up or connected to either villages or even cities – which were just collections of villages – in India, Pakistan or Bangladesh. Aunties were the guardians of local stories, myths and downright untruths as well as, more worryingly, often being the arbiters of good behaviour and religious observance – especially amongst women and girls. Aunties arranged marriages, attended the births of children and sometimes even prepared the dead for burial or cremation. Most of the time aunties were there to help the younger folk, but sometimes, some aunties maybe of a jealous turn of mind, would set out to discredit a young person and then that, usually girl, was in big trouble.

Mumtaz had, she knew, been lucky with her aunties. And although some of them had been instrumental in getting her together with her late husband, all of them had been horrified that he had turned out to be such a cruel and reckless person. In all she had eight real aunties – two on her mother's side and six on her father's. But there was a whole cohort of other older women, once resident back in her grandparents' village in Bangladesh, who were also aunties. One was the younger sister of her maternal grandmother's best friend. In her seventies now, Miraya Acharya or 'Auntie Mir' as Mumtaz knew her, lived with her son and daughter-in-law in a rather ugly house on Clarence Road, Manor Park.

Although she rarely left the large sitting room she occupied in solitary state, save for her chihuahua dog, Pepe, Auntie Mir was someone who knew everyone and, more importantly, their business.

Auntie Mir's son Krishna was at home when Mumtaz called. Usually people didn't just turn up to see Auntie Mir unannounced but Mumtaz knew that she was the exception because of her job. In Auntie Mir's mind, private investigation was as important as 'police work' and that was sacrosanct. It was also, she hoped, a wonderful source of future gossip.

81

The principle motif of Auntie Mir's sitting room was religious statuary. Not for the first time, Mumtaz marvelled at how alike, in their love of images, the Catholics and the Hindus were. Auntie was particularly fond of the God Shiva who, to Mumtaz's way of thinking, was really very alarming.

When she saw her, Auntie Mir said, 'Oh, Mumtaz! How lovely to see you!'

She spoke with a really posh British accent, which was even a little bit clipped. Auntie Mir was, as she never ceased telling people, a Brahmin, a very high caste Hindu.

Mumtaz kissed her auntie and then sat down at her feet like a good 'child'. Auntie Mir took in a deep breath and then yelled, 'Krishna! Tea and sweeties for Mumtaz!'

Then she clapped her hands to emphasise the request. Mumtaz knew that Krishna's wife, Sangita, a lawyer, merely tolerated Auntie Mir. A very modern and independent woman, Sangita had she been home, would have screamed blue murder at her husband had she heard his mother ordering him about. But she was at work.

A period of exchanging of family news happened next. This continued until Krishna arrived carrying a vast tray on which were placed a teapot, teacups and vast plates of traditional mithai sweets. Made from many ingredients including condensed milk, coconut, grated carrot and honey, the mithai came in so many colours and shapes, looking at them for too long made your eyes tired.

Mumtaz poured the tea while Auntie Mir prodded her to begin eating sweets immediately as she was 'too thin'. Mumtaz complied, although attempting to keep up with Auntie Mir in the sweet eating stakes was impossible. She was a machine.

Tea poured and two sweets eaten, Mumtaz said, 'Auntie,

dear, as I'm sure you have guessed, I have come to see you out of love but also out of a need. I have to solve a mystery.'

Auntie Mir's eyes widened, even though she couldn't talk because her mouth was full of mithai.

John Saunders left his hotel at 1.30 p.m. Harewood Row, the road his hotel was on, was right by the Tube station. But John didn't get on the Tube. Instead he walked down to the A501 and sauntered across to Marylebone High Street. Eventually, after dithering in the churchyard of the parish church of St Marylebone, he went into Daunt's Bookshop.

Rob Turner had only been working for the Arnold Agency for three months. Like Lee Arnold, an ex-copper, Rob hadn't been able to adjust to a new life in the Hertfordshire countryside when he'd retired and so had come back to both London and work. Although, admittedly the latter was only something he did when he wanted to. So far, this gig had been boring. Rob sent a text to Mumtaz to tell her John was on the move. This Saunders bloke must've slept in for bloody hours. Now in a bookshop he was nosing around in the non-fiction section when Rob caught up with him.

Not what anyone would have called a reader, Rob nevertheless found the bookshop itself really beautiful. At the back of the place was a big arched window, which was stunning. Saunders, however, seemed to be oblivious to anything except the books. Rob picked up a book by Martina Cole because she was one of his wife's favourite authors. But he only glanced at it. Saunders it seemed was looking at a load of stuff about the history of America.

The things men did! Suze, who Lorraine had finally put in a cab after she'd made a twat of herself with that bloke at the club, had called her to let her know what her husband Colin had done.

'That bloke last night,' she sobbed down the phone, 'he wasn't a policeman at all!'

'So what was he?' Lorraine asked. She had to go out and sort her own shit soon and so she was only paying Suze scant attention.

'A private detective,' Suze said. 'Colin sent him to catch me out! What am I gonna do?'

For a moment Suze didn't really understand, then she said, 'What, to sort of . . .'

'To make me chat him up,' Suze said.

Not that there'd been any 'make' about it.

'The bastard's been trying to catch me out for months,' she continued. 'Wants a fucking divorce, no strings attached. Not having no kids, I could lose the lot! Me house, the car, everything! Cunt!'

It would have been easy to be judgemental. Suze had been playing around with other men for over a year. But Lorraine was sympathetic. 'You gotta keep your nerve,' she said.

'What?'

'Tell your old man the bloke put his hands down your knickers.'

'He's got a recording!' Suze wailed.

Ah.

'There's me on there offering him a blow job!'

Lorraine had wondered, knowing Suze as she did, why the bloke had let her down at the last minute. Cruelly she wondered whether it had something to do with Suze's lack of muscle tone.

'So what's Colin say?' Lorraine asked.

'He wants a divorce! Says he's been watching me for yonks. Says he knew I was up to something. Lorr, he's saying he wants me out of the house!'

'He can't do that.'

'Yes, he can,' Suze said. 'I mean, I'm not like you, I don't have kids. And I've never worked. He says his brief has told him that he can prove it ain't my house at all.'

'Shit.'

'I mean, I know you got troubles of your own, but could I come round?'

'You can, but not now,' Lorraine said. 'I have to go out.'

'Oh.' She sounded crushed.

'You can pop round later,' Lorraine said. 'I've just got to do a bit of business.'

It wasn't as if she wanted to. She didn't. But if she didn't pay something today, then the interest was going to rack up something rotten.

'Tell you what,' Lorraine said. 'Why don't you come round this afternoon at about four? The kids'll be out and we can have a bottle of Prosecco.'

Suze sighed, obviously relieved. 'Thanks, Lorr,' she said, 'that'd be great. You're a lifesaver.'

'All right, babe.'

When she ended the call, Lorraine went upstairs and looked at her handbag collection. She didn't want to sell any of them, but she'd have to pick one . . .

'The thing you Muslims have to understand is that caste is a complicated issue,' Auntie Mir told Mumtaz. 'In very simple terms, Brahmins are at the top of the tree and Dalits at the bottom.'

'Dalits are untouchables?' Mumtaz asked.

'Yes, but we don't use that word any more, even if we think it. Now, in between these two high and low castes are firstly the Kshatriyas, the warrior and ruler class, then below them the Vaishyas who farm and they are merchants. Then come the labourers, the Shudras then the Dalits. We Brahmins are the priestly, intellectual class, you see.'

'Yes.' There were such divisions within Islam, in fact within every religion but, Mumtaz always felt, the Hindu system was the most famous.

'So this chap, Patel, you ask whether he can be a Brahmin? The answer is no,' Auntie Mir said. 'Patels are ambitious people but originally they were from the Shudra caste. An honest working caste, but lowly.'

'So he couldn't have been a Brahmin?'

'No, no, no, no, no! No, darling, I think this man lied. It's easy with white Europeans. I mean, what do they know? I could tell them I was a Mughal empress, they'd know no different. This man who was a friend of this Patel, he was white?'

'Yes.'

She shrugged. 'So there it is,' she said. 'Where did they meet this Patel and this other man?'

'They worked as stewards on a trans-Atlantic liner.'

'Hah! Well that confirms it! No one of high caste would do such a job!'

Auntie Mir was a terrible snob. But then, in spite of not having much more than the clothes she stood up in when she first came to the UK, she had been told by those around her that she was special for her whole life.

'And anyway, what do you want me to do, dear?' Auntie Mir asked Mumtaz.

When she said it, it sounded so lame.

'This Mr Patel . . .'

'The steward.'

'The steward, he lives or lived in Manor Park,' she said.

'And you think I know him?'

The only way forward was flattery and, as it happened, the truth.

'You know everyone, Auntie.'

The old woman smiled. As she patted her hair, all her many gold bangles jingled.

'As soon as I was told this man came from Manor Park, I thought of you,' Mumtaz said. 'Now he would be probably about sixty or seventy. I'm sorry I don't even have a first name but . . .'

'Patel, sixty, seventy . . .' Auntie Mir nodded. 'I will think on it and make some enquiries,' she said. 'So many bloody Patels so little time, isn't it?'

Lorraine got a cab, which Lee followed. From her home in Gidea Park she headed off towards Romford. The cab came to a halt outside a pawnshop, which Lorraine dived into carrying something in a plastic bag. When she came out the bag had gone. Then she got back into the cab and Lee followed her all the way to Langdon Hills. Same house as before.

Once Lorraine's cab had disappeared down the road, Lee turned his engine off and sat. He'd got up rather too close to Lorraine during his wooing of Suze Dean. As far as he could tell, Lorraine had been tipsy rather than drunk, like Suze. And the place had been heaving with bodies and howling with noise. Would or could Lorraine recognise him? It was probably unlikely but not impossible. Thinking about it made Lee sink down a little further behind his steering wheel.

He sat like that for about five minutes before he began to feel sleepy. Going out to that sodding club wasn't what he normally did and so he was tired. Lee opened the driver's side window, which was when he heard the screams. More like crying to start with, a woman's voice quickly escalated in volume until she was howling.

Lee sat up. It was coming from the house Lorraine had gone into. It sounded like someone was in pain. He waited a few seconds to see whether the noise abated. It didn't. Lee opened his door and got out of his car.

If someone, Lorraine or whoever, was in some sort of trouble in that house he had to help. Even if Lorraine recognised him, he just had to. If anything, the screams were louder now and, after locking his car, Lee began to move towards the house, breaking into a trot. He was halfway up the long garden path, when the front door flew open and he found himself looking into the eyes of a man probably in his early forties, who was red with rage. It took Lee a moment longer to see that a woman had barrelled out of the door and into the front garden.

The man, who had a squeaky voice, like famous Essex comedian Joe Pasquale, Lee thought, said, 'Can I help you, mate?'

Lee used an old technique.

'Sir, have you ever considered taking Jesus into your life?' he said.

The man, who was short, dark and stocky, looked at him with an expression of complete disdain on his face and said, 'Fuck off!'

Then he closed the door.

Lee watched as Lorraine Pritchard, blood up her arms by the look of it, ran down the road and disappeared into a copse of trees.

'I bloody can't stand Birmingham,' Dexter said.

They'd passed the Bullring Shopping Centre at least three times and yet still he wouldn't let Shazia drive. Although she hadn't been driving as long as her boyfriend, she knew, as did he, that she was the better driver. She was certainly more patient.

'Fuck it!'

She put a hand on his arm in lieu of asking him why he'd left the satnav behind. But then he knew he'd been a dick and didn't need her to tell him. Eventually, red-faced and frustrated, Dexter pulled into the car park of a drive-in McDonalds and slumped across the steering wheel.

'Where the fuck are we?' he said.

Shazia looked at the map. 'We need to get to the A38,' she said. 'We're not far.'

He looked up at her through a haze of wild blonde hair.

'I'll need a minute.'

'I can do it if you—'

'No!'

'I don't mind . . .'

'It's OK,' he said. 'Just . . . You know it's a strain . . .'

'Which is why I offered,' Shazia said.

'Like I'm not capable . . .'

'No!'

Now she was angry. He was being so 'blokey' about it. Her father had been the same. He had always done the driving leaving her mother and later Mumtaz – both perfectly capable drivers – fuming in silence. Well, that wasn't happening here. She said, 'I know you're perfectly capable of driving but you're also really tired now.'

'I'm not nervous or anything, you know!' he said.

Shazia couldn't help herself. 'Dex, don't be dick,' she said.

'Me!'

'Yeah. Look I know why you don't want me to drive,' she said. 'Just admit it.'

'Admit what?' Then Dexter suddenly realised. 'Oh God, not toxic masculinity again!'

'The driving thing is a typical example,' Shazia said. 'Cars are like, well . . .'

'If you say the word "penis" I will lose my shit!'

'Men always think that women can't drive! My father was like that and it's bollocks! It's one of the ways men continue to oppress women. If I don't pull you up on it . . .'

'Oh, the fucking world will come to an end!'

She said nothing. He'd been driving, badly, for over three hours and now he was exhausted and pissed off. It would make sense for her to take over now. But why had it turned into a row?

Eventually, for want of anything more constructive to do, Shazia said, 'Look. Do you fancy a Big Mac?'

He looked up at her. She could see he wanted to remain being angry, but he also really liked McDonald's. After sighing a couple of times, he said, 'Only if I can go large.'

Lee called his client while driving around to see if he could find Lorraine Pritchard. He couldn't. When her husband answered his phone he said, 'Lee, mate. How's tricks?'

Lee quickly told Jason what he'd witnessed and said, 'Whatever you may think about your missus, this bloke roughed her up good and proper. Personally, I'd have words with her.'

'Why?'

'Because this is assault,' Lee said. 'It's criminal. Whether she's borrowing money from the people in that house I don't know . . .'

'Find out who they are but don't interfere,' Jason said. 'I just need names and then I can sort it out from there. Truth to tell, I don't give a shit what happens to her. The kids are a bit different, but her I couldn't give a stuff.'

Lee sighed. Matrimonial work did his head in, but it was still his bread and butter, worst luck.

'I'm off to see Terry of Tel's Wheels tonight,' Lee said.

'Well, use your best spiel on him,' Jason replied. 'If Lorraine's seeing Tall Tel, then there has to be more to it than just a social call. None of her family could stand him and that includes Lorraine.'

Lee saw a figure emerge from the copse where he'd last spotted Lorraine. It was her and he felt relieved. But she was still crying and also, by the look of her, bleeding. In his copper's brain he wanted to call his old colleagues. But that wasn't his job and he knew that neither Jason nor his missus would thank him for it.

'You still there, mate?' Jason asked.

'Yeah. Yeah.' Then he said, 'I've just seen Lorraine. She's still with us. On her phone . . .'

'Spending my money on cabs . . .'

'I imagine so,' Lee said. 'I'll follow her.'

'All right.'

Lee ended the call. He was pretty certain that the bloke he'd seen throw Lorraine out of that house hadn't been the registered owner, Barzan Rajput.

SEVEN

To say or not to say? That was the question.

Suze had turned up at Lorraine's house at four-thirty to find her friend covered in cuts and bruises. Unusually Lorraine, who generally made a big fuss if she got so much as a broken nail, didn't say a thing about it. Returning from the kitchen with a bottle of Prosecco and two glasses, Lorraine said, 'So tell me all about it, babe.'

'All about . . .'

'Colin and his private detective,' Lorraine said. 'What did you think . . .'

'Oh! Oh yeah,' Suze said. 'Well, he's got me, ain't he? Now he's got proof I've been up for it . . .'

'Not proof you've done nothing,' Lorraine said.

'No, but . . .'

'To do you for adultery, he needs proof you done something!'

'I don't think he does, though. I think it's about intent or something . . .' Then unable to contain herself any longer she said, 'Lorr, darlin', what's happened to you?'

'Oh . . .'

She reached a hand out towards her, which Lorraine took.

'Oh, it's nothing . . .'

'Jason . . .'

'Oh no, it's not him,' she said. 'I . . . I met this fella, some time ago. He likes it a bit rough . . .'

'Well, there's rough and there's rough!'

Lorraine took her hand away. 'It's all right. Don't wanna talk about it.'

'Yeah, but—'

'I don't!'

The force she spoke with made Suze jump.

'Sorry. Sorry.'

They looked at each other and then Suze said, 'Well, if you do want to talk . . .'

Lorraine waved a hand. 'No,' she said. 'Like I say it's nothing and anyway I've finished with him now. It was just a fuck. Know what I mean?'

All his life Fred Harper had been fascinated by the underworld. As a kid back in Ilford he'd made tunnels in the back garden, which he'd then 'investigated' with his younger brothers. It had driven his parents round the bend. His mother, on finding one of his tunnels underneath her begonias had said, 'What you doing, you daft ha'porth? Trying to get to Australia?'

But Fred carried on tunnelling. And, when he failed all his 'O' Levels at school and his parents told him to go out and get a job, he made sure it was under the ground. Fred had been a

London 'flusher' for over forty years. Flushers were a small but extremely efficient band of men who cleaned out the sewers beneath the capital, checked for damage and, more latterly 'fatbergs'. He loved it.

Fred and his mates had been working in the West End all morning, when Norman, Fred's guv'nor had said they needed to do some work on a massive fatberg underneath Regent's Park. They'd been having a go at it for weeks. Shifting the bleeder was still going to take some time. It was late and hopefully, they'd be knocking off soon. Fred was looking forward to getting home to his small house in Wandsworth and the network of tunnels he had been constructing underneath his back garden for twenty years. In truth it had actually moved beyond his back garden now and into the road behind his house, but he didn't publicise that.

Norman was moaning as usual. He didn't have the feel for the job that Fred did and he was political.

'All this fucking fuss just for some fucking great orange twat!' Norman said as he shuffled along the tunnel, Fred and the latest addition to the team, young Dylan, in tow.

'Well, he is the President of America,' the boy said. 'I mean whatever we might think about him . . .'

'He's an arse'ole,' Norman said. 'And anyway, Dylan, thought you'd hate the bastard. I mean coming after your mate Obama . . .'

Dylan was mixed race – something Norman referred to a lot.

'Oh, I don't like Donald Trump,' Dylan said. 'But I mean, what if something did happen to him while he's over here? They'd probably invade or something.'

'Like to see 'em try!'

Fred, at the head of the trio remained silent. There was no

arguing with Norm when he had the bit between his teeth. Proper old leftie he was.

It was well known that in the tunnels you had to have eyes everywhere. Up above in case something or someone (a rat) was about to hit you on the head, to the sides in case the walls looked dodgy or some massive flush was on its way from a public bog and down below where you were putting your feet. Of course things happened. Sometimes a bit of brick fell down and smacked you on the shoulder or you banged your head against a fucking great lump of hardened trans-fat or you tripped. The latter was the most dangerous because to trip in a wet tunnel heaving with piss and shit, especially if you had your mouth open, meant a trip to the hospital. In forty years that had never happened to Fred. But there was always a first time for everything and this was his time. He was in the shit, literally, before he even registered he'd slipped, but then that was how it was. Other blokes had told him about their experiences over the years and suddenness was a regular feature.

What Fred hadn't been expecting, however, was that his fall would bring him face-to-face with a human corpse.

He picked her up in a taxi. She hadn't been expecting him or anyone else. Brenda had been booked to do a double shift, her usual wards, plus a deep clean on the breast unit, and so she was knackered.

'How did you know I'd be here?' she asked her brother as she got into the cab.

'Desmond told me,' he said. 'I rang him earlier.'

John rarely talked to Des and so she was glad at least some communication was happening.

John continued. 'I'd like to go down to the Woolwich Tunnel before we go back to your place, if that's OK.'

'Thought you wasn't seeing us today.' She shrugged. Then she said, 'S'pose so. What for?'

'I'd like to walk through it again. With you I feel it will bring closure to the experience.'

The experience! She hardly thought that what amounted to his kidnap and the subsequent grief it had caused all those years ago could be called an 'experience'. At the time it had been a fucking disaster. Their mother had blamed Brenda for what had happened for years.

But Brenda said yes to John's request. She hadn't been through the old foot tunnel for years and the walk would do her good. But once down in the, admittedly much cleaner than she remembered, tunnel, she began to regret her decision.

Before John had returned she recalled a conversation she'd had with Des's middle son who was interested in science fiction and the occult. This had been some years ago when the boy, who had been unemployed at the time, had spent most of his waking hours on weirdo conspiracy websites.

He'd brought up the subject of the Woolwich Foot Tunnel. He'd told her, 'Some people reckon it's a portal to a different dimension. When it was being renovated, some of the workmen said they actually lost time when they were down there. Like hours and that.'

The kid was a space cadet and so Brenda hadn't given it much thought. But now she was in the tunnel again it came back to her. When John had gone missing back in 1976 some people had come up with some pretty wacky ideas about what might have happened to him. At least two spirit mediums had gone down there to try and make contact. One had even stated, without any doubt at all, that John had travelled back in time to the nineteenth century. Daft bleeder!

Now, as they walked underneath the river towards South Woolwich, Brenda said, 'How does it feel being down here again after all this time?'

John didn't show much emotion anyway and so he just shrugged. It was like being with a fucking robot sometimes. Then he said, 'How do you feel?'

'Me? A bit creeped out to be honest,' she said.

'Creeped out about what?'

'Well, there's the fact that you disappeared for decades after coming down here . . .'

'But now that's been explained.'

'Yes, but . . . John, you do know there's stories about this place, don't you? About people coming down here and losing time.'

'What do you mean?'

'Well, coming up hours after they thought they would. Some sort of time machine thingy.'

He snorted. 'There's no such thing,' he said.

'How do you know? There's people who've been really shook up by this place.'

'I know,' he said, 'because I believe in the Lord Jesus.'

That again!

'All these silly theories are just forms of devil worship,' he said. 'Belief in fairies and ancient gods, Halloween, aliens, time travel, it's all on the same continuum. We're meant to believe in the one true God and his son who died for us, Jesus Christ. So when people don't do that they look for other false explanations, like this.'

'John, I don't think that people think this place explains why we're here or nothing,' Brenda said.

When she'd been a kid, Brenda could remember how the old tunnel dripped as water from the outside oozed in. She'd always been afraid that it was about to let the Thames flood in and, in truth, she still thought that was possible. Because, theoretically, it was.

Brenda sniffed. Place still smelt of piss too. What hadn't happened in the past was that you got passed by some hipster on a bike wearing a bright blue helmet and what looked like body armour. They both watched him speed in front of them and Brenda was tempted to call him a 'tosser'. But she stopped herself. John wasn't keen on abuse, probably because 'the Lord' didn't like it.

When they reached the lowest part of the tunnel, Brenda said, 'Tell me about your parents in America.'

'What about them?'

'What are they like?'

He said nothing so she tried again. 'What do they do? I mean I know they do charity work and—'

'That's what they do,' John said. 'They endow charitable foundations.'

'Who do—'

'Provide assistance to refugees in places like Iraq,' he said. 'They endow community projects all over the world. In one country it might be a community school, in another they pay for wells to be dug so people can access clean water.'

'Do all of these projects just do stuff for Christians?'

'No,' he said. 'Although we work through Christian organisations and, where Christians are persecuted, we help out.'

A woman walked past them in the opposite direction, looking miserably at a mobile phone that clearly wasn't getting any reception. It was warm at the lowest point of the tunnel and Brenda began to sweat.

'So, do you like, have a job with them?'

He stopped, turned and looked at her. 'I told you,' he said. 'I am extremely active within the projects. When I've finished reacquainting myself with you and your family I will go back to work.'

'But why now, John?' she asked. 'Why did you leave it so long to come and find us? Dad died years ago and you've known all along those people ain't your real family.'

'I know they love me,' he said. 'I didn't want to disturb them by coming here.'

'Didn't you miss us all them years ago when Dad took you?'

'Yes. But I trusted him, and he did the right thing.'

'Did he?'

'The Gustavssons have given me a brilliant life,' he said. 'I would never have become anything here. I think our father took me away for my own good. Don't you?'

'I don't know.'

'Well, look at me, Brenda, I have a great life and, more than anything else, my US parents brought me up in fear of the Lord and for that I am grateful. Money isn't everything, freedom in one's own mind is what is important.'

But Brenda, try as she might, couldn't see how being indoctrinated day and night into any kind of belief could be a good thing. And, what was more, she couldn't see how an old reprobate like their dad would do such a thing, unless there was also something in it for him.

Not knowing the Romford area well was a bit of a handicap. The bloke he'd seen throw Lorraine out into the street had been white and so it was unlikely, although not impossible, that he was a member of Mr Rajput's family. So was he a landlord?

Years ago, when he'd still been boozing, Lee had a short relationship with a woman who worked for Romford Social Services. Poor Alison had been a nice girl, but his drinking had been too much for her and so it hadn't lasted. But they'd kept in touch and she was now married to a bloke from Kent. She still worked for Social Services and sometimes she helped her old mate Lee out with issues that touched on the role of social work in the community. On the basis that social workers often knew a lot of the local landlords through their clients he rang her up. As usual she was drowning in an unreasonable caseload.

'Sorry, man,' Alison said. 'If I had balls I'd be up to 'em. Give me the name anyway, I'll see what I can do.'

'Barzan Rajput,' Lee said.

There was a pause, a strange silence that was not usually something that Alison did.

'Ali?'

He heard her take a deep breath and then she said, 'Really?'

'Yeah,' he said. 'Owns a house up Langdon Hills. Seems he rents it out. Why?'

She was in the office and so he understood she couldn't use actual names.

She lowered her voice. 'If it's the same man I know, he owns a load of property in Harold Wood. Multiple occupancy. I thought he was strictly downmarket. But Langdon Hills . . .'

'Out of his league?'

'Oh no,' she said. 'Lives in a converted farm in Bulphan. He's loaded but the property he usually buys to rent out has always been doer-upper. Not that he ever does any of them up . . .'

'So this might not be the same bloke?' Lee said.

'Possible. Let me ask around.'

And then she ended the call. Lee was knackered and wanted to finish up for the day but he still had Tel's Wheels to visit. He headed for 'downmarket' Harold Wood.

'ID?'

That was usually a bit of a problem when people had drowned. But this guy had clearly been an organised type. He had his driving licence and bank card in a ziplock bag. This was just as well, considering he was covered in piss and shit.

Sergeant Paul McCulloch was used to dead bodies. Like most parks in London, Regent's Park had its fair share of drug and alcohol deaths, suicides and even the occasional murder. But this underground event was a new one on the sergeant.

A Norman Jaques, leader of a team of sewer flushers, had made the call. Said he'd found a dead body in the sewer underneath the park. McCulloch and Constable Rich had met the flushers at the entrance to the sewer where the two of them had been obliged to put on boots, coveralls, masks and gas monitors. Right palaver, especially when it came to McCulloch's outfit, which only just fitted. At six foot five, he was one of the Met's tallest officers.

When they got down there a man called Fred handed him the ziplock bag and said, 'Found this floating between his arm and his body. Don't know whether it's his.'

'We'll see,' Paul said and put the bag into one of the very tight suit's pockets. A young lad, about the same age as McCulloch's own boy stood about looking distressed and a bit useless.

McCulloch took pity on him. 'You go up, lad,' he said. 'There's my Constable Borowski up there. You tell him what you saw.'

The kid didn't have to be asked twice. When he'd gone,

McCulloch said, 'So, assuming he's not one of you, any idea why he might have been down here?'

Fred and Norman looked at each other and then Fred said, 'It's rare we get someone just wandering into a sewer. But from his gear and the fact that he's wearing a monitor, I'd say he's probably – was probably, an urban explorer.'

Norman nodded. Then he said, 'They're mostly young blokes.'

Although the corpse was lying on its side, it seemed likely, with its brown hair and slim physique, that it was a young man.

'Sodding nuisance, they are,' Norman continued. 'Don't know what they're doing a lot of them. Although he's got a monitor on and so not clueless. No helmet, though. Coming down here and pratting about.'

'Why do they do it?'

'Dunno.'

But Fred said, 'Well it's interesting, innit? I mean, it's a bit smelly down here and that but I wouldn't do nothing else.'

'Yeah, but you're strange,' Norman said. Then he turned to McCulloch. 'I think it's something to do with being the first to get in somewhere you shouldn't. I have met a couple of 'em over the years. Never turned up dead before, though.'

'Do you know if they come down on their own?' McCulloch asked.

'Not usually.'

'Ain't safe,' Fred said.

'But it happens.'

'Oh yeah.'

McCulloch looked at the body on the bottom of the wet, slimy sewer. What a place to end up and what a way to go, drowning in shit. However, because of where the corpse was there were other considerations. He knew the flushers would understand, after all that was why they'd been down there at this particular point in time. That fatberg could be embarrassing if it, indirectly, blocked Trump's toilet.

'I'll have to let anti-Terror know,' McCulloch said.

Norman nodded. 'I guess you do,' he said. 'What with the president coming . . .'

'And staying in the park,' McCulloch said.

'Ambassador's residence, we know,' Fred put in.

McCulloch nodded. 'Whoever this man is we need to check him out thoroughly,' he said. 'Was he alone when he fell over and drowned? I mean that can happen . . .'

'Oh yeah, if you can't get up, you bang your head or something . . .'

McCulloch looked at the corpse's driving licence through the ziplock bag and murmured, 'Lives in Newham . . .'

Terry Gilbert was in the small shed that constituted his office when Lee turned up. It was a real old-fashioned set-up with Terry smoking at his desk, hunkered over an ancient handwritten ledger. There was a girlie calendar on the wall and the place smelt of smoke, engine oil and pizza. It was like being in a seventies theme park.

'Hello, mate,' Terry said when he saw Lee, and the two men shook hands. Now he was standing up, Lee could see that Terry was even wearing a sheepskin coat – the staple of the used car salesman circa 1975. 'Come to have a dekko at that Picanto?'

It was a nice-looking little car, very clean and, when Terry took him out for a test drive Lee had to agree with him that it ran well. When they got back to the office Terry asked Lee what he thought of the vehicle.

'Lovely little motor,' Lee said. 'But as I said on the phone, it's a bit rich for my blood. I mean, is there any movement on price at all?'

Terry took a sharp intake of breath. 'I can do her for seven, seven fifty but that's bottoms,' he said.

Lee nodded but he didn't commit himself. Eventually he said, 'Fact is, Tel, I've a bit of a cash flow problem at the minute. I'm selling a flat I own in Forest Gate and I'm waiting for the money to come through . . .'

'Oh.' Terry shook his head. 'I'm not being racist, but I bet that's Asians you're waiting on money from.'

Lee hated conversations that proceeded along the 'I'm not racist but' channel, but he just nodded. Terry could make of that what he would. It was a complete fabrication, anyway.

Terry said, 'I know it's a bit old school, but we're mainly cash and bankers' drafts here. I'm not keen on credit cards and I know that's probably cutting me nose off to spite me face . . .'

'I don't have a credit card,' Lee said. 'Until this flat sale goes through, I don't have much. Mind you, once that's done and dusted I'll be flush.'

'Mmm.'

Lee offered Terry a fag, which he took and they both lit up.

'Tell you the truth, I've been down on me luck for a while,' Lee said. 'Divorce. The lady I'm getting the car for ain't strictly me wife, not yet. Got fleeced by me ex.'

Terry shook his head.

'Lost me house and everything,' Lee continued. 'Only just back on me feet again, to be honest. Lucky to have my new missus in tow, which is why I wanted to buy her a motor. She's been so good to me and she could really do with a nice set of wheels to make her life easier.'

This time Terry nodded. Then he said, 'Well, look. You strike me as a nice geezer and I hear you about your divorce. Never been through it meself, but one of my boys has and he got twatted, I can tell you. It's all stacked against the men these days, everything.'

'I know it's—'

'So look, I'd like to help you and so . . .' He shook his head again as if trying to dislodge something. 'I know some people,' he said. 'I mean the interest's high and that, but if you just want cash for a short time . . .'

'Well . . .'

'You can say no. I mean it's kosher. I'll be honest, I've used them myself when things have been a bit moody. Means you can have the car for your lovely missus now.'

Lee had to suppress his excitement. He said, 'Well, I s'pose . . .'

Mumtaz was getting back to basics. So far she knew that the man claiming to be John Saunders was the same person as the Gustavssons' son. This meant he was very rich. He was also apparently very religious too. He and Brenda had submitted to home DNA tests which had proved positive. However, that could be a problem as not all such tests were reliable. Although Brenda said she wanted to know whether this man was her brother *for certain*, she was already pretty sure that he was. The thing she was interested in was why he was in London now. Why come home after all these years? With his money and connections he had to have been able to find Brenda for years.

Mumtaz had found John a very rigid and cold man. The way he was made her wonder whether he might have a form of autism. When Brenda had described John as a child, he had sounded very like a boy Mumtaz had been to school with who was diagnosed with Asperger's syndrome. This could explain why he had turned up when he did, because it made sense to him – if not to everyone else.

In a way Mumtaz felt a bit of a fraud taking Brenda's money. She'd made some enquiries but those had so far been simple. And while she could understand why Brenda didn't want some random stranger joining her family, she couldn't imagine why John would wish to harm them. Maybe he was simply just trying to convert them to Born Again Christianity?

Perhaps Brenda was motivated, albeit unconsciously, by guilt? After all, while she didn't exactly 'lose' her younger brother, she was there when their father took the boy. And whenever someone 'came back from the dead' there were always those who retained their scepticism.

Reg Saunders had sold his son. Did John know that? Did Brenda? Either his first motive in doing this had been to give the boy a better life or it had been to get more money for himself. He'd been an alcoholic and so it was possible he had simply obtained that money to feed his addiction. But then again maybe there had been a deeper reason. Maybe he'd been in debt to the sort of people who would break your legs if you didn't pay them back?

If it was the latter, then Reg had gone to some elaborate pains to do that.

The office phone rang and Mumtaz picked it up. It was Lee and he sounded happy. When she asked him how his case was progressing, he just said, 'Bingo.'

EIGHT

Dexter's mate Pete shared a house with four other students. Less than a mile from the university campus, they lived in a dingy red-brick house, which had a small, untidy back garden. On a street that seemed to house hundreds of other students it was messy, noisy and smelt of garlic and smoked paprika. While nowhere near being some sort of tidy freak, Shazia recognised it was too much for her and so she went outside to watch a group of Pete's mates build a bonfire.

The plan was to cook baked potatoes underneath the fire while holding shovels over it containing things like peppers and courgettes. Pete's house was totally vegan and so Shazia would have to go without her beloved chicken. Booze, however, was plentiful, and she had started drinking Bud as soon as they'd arrived. Later, Pete had told them, they were going to burn an effigy of Donald Trump that some art student girls had made.

So far, most of Pete's mates were white. One black girl had rocked up earlier with some vegan sausage rolls and then left and there was a very severe-looking Asian boy rolling joints in the kitchen. But Shazia felt out of place. The reality was she was looking forward to seeing Mumtaz. It would have suited her down to the ground if they'd just driven home to London. But Pete was Dex's best mate and so they'd had to stop in Birmingham.

Were she honest with herself, Shazia was starting to have misgivings about the demo in London. Who knew what would happen and if she did get arrested by the police, what then? Demonstrating against Trump and his policies against Muslims particularly was important but if it messed up her plans, what then? She needed to discuss it with Mumtaz. And although she might not know what to do either, at least as a fellow Muslim she would understand how conflicted the whole issue was.

It was close to midnight when Vi Collins rolled up at Lee Arnold's door. Armed with a bottle of Diet Pepsi for him and a nice rose for herself, she made no bones about why she was there.

'I've been feeling horny all day,' she said as she stepped across the threshold.

At nearly sixty, Detective Inspector Violet Collins was tall, slim and fond of wearing little tailored suits with shoulder pads. Dark like her Jewish mother, she was a good-looking woman, if heavily lined by decades of smoking. She was also what she liked to call Lee's 'fuck buddy'. In other words, they had no-strings sex as and when they wanted. This had started years before when he'd been in the Job too and had only ceased during the short time he'd been with Mumtaz.

When she walked into Lee's living room, his mynah bird Chronus, who she'd given to him when he was getting off booze and drugs, winked at her.

'Hello, you scruffy old bugger!' she said as she affectionately stroked the bird's head.

Then she went to bed with Lee.

After sex, when they were both lying naked on his bed, she told him about her day.

'Bloody paperwork,' she said. 'Bored shitless until early evening.'

'What happened?'

She lit a fag. 'Got a call from Counter Terrorism.'

Lee sat up and drank some water. 'Should you be telling me about it?'

'Probably not.' Then she continued. 'Some bloke from Canning Town's been found down a sewer underneath Regent's Park. Dead. Drowned in shit, apparently – after a blow to the head.'

'Christ! What was he doing in a sewer?'

'What you call an urban explorer,' Vi said. 'They go into places they shouldn't and then take pictures they put on Instagram or something. When this officer gave me his name it rang a bell.'

'What for?'

'Got in a fight up at the old hospital on Samson Street,' she said. 'Just before they demolished the place he got in and had an altercation with a security guard. Give the poor git a broken nose. Posh boy, you know. Lives in one of them new flats overlooking the flyover. All vegan and yogurt knitting.'

Lee laughed. In recent years a lot of middle-class people had moved into the London Borough of Newham, bringing with them some distinctly un-East End habits and a lot of money.

'Anyway, I had to go and tell his flatmate, prepare him to identify the body.'

'So why were Counter Terrorism involved?'

'Because Trump's due to stay at the US Ambassador's residence in London, which is in Regent's Park. Winfield House. Course the plods up there have been checking under, around, above the fucking place for weeks. Then suddenly chummy turns up in the sewers. Team of flushers, sent down to clear the place for Trump's bowel movements found him.'

'Shit.'

Vi laughed. 'Exactly,' she said.

'Was he on his own?' Lee asked.

'Well that's the sixty-four-million-dollar question, isn't it?' Vi said. 'He was found dead on his own. Either someone hit him or he had an accident. But whether someone else had been down there with him or is still down there isn't yet known. I imagine Counter Terrorism'll give the whole system a good going over now. And talking of goings over . . .'

'What?'

'You and Mumtaz . . .'

'That's still over since last time you asked,' Lee said.

She sighed. 'Well it shouldn't be, kiddo. You know that, don't you?'

'Vi!'

'I can see it in your eyes,' she said. 'The sadness. Do something about it. I'll always fuck you as you know, but she's special. Don't let it end like this.'

Brenda couldn't sleep and so she got up and went downstairs to make herself a cup of tea. Des was snoring his head off and, while she was used to it now, it was not helping on this occasion. His kids always seemed to want to talk to him on his own whenever they were about and they wore him out. Des's first wife had died before Brenda had met him and, although his lot had taken to her right away, they still felt there were some things they only wanted to share with their dad – which was natural.

Earlier she'd made dinner for the usual cast of thousands and so by rights she should be tired, but she wasn't. Haunted by that strange little trip she'd made with John through the foot tunnel, whenever she closed her eyes she could see it again. Was there anything she could have done to stop what had happened there back in 1976? Aside from seeing her dad take John away there wasn't. But she'd been facing in the wrong direction. She'd missed them. But what else had she missed?

Reg had left her mum by the time he took John and so the family didn't see him very often. She'd bumped into him a few times on Rathbone Market but he'd always been drunk and she'd tried to avoid him in case he asked her for money. Then he'd disappeared. No one had ever even suggested that Reg had taken John. When the police had asked her mum whether that was a possibility back in '76 she'd laughed. The boy had irritated Reg, and anyway, he couldn't look after himself much less a kid.

Looking back, in some ways, John had been very like Reg. The way he just wandered off sometimes, talking to himself . . . Brenda had always put the way Reg had been down to the drink, but maybe there'd been more to it than that? Her mum had reckoned that her dad had always been a bit 'barmy', as she'd put it. And Brenda's memories of her father's family were of a group of people who she had always felt were cold but at the same time fussy. Nanny Saunders had had a thing about things going in specific drawers and cupboards. If something was put away wrongly she lost the plot.

111

But none of this solved the mystery of why John had reappeared now. He'd travelled on a US passport and Brenda wondered how he'd got that. He'd never had a UK passport as far as she knew, although she supposed Reg must have got him one before he left the country. His 'rich' parents in the States must have organised his US one. Money, as usual talked, and she wondered who they'd had to pay off in order to make their 'son' American.

All of this made Brenda feel bad. John was and remained an oddball. The fact that he suddenly wanted to see his blood relatives wasn't suspicious. That he creeped her out wasn't anything new, she'd always felt awkward around him. Then again, when he'd been a kid, especially when Brenda had still been at home, she'd always know when John was concealing something. Now she couldn't shake that feeling, no matter how hard she tried.

Alcohol is said to loosen the tongue. Shazia knew this for a fact because her father had always talked and talked and wept and screamed when he'd been drunk. Now she was well on her own way to intoxication, talking to a girl called Rabia.

The two young women had met when Rabia had come to sit with Shazia round the bonfire in the garden. An art student, like Pete, Rabia came from a very liberal family who lived in West London. And although Shazia hadn't wanted to 'over share' about her own situation, she'd found herself, under the influence of Budweiser, doing just that.

'My dad gambled,' she'd told Rabia as the two of them snuggled up close to keep warm. 'He borrowed money from these gangsters and still owed them money when he died. My stepmother is still paying them back.'

'What gangsters?' Rabia asked. 'Like on council estates?'

'No. These people, the Sheikhs, they're like, organised crime, you know? Not like kids on bikes selling wraps of coke on street corners.'

'Oh. Can't your stepmother report them to the police or something?'

Mumtaz was currently at peace with the Sheikh family. To some extent they had lost part of their hold over her when she confessed to Shazia that she'd allowed her father to die when Naz Sheikh had stabbed him. Mumtaz had watched her abusive husband bleed out in the grass on Wanstead Flats. Also being close to her boss Lee Arnold protected her – although Shazia understood that Mumtaz and Lee were 'on a break' at the present time.

Shazia said, 'It's complicated.' Which it was.

She looked back towards the house and saw that Dex and Pete were dancing in the kitchen. They were arse'oled. Dex had been drinking since the moment they arrived and would have the most monumental hangover in the morning. So would she if she didn't stop boozing. Shazia put her latest bottle of Bud down on the ground. That was quite enough of that. Someone had to drive in the morning and that was not going to be Dex.

They could stay another day of course, if they wanted to, but Shazia was keen to get back to her amma. Mumtaz was worried about her going on the anti-Trump march and, since her own misgivings had surfaced earlier, Shazia was no longer as desperate to go as she had been. It made her feel bad and she desperately wanted to talk it over with someone other than Dex.

Rabia's phone beeped to signal she had a message. She took it out of her pocket, read the screen and then said, 'Oh my God!'

'What is it?' Shazia asked.

'My dad reckons that someone's already been found trying to get to Trump!'

'But he hasn't even arrived.'

'No, but . . .' She read a second message. Rabia's father was a barrister who worked out of a very prestigious set of chambers in the City. 'Oh, just some guy found dead in the sewer underneath Regent's Park,' Rabia said.

'So?'

'It's where Trump is staying,' Rabia said. 'The American ambassador lives in some mansion in Regent's Park. My dad doesn't want me to go to the demo, but I'm going.'

'Me too,' Shazia said.

NINE

Henry Dubray had been a minimalist sort of a man. He'd bought his flat in Canning Town outright back in 2017 and, according to his flatmate, Boris Jacobson, he'd not been into clothes or going out or accumulating stuff.

'He worked for a start-up based around an app designed for flat-sharers.'

Vi Collins didn't understand much of what Boris had just said but she had no doubt the officer in the flat with her did. Counter Terrorism Command (CTC) had swept in as soon as Henry Dubray's address had been confirmed. They'd taken away all his computers, phones and personal effects leaving his flatmate in a space that was so empty it echoed.

Chief Inspector West, whose actual role within the CTC he hadn't specified said, 'How did you know him?'

If anything, West's voice was posher than Boris's – which was a feat in Vi's opinion.

'We met at Durham,' Boris said. 'We both read English, both ended up in tech.'

'What do you do?'

'I'm a software engineer for Google.'

'Nice.'

West was probably about forty-five, dark, tall and to Vi's way of thinking as fit as fuck. But he was also CTC, which was halfway towards being a Spook in her eyes. And she had fifteen years on him.

West, who had been wandering around the open-plan flat, sat down opposite Boris.

'Tell me about urban exploration,' he said.

'Don't do it myself,' Boris said. 'I ride my bike but that's as physical as it gets. Henry was the outdoorsy one. He got into climbing at uni. Used to go up to the Lake District, walking, climbing, snowboarding. I know he always liked old, hidden places and I did go on one of his urban exploring gigs back when we first came to London.'

'Which was?'

'2014. We lived over in Walthamstow at first. Henry got in with some guys who got into an old psychiatric hospital and I went with them. They were really serious about it and did a lot of photography, taking mood shots and pictures of smashed up toilets and sluice rooms. It wasn't for me, but Henry loved it.'

'Did Henry stay with that group in Walthamstow?'

'No. He did his own thing,' Boris said. 'You'll see from his laptop that he uploaded thousands of pics to Instagram. A lot of people followed him.'

'Did any of them get in touch?'

'Yeah. It's a big interest. People'd ask him sometimes to take them places.'

'And did he?'

'Sometimes. If he liked the idea himself.'

'Did he say anything about where he was going yesterday?'

'No,' Boris said. 'I left before him.'

'And when he didn't return here last night?'

Boris shrugged. 'Sometimes one or other of us spends the night elsewhere. We're not joined at the hip.'

West nodded, then he said, 'Girlfriends?'

'Not at the moment,' Boris said.

'Neither of you?'

'I'm just enjoying being single,' Boris said. 'Google's a very social place to work, I don't want any ties. Henry? Well, he was having a thing with a girl from here, actually. Somewhere on the council estate.'

'Do you know her name?'

'No. I saw her once, she was mixed race. Pretty, seemed nice.'

'Meaning?'

'Bit of a headcase from what Henry said. Really possessive, checked his phone. He couldn't bear it. They split up recently. Two weeks ago, maybe . . . He wasn't still with her when he, you know, he . . .'

The young man lowered his head. Vi was inclined to judge blokes like Boris and Henry harshly because they were posh and were incomers to what had once been a solidly working-class area. But the poor kid had just lost his mate and so of course he was upset.

'Do you know whether this girlfriend ever went with him on his urban exploration trips?' West asked.

'No. He told me she didn't like that sort of thing.'

'What about politics?'

West was firing questions rather than asking them. But then Vi could understand that. Counter Terrorism had to move fast, especially when the threat was to someone as high profile as Trump. Christ, what a circus! Millions of pounds spent protecting some bloke who talked about grabbing 'pussy'.

'Mine or Henry's?'

'Both.'

Boris's face was now red, and he kept licking his lips as if his mouth was dry.

'I dunno,' he said. 'Broadly left wing, I suppose. I don't belong to any party as such and neither did Henry, as far as I know. I know he was in favour of more green initiatives like renewables, but that was about it.'

'Do you know what he thought about President Trump?'

'I think he laughed at him, mostly,' he said. 'I mean he's a bit ridiculous, right?'

West didn't say anything.

If these 'loan providers' were so 'kosher' then why were they meeting them in a scroggy cafe like Pat and Ed's on Romford Market?

Terry, who'd gone up to the counter, returned with two big mugs of tea and said, 'Egg sandwich is coming.'

'What you having?' Lee asked.

'Beans on toast. Gotta watch me cholesterol, apparently.' Terry sat down. 'Now the bloke we're meeting is Maltese but he's all right. He's got businesses all over the shop. He's helped me out a few times.'

Terry hadn't said where this bloke lived. If it was the bloke from Langdon Hills, then would he recognise Lee? They'd only clapped eyes on each other for a second or two but Lee was pretty sure he'd recognise him.

Lee supped his tea, which was dense and dark and, once he'd loaded a pile of sugar into it, just how he liked it.

'He's called Steve,' Terry continued. 'I won't give you his surname in case you decide against it.'

This was getting less and less 'kosher' by the second. But Lee just smiled. Terry said, 'Course, I hope it works out for you. I'd love you to have that little Picanto. Not often you see something like that in such good nick.'

Typical car dealer spiel. But what was in it for him, Lee wondered? And if, as he speculated, Terry had got his niece involved with this man, how much did he know about whether she could afford the interest?

Their food had just arrived when a short, wide, dark-haired man entered the cafe. Lee recognised him immediately.

Aunties could appear somewhat unmoving, a little like some of the Hindu goddesses some aunties worshipped. But that was just an illusion. Aunties were always deep thinkers and, although they appeared to move for very little aside for sweets and tea, they got things done.

'Mumtaz, darling,' Auntie Mir's honeyed voice poured down the phone. 'How are you this morning, my dear?'

'Oh, I'm fine, thank you,' Mumtaz said. 'Shazia is coming home today to stay for a few days.'

'Oh, how nice! And how is she getting on at Manchester, isn't it?'

'Very well.'

It was possible that Auntie Mir had some information about Mr Patel the ship steward who had worked with Reg

Saunders. But family news had to be attended to first.

'And will she visit your parents while she is home?' Auntie Mir asked.

She wasn't planning on doing so and Mumtaz wasn't about to force her, but she said, 'I expect she will, yes.'

'She's a good girl,' Auntie Mir said and then she changed the subject. 'Now, Mumtaz dear, I have been making some enquires about this Patel fellow of yours who worked on cruise ships.'

'Oh, Auntie, thank you so much!'

It was important to be effusively grateful. Most aunties worth their salt appreciated that, even though they would never admit it.

'Yes, well, Mumtaz, my dear, what else is an old woman like me for if it's not to help the young, eh?'

'Yes, but Auntie you—'

'Anyway,' Auntie cut in. 'This Patel I have found out about is the father of the wife of the chap who runs the off licence on Little Ilford Lane. I don't go to such places myself but Mrs Bhaskar who lives at number thirty-five has a shameless daughter who has a lot of "Prosecco O'Clock" signs in her kitchen. I wouldn't put up with it myself, but what can you say? The point is that this Patel is a man of seventy who used to work on cruise liners as a steward. His given name is Akaash and he lives with his daughter and the off-licence man in the flat above the shop. That's *Vape and Booze* on Little Ilford Lane. Although they also sell some groceries for the sake of appearance. You must go to see him at two o'clock this afternoon. Mrs Bhaskar's daughter says he has diabetes so don't take anything sweet.'

This was typical of a determined Auntie on a mission. Not only finding a possible candidate for investigation but making an appointment for Mumtaz to see him too. If he turned out to be

120

the wrong person, however, that wouldn't be Auntie Mir's fault and Mumtaz would have the cringeworthy job of apologising to her for something over which she had no control.

But she sucked it up. 'Thank you so much, Auntie,' she said. 'You are a miracle worker.'

'Ah, not miracles my dear child,' the old woman said, 'contacts and determination.' Then in a moment of uncharacteristic black humour she added, 'And also of course, at my age, no one is going to say no to me.'

Then she cut the connection. John Saunders was with his sister today. Brenda, her husband, some of their children and John were all going on a boat trip from Tower Bridge to Westminster Bridge. The trip which John claimed he'd done before as a child included lunch and drinks. Having met John once, Mumtaz was inclined to wonder whether he'd enjoy something like that. He didn't drink alcohol and didn't strike Mumtaz as the type of person who enjoyed being around a load of kids. Maybe he'd amuse himself looking at the city's many churches . . .

Were he in fact Maltese, 'Steve' had no sort of accent – apart from Estuary. As soon as he'd seen Lee and shaken his hand, Steve had furrowed his brow and said, 'Have we met somewhere? I feel I've seen your face . . .'

'Not that I know of,' Lee said. 'Spend much time in Forest Gate, do you?'

'That where you come from?'

'Yeah.'

'Not often over that way, to be honest,' Steve said.

Lee was tempted to ask Steve where he came from, but then he knew the answer to that already. Steve, on second viewing, looked much less menacing.

'So, Tel here tells me you want to borrow some dosh,' Steve said.

Terry and Lee's food arrived then. As the waitress put the plates down in front of them, Steve said, 'Sausage sandwich please, darlin', and a large cuppa.'

The waitress smiled and said she'd get onto it right away.

'To buy a motor . . .'

'That lovely little Fiat I've got . . .'

'Yeah, Tel. Shut up will you, mate,' Steve said. 'The man's talking.'

Lee watched Terry's face burn with embarrassment.

'I've got a bit of a cash flow problem,' Lee said. He pushed a piece of paper across the table towards the man. His cousin Frank, a barrister's clerk, did a really good fake solicitor's letter. 'This property I'm selling—'

Steve pushed the letter back. 'Don't wanna know your circumstances, mate,' he said. 'How you pay me back is up to you. In the meantime, you pay me my interest and we'll all get along fine.'

'I need eight grand,' Lee said.

Steve nodded. 'We can do that.'

'When?'

'Whenever you want. Whaddaya do for a living?'

In situations when he had to be needy but working, Lee always resorted to the same profession.

'Sales.'

Steve shrugged. He'd heard that answer before. 'All you have to do is sign an agreement.'

He took a crumpled piece of paper out of his jacket pocket. It was standard loan shark fare where the 'client' gave all his or her details and the lender almost none.

'What term did you have in mind?' Steve asked.

'Six months,' Lee said.

'We can do that.'

'What interest rate do you charge?'

Steve's tea and sandwich arrived. He took a mouthful of sausage, which he spoke through.

'I'd have to work that out,' he said. 'Depends on a lot of factors, whether you own your own home, employment and that.'

Bullshit, but Lee played along.

'Course. When could I have the money?'

'Whenever you like,' Steve said.

'Your missus could have that motor today,' Terry put in.

What was in it for him? Lee had heard a lot of stories about how some people had been lured into the clutches of loan sharks by existing clients. Sometimes they got 'paid' by the lenders for this. Sometimes they reduced their interest rate by a couple of percentage points. Had Terry maybe lured Lorraine in like this?

Lee picked up the 'agreement'. 'I'll have to have a think about it,' he said.

Steve snatched the document back, his face now dark with annoyance. 'Well you won't need this,' he said. 'Let Terry know what you've decided and we'll talk again. I thought you needed this money now. I don't waste my time meeting people who ain't serious about doing business.'

Quick to anger, Steve was quite a piece of work. But Lee knew that, strictly, his business wasn't breaking the law even if what he'd seen this man do to Lorraine, had been.

'And I can't hold onto a lovely little motor like that forever,' Terry said. 'I mean, mate, you know I wouldn't give you a bum steer, this is a good offer, I'd take it if I was you.'

Coming on all chummy as he felt his commission or whatever he thought it was, slip through his fingers.

Lee got to his feet. 'I'll call you Monday,' he said. 'If the motor goes, it goes.'

'Dunno when I'll get something that tasty again,' Terry said.

Lee threw a ten-pound note down on the table to cover his food and drink. Then he said to Terry, 'Catch you Monday.'

Steve put a very muscular hand on Lee's arm. He said, 'My offer might not be on the table come Monday, pal.'

'I'll—'

'Interest rates can go up as well as down . . .'

Lee pulled the man's hand off his arm.

'One way or another,' he said, 'I'll get it sorted – pal.'

The kids and grandkids were demolishing the buffet down below with Des. John alone was up on deck. Was he trying to reacquaint himself with his city? Or was he just up there thinking about nothing? Brenda decided to join him.

Leaning on the balustrade beside him she said, 'What you thinking?'

He shrugged.

'It must be strange for you coming back here after all these years,' she said.

She didn't expect him to answer, but he did.

'I came to England in the nineties,' he said. 'We went to Cambridge. My dad had business there.'

'At the university?'

'Our foundation provides bursaries for poor theology students.'

Brenda didn't know exactly what a bursary was, but imagined it was some money to help with fees. None of her kids had gone to university. Not because they weren't bright, quite the opposite. They'd all realised very early on that they had to work as soon as they could to bring money in.

Looking at John in profile, Brenda felt she did recognise his face. A bit. 'Why didn't you come and see me back then?' she asked. 'When you went to Cambridge?'

'Because I didn't come to England for that reason at that time.'

'You could've made a detour.'

'I could've but I didn't,' he said.

'John, why are you here now?' She'd asked him before but it was a question that just wouldn't go away. Hence her involvement with the Arnold Agency. 'I'm asking why now,' she continued. 'I mean you – forgive me – you say you want to leave all this money to my kids when you die, but you hardly speak to them. Look, mate, I'm worried, all right? I get the feeling you're not telling me everything. Are you sick or something, is that it?'

'No,' he said. He was quite unmoved by what she'd just said. But then he'd always been like that.

She sighed. Passing by St Paul's Cathedral she was struck by how many huge buildings had sprung up around it in recent years. She'd just settled her mind to the idea that John wasn't going to say anything more when he spoke again.

'I don't want you to think badly of me,' he said.

'Badly?'

'When I'm gone.'

Brenda had had enough of this. 'John, mate, if you're dying then fucking well say so! I know they do things different in your country but surely if you are about to pop your clogs . . .'

'I'm not dying, Brenda.'

'Then why all this "when I've gone" routine?'

He didn't answer.

Angry now, Brenda said, 'Listen, John, I know you was

always like this and so I know I have to put up with it. But you are hard work, you know. And you bother me, mate, you do.'

'Bother you how?' he said.

This time she shrugged. 'I dunno,' she said. 'If I knew the answer to that . . .'

'I do love you, you know,' John blurted.

Brenda looked at him but failed to find anything she would call love in his eyes.

Back within the more familiar confines of Forest Gate nick, Vi Collins was telling her deputy, Sergeant Tony Bracci, about her recent brush with Counter Terrorism over in Canning Town.

'People like Chief Inspector West don't give much away,' she said as she finished her 'posh' coffee and then flung the paper cup in the bin.

'So he never told you much about this Henry Dubray, then?' Tony asked.

'He didn't but his flatmate, Boris Jacobson, did. Typical newcomers to Canning Town – university educated, work in tech, leftie. Henry liked doing this urban exploring while Boris just tits about at work and on his bike.'

'Any connection to anti-Trump stuff?'

'If there was, West wasn't going to tell me,' Vi said. 'His mate said that Henry found Trump funny, but who don't?'

'Yeah, but he's all for putting his country first and I admire that,' Tony said.

Tony, the grandson of Italian ice merchants based in Barking, had always been to the right politically. Ten years Vi's junior, he respected 'the boss' but also feared her a little bit too. Vi was old school Labour and didn't mind who knew about it.

126

'If you was a woman or you had a bit of sense in your head you wouldn't admire someone like him at all,' Vi said. 'Sticking his hands where he shouldn't, talking about women like we're fucking bits of meat . . .'

'Oh, I don't like all that,' Tony said. 'I like how he's patriotic. And he don't care. I mean you can't be a patriot these days and—'

'Oh, grow up, Tony!' Vi said. 'Since when did anyone threaten to duff you up because you're a patriot?'

'Well, no, but—'

'But nothing. Now look, this whole thing is on Counter Terrorism's plate for the time being. If this posh kid did mean Trump harm, then they'll have to deal with it. If not, he'll land back on our manor.'

'Yes, guv.'

Tony was glad the conversation about Trump was over, even though he'd started it.

Vi got up from behind her desk and walked towards her office door.

'Anyway,' she said. 'One thing's for sure, if Counter Terrorism weren't aware of that sewer underneath Regent's Park, they are now. By the time Trump leaves there'll be plods covered in shit as far as the eye can see.'

Then she went outside for a cigarette.

TEN

'You really need to speak to my brother,' Akaash Patel told Mumtaz. 'Reginald Saunders was his friend, not mine. To be fair, Yogesh, my brother, and I were not close back then.'

'Are you now?' Mumtaz asked.

'No. He's dead.'

He didn't seem upset about it, but then if they hadn't got on why should he be? Mumtaz rather admired Akaash's honesty. Often, people felt duty-bound to extravagantly mourn lost family members, whether they'd liked them or not.

'But I remember Mr Saunders,' Akaash said. 'A bit of a rogue – which was why he liked Yogesh. Two peas in a pod. Yogesh used to have fun with him, told him he was a Brahmin. Well, he had to keep his story straight. All that "high caste Indian" rubbish impressed all the white ladies on the ships. I let him get on with it. I was there for the money and only that, myself.'

'So did Mr Saunders, did he . . .'

'Oh, I think he may have slept with a few of the lady guests, yes,' Akaash said. 'Unlike my brother who slept with anyone who would have him. But then he was a good-looking man and so why not? I hope I haven't shocked you?'

'Not at all.'

'That's good.' He smiled. His teeth were dark brown from chewing betel. He reminded Mumtaz of her grandfather who had also indulged that habit.

'Mmm.' Then he said, 'One thing I do remember about my brother and his friend Reg was how some years later, must have been in the mid seventies, Yogesh found him as a passenger on board his ship. As you know, I am sure, Mr Saunders had been dismissed by P&O. I suppose they couldn't stop him becoming a passenger . . .'

'Were you still working on the ships then?' Mumtaz asked.

'Oh no. I had managed to get a job at Tate & Lyle's by then. I never liked the life at sea, unlike Yogesh. I just did it until something better came along.' He shook his head. 'You know, you asking about Mr Saunders now, if I think about that, it is very odd. He was a drinker and never had any money, as I recall. Then suddenly he's on a cruise – with his son, apparently. That did not strike me as strange at the time, but it does now.'

'Did your brother comment on it?'

'I don't remember. Knowing Yogesh, if the man bought him drinks and gave him tips he was not going to worry about where that may have come from.' He frowned. 'What I do remember him saying, though, was that Mr Saunders made friends with a very rich American couple that Yogesh had seen before when he and Mr Saunders worked together.'

'Mr Patel, do you know about how Mr Saunders' son went missing in 1976?'

'The little boy? Was that after the cruise?'

'John Saunders disappeared in July 1976,' Mumtaz said. 'Is the cruise you're thinking of one to New York?'

'Yes,' he said. 'Not many go from Tilbury, mostly they go from Southampton. There used to always be one at the beginning of the summer and another one at the end. May or the end of August.'

'Do you know which?'

'Well, it must have been May because you say the boy disappeared in July . . .'

'Yes, but putting that aside,' Mumtaz said, 'how do you remember that conversation with your brother? To you, does May or August sound about right?'

He thought for a moment and then he said, 'August.' This was followed by a moment of deep thought after which he added, 'Oh, and he didn't use his real name on that cruise. Up to some mischief, I imagine. I wish I could remember what it was, but I can't. Yogesh would have known . . .'

'Where's Des's son?' John asked.

'Lennox? He's down at the buffet stuffing his face, same as all of the kids,' Brenda said.

'No, the other one.'

Brenda realised he was talking about Des's second son. 'Dylan? He's not feeling too good today,' she said. 'And don't ask me what it's about because he don't tell me nothing. Not that he needs to. Not my kid. Any case, he's an adult. I mean you've not seen my eldest two once since you first turned up.'

John turned back to look at the northern shore of the river again.

'You know,' he said, 'I could always remember my old life. I never spoke about it to Mum and Dad, but I never lost it.'

Brenda moved closer to him, their shoulders touching. 'Did you ever ask them if you could come back?'

'No.'

'Why not?'

'It didn't make sense,' he said. 'I thought it through. Here I was poor and I was always going to be. There I had everything.'

'You thought that through at ten?'

'Mmm.'

Brenda shook her head. She had never and would never understand her brother.

'John, do you know what the arrangement between our dad and your parents was?' she asked. 'I mean why did he give you away or did he . . .'

'So I could have a better life, I told you.'

She shook her head. Knowing her old man, money must have changed hands. And yet if it hadn't, maybe that was worse? For her . . . Why hadn't Reg ever felt that she had needed a new start? Why hadn't she qualified for getting away from his boozing, her mother's indifference and spam fritters? Was it simply because the old man had been a sexist pig as well as a drunken waste of space?

Eventually Brenda said, 'So what're your plans, then, John? I mean, I s'pose you'll go back to America . . .'

'There's still a lot of work to be done,' he said.

'What? Converting people . . .'

'Showing them the way, yes,' he said. 'A person's life has to mean something. Mine still has much to do.'

Brenda wasn't a stupid woman. She hadn't had any sort of education, to be honest, and had left school at fifteen with

131

no qualifications. But she'd learnt a lot over the years. On her own and only, in recent years, with encouragement from Des, she'd done a lot of thinking and a lot of looking stuff up in books.

John was, she knew, being evasive. She also knew that he felt she hadn't noticed. But she had. There remained a very good reason why she'd engaged the Arnold Agency. She reminded herself to call Mumtaz when she had some time on her own.

He'd managed to catch sight of 'Steve's' surname on that greasy, hooky agreement before the man had ripped it out of his hand. Lee found a lot of Steven Galeas online. A common Maltese surname, Galea took up a lot of Internet space and entries for Steven Galea specifically were numerous. Steven Galea the accountant, Steven Galea the restauranteur from Doncaster, Steven Galea, actor – it went on and on.

His mobile rang. He looked at the screen and saw that it was his old flame, Alison from Romford Social Services.

'Hello, Ali.'

'Lee.' she said, 'I'm down Lakeside with the old man so I'll have to be quick . . .'

He could hear the familiar sound of people talking, a tannoy and kids going mad with boredom in the background.

'You asked me about that property of Barzan Rajput's in Langdon Hills,' she said.

Where, if Lee was right, Mr Galea and his wife or whoever she was, lived.

'Yeah.'

'Turns out old Barzan rents that gaff out to his son,' Alison said. 'Anjam, thirty-nine. It's he who, officially, lives there.'

'With anyone else?'

'Dunno. Maybe he's moved some poor besotted female in. He's a good-looking bloke even if he is a wanker.'

'In what way?'

'Thick as shit,' Ali said. 'I'm not surprised daddy had to set him up with somewhere to live. Couldn't find his own arse'ole with a compass.'

Lee thought for a moment and then said, 'The name Galea mean anything to you, Ali?'

'Galea? No,' she said. But then she corrected herself. 'Hang on, there is a hairdresser just off the market, Rosemary Galea. Don't know nothing about it. My sister cuts my hair.'

'OK, thanks Ali,' Lee said.

He heard her laugh. 'You owe me one,' she said and cut the connection. He'd have to take her out to lunch sometime. Anything Chinese.

Lee put his chin in his hand and sparked up a fag. Chronus the mynah bird grumbled on his perch and, with a resentful glance at Lee's cigarette, he put his head under his wing.

Could birds be pertinent in this situation, Lee wondered? He hadn't seen anyone who could have been Barzan Rajput at the house in Langdon Hills. Just Steve Galea and some woman. Was Ali's 'wanker' subletting to the couple and living elsewhere or was he actually sharing with the Galeas? Or – was this a case of cuckooing?

Cuckooing usually happened where a vulnerable person was living alone in a property. Said vulnerable person then suddenly finds they are making really good new friends who proceed to move in on them, often taking over both their homes and their lives. Then the abuse would begin. Generally, those 'cuckooing' a property would use it to either grow or deal drugs or both. But cuckooing could be used for other illegal purposes too. Maybe the Galeas were using Anjam and his house from which to run their dodgy loan company?

But if they were, this opened up questions about whether Anjam's father knew or not. Maybe he did and it all happened with his blessing. Or perhaps he didn't. Perhaps this was an apparently rather inept son's way of trying to run a business of his own?

Mumtaz left a message for Brenda Joseph. She asked her to call when she had some time to herself. She'd have to tell her what she'd learnt so far about the 'sale' of her brother, however painful. As she walked up the garden path to the front door of the flat, a car pulled up and Shazia got out.

'Amma!'

The two women flew into each other's arms.

'Oh, darling, you're early!' Mumtaz said as she stroked her daughter's face, brushing strands of hair away from her eyes.

'Is it a problem?'

'No! No, not at all! It's a lovely surprise!'

They kissed and it was then that Mumtaz realised that a pale young man was standing behind Shazia carrying a rucksack.

'Oh, Amma, this is Dexter, he, er, we drove down in his car . . .' Shazia said. Mumtaz saw the girl turn her eyes down when she said his name. This was the boyfriend she didn't officially know about, but had rightly surmised existed. Tall and very slim, he had a nice smile even though the bags underneath his eyes and the slight whiff of alcohol that was coming off him were unmistakeable. This boy had had a rough night.

Mumtaz offered him her hand. 'Pleased to meet you. I am Mumtaz.'

'Hello.'

He had a nice voice, slightly posh, that he was trying to cover up.

Dexter looked at Shazia and said, 'Er, I'd better get over to Mum and Dad's . . .'

'Oh, don't you want to come in for a cup of tea, first?' Mumtaz asked.

The whole situation was awkward but Mumtaz knew that she was taking just a little pleasure in the young folks' embarrassment. She loved Shazia but the girl's reddening cheeks were amusing her.

'Oh, er, no thank you,' Dexter said. 'Thanks. I, um, my parents live over in Notting Hill and . . .'

Notting Hill, eh! Shazia had done well for herself!

'. . . parking's a bit of a problem round there. You have to get in early and Dad has to get me a permit and . . .'

'It's all right,' Mumtaz said. 'You don't have to explain.' She put a hand on Shazia's shoulder. 'Thank you so much for bringing Shazia home, it's very kind of you.'

'It's . . .'

'Will you meet up on Monday for the demonstration?'

'Yeah . . .'

'Amma,' Shazia cut in. She took her rucksack from her boyfriend and said, 'See you on Monday.'

Mumtaz saw the boy go to kiss Shazia, but the girl turned away. Once Dexter had driven off and the women were inside the flat, Mumtaz said, 'You do know, I know he's your boyfriend, don't you?'

She saw the girl pale.

'How?'

'Shazia, you're a lovely young woman, of course you have a boyfriend,' she said. 'And of course I've heard a man's voice in the background when you've phoned me.'

135

'Oh God!'

Mumtaz smiled. 'And it's OK,' she said. 'I'm not your father . . .'

'Thank God!'

'And your late mother, from what I have heard, would just have been happy that you were happy.'

Mumtaz hadn't known her husband's late wife, but she'd been told that she was a kind woman who had loved her daughter.

Shazia put her bag on the floor and sat down in one of the living room chairs.

'It's just all a bit confusing, you know?' she said.

'What is?'

'Everything. I mean Dex is white . . .'

'Shazia, you love whoever you love, you know that. That's—'

'So why aren't you with Lee?'

It was a fair point and Mumtaz knew it. She wasn't with Lee because, although she knew that her family liked him, she was conflicted. She was a Muslim woman who, in spite of her first marriage turning into a nightmare, even now expected to marry a Muslim man. She didn't know whether she could live her life in two worlds. She also knew that she couldn't and shouldn't transfer her own feelings about that to anyone else. Especially not to Shazia.

She said, 'I don't want to talk about this right now.'

'So when do you want to talk about it?'

Mumtaz shook her head. 'You know I have misgivings about you going on this demonstration . . .'

'Don't change the subject!'

They looked at each other in silence. Shazia had been home for no more than a few minutes and already they were arguing.

* * *

'Ruby Henderson?'

Small and thin, wearing way too much make-up, in Conor West's opinion, she held a small child by the hand and smoked a cigarette. Music pounded out of a room somewhere, Jay-Z.

'Who're you?' the woman asked.

West and Sergeant Khan took out their ID.

'Counter Terrorism,' West said. 'Can we have a word, please?'

The woman, winded at first, eventually yelled over her shoulder, 'Kian! Turn that down, will ya!'

Nothing happened and then the woman, Ruby, said to the officers, 'You'd better come in.'

She led them through to a very large living room that contained a sofa, a TV and a laptop computer. The music was coming out of the latter. A young, mixed-race male was sitting on the sofa wearing a pair of headphones. Ruby went over to the laptop and turned it off. West experienced what felt like the removal of pain.

Ruby didn't offer them a seat, but pushed the young man off the couch and sat down. The boy gave the officers a tired look and then sloped off. He was eighteen at the most and so probably of no interest to West. This was about Ruby Henderson who, her records showed, was forty and probably the kid's mother. The small girl whose hand Ruby had been holding ran off back into the hall.

'What do you want?' she asked.

'I don't know whether you're aware Miss . . .'

'Mrs.'

'Mrs Henderson,' West continued, 'someone called Henry Dubray, with whom we believe you have been associated, has been found dead.'

In spite of the heavy make-up, West saw all the colour drain from Ruby's face.

'This information isn't yet in the public domain and I'm sorry to have to be the one to tell you, but I'm afraid we have to try and find out who killed Henry as a matter of urgency.'

'Killed him?' She looked up, her eyes full of fear. 'You sure?'

'It's a possibility,' West said and, uninvited, he sat down next to her on the couch. She smelt of stale fags and cannabis, but that wasn't West's problem.

'Can I call you Ruby?' he asked.

He saw Khan take a wooden chair from just inside the kitchen and sit down.

'Yeah.' She was crying now. 'What happened?'

'I told you—'

'He wouldn't have had anything to do with terrorism!' Ruby said. 'Why would he?'

'We're not saying he did,' West said. 'But we think he may have come into contact with people who have.'

'Who killed him?'

'We don't know. Now my understanding is that you were going out with Mr Dubray until a few weeks ago. But looking over his phone records, we can see that you spoke on the phone last Tuesday. Can you tell me what that was about?'

Ruby took a handkerchief out of her pocket and dried her eyes. 'God knows,' she said. Then catching her breath, 'We finished a few weeks ago. He was a nice bloke but a bit immature. I ended it. We probably spoke about some stuff he left round here.'

'What stuff?'

'Oh, just some of the books he had about exploring,' she said. 'He liked to go into old ruins and sewers and stuff. I never got it – that was one of the problems we had. But Kian was interested.'

'Kian is your son?'

'Yeah. Do you want me to get him?'

'Yes, please.'

It wasn't an easy thing to say, but when Mumtaz told Brenda Joseph she believed her father had actually sold her brother, she wasn't surprised.

'He was a drunk, what can you say?' Brenda said. 'He was lazy and stupid and selfish. But he was me dad and . . . You know, Mumtaz, I've probably spoken to John more in the last couple of days than I have before and I think I'm probably more confused than I've ever been about him.'

'How do you mean?'

'He keeps talking as if he's going to die,' she said. 'Says he wants me to think well of him when he's "gone". I asked him straight if that was what was happening, but he said he was all right. Then I asked him what he was doing next, with his new parents' charity work and that, and all he'd say was that there's still a lot to do.'

'Brenda, I know this is going to sound a bit crazy, but trust me on this,' Mumtaz said. 'I studied psychology and sometimes the strangest things can have some value. John's a mystery, but what is your fantasy about why he's here? What do you think about him coming here now?'

Brenda thought for a few moments and then she said, 'I think he's come to take his revenge.'

'On whom? You?'

She paused. 'I don't think so. But underneath all the God stuff, you know I think he's angry.'

Mumtaz had felt that about him too. When she'd met him in the cafe it had come through. People talked about 'muscular' Christianity, but this was more than muscular, this was . . . She didn't have words that really encapsulated it. Fanatic?

'I don't really know why,' Brenda continued. 'I mean, he got the best end of the deal however he got there, didn't he? Rich parents, travel, not having to worry about the daily grind.'

'But he was rejected,' Mumtaz said. 'By people who were poor but who, nevertheless, were his family. Your father sold him to get money for drink. That has to be the ultimate betrayal. That you weren't part of that doesn't necessarily mean you're off the hook in his mind.'

'So you do think he means us harm?'

'I don't know,' Mumtaz said. 'But I do agree he has an agenda.'

'So I wasn't wrong to call you in, then?'

'No. I just haven't yet worked out how I can actually help you.' Then she said, 'I spoke to an Asian man who claims to be the brother of Mr Patel, the "high-ranking" steward your father worked with. He wasn't high-ranking at all, but that's irrelevant. Your Mr Patel passed away, but his brother does remember him telling him that he'd come across your father travelling with a young boy who he thought was your brother. But he wasn't travelling under the name Saunders.'

She heard Brenda sigh.

'I know this must feel like disappearing down a rabbit hole . . .'

'Because of how he was with debts and that, Dad did use other names,' Brenda said. 'He had nicknames, like most East End blokes of his generation. "Frog" was his main one, for "Frog and Toad" – road in the old rhyming slang.'

'Why?'

'Because whenever he was going down the pub he'd call out to Mum, "I'm just off down the Frog." We all knew what it meant and so did his mates.'

'Would he call himself Mr Frog . . .'

'Nah!' she laughed. 'I was just giving meself some time to think. We did have someone call one day asking for a Mr O'Connell. That was Dad. Mum went mad when he got home because O'Connell was her mum's maiden name and she thought this bloke had come round after one of her uncles.'

'Do you think he might have used O'Connell when he left the country with John?'

'Maybe. Mind you, he would've been a bit of a doughnut to do so. But then he was a doughnut . . .'

'Brenda, I think your dad and John sailed to New York from Tilbury in August 1976,' Mumtaz said. 'I can, with your permission, have a go at getting hold of the ship's manifest . . .'

'But what will that tell us about why John's here now?' Brenda asked.

'Maybe nothing, maybe something. His movements so far aren't giving us much. When he's not with you he goes into bookshops, parks, he seems to be interested in history. He doesn't talk to people. He doesn't buy anything.'

'That sounds like John,' Brenda said.

But Mumtaz was unsure. That operative assigned to John Saunders had wondered whether he had rumbled him. And operatives with a lot of experience, like Rob Turner, did not get feelings like that about people for no reason. At the moment, apparently, John was walking through the Woolwich Foot Tunnel . . .

ELEVEN

Some high street shops were tatty, dusty and smelt a bit. Such places, to a person who was compulsive about cleaning, like Lee Arnold, were disturbing. What, however, was even more unsettling was the kind of high street business that looked as if it clearly wasn't something it wanted to be. Such a place was High End Lettings on Whalebone Lane, Romford.

While outside, the facade was all black glass and plasma screens exhibiting new properties to let in hyper-real colours, inside – if one ignored the great bank of black sofas along one wall – it was like a low-rent benefits agency office. And while the desks at which the 'letting executives' worked were crammed with tech, their clients sat nervously on the sofas in various combinations of dirty tracksuits, back-to-front baseball caps, stinking trainers and visible thongs. There were also babies. As Lee entered the place, he found himself cringing. According to

Alison, Barzan Rajput was a slum landlord and this display of human misery seemed to confirm that.

'Can I help you, sir?'

A young Asian woman, smartly dressed and with a fixed smile on her face, popped up beside him. No doubt a 'letting executive'.

Lee smiled. 'I'm looking for a house to rent,' he said. 'Four beds, ideally. I've got a new job in Basildon and I want to move a bit further that way.'

'Where do you live now?' the girl asked.

'Newham,' he said. Nice and non-specific.

She put a hand on his shoulder. 'If you'd like to come over, I can have a look on our system for you.'

When he finally came downstairs, Kian Henderson was subdued. No longer, apparently, the sulky teen he'd been earlier, he sat down next to West and said, 'Mum says someone shanked Henry.'

His mother, close behind him said, 'I didn't say he was shanked, Kian. Don't make it worse than it is.' She looked at West. 'All these stabbings, the kids automatically think that if someone's dead, they've been knifed. Henry's dead, Kian, I don't know how.'

Kian looked at Khan. 'How'd Henry die?'

West said, 'We can't tell you. But if you liked Henry you can help us by telling us a bit about this urban exploring he used to do. Did you ever go with him, Kian?'

The boy looked at his mother who said, 'I told him he couldn't.'

West looked at the boy and waited. Kian averted his eyes from his mother's face.

Eventually Ruby said, 'I know you done it, Kian, and so you

might as well tell him. Henry's dead and, though we wasn't going out no more, I'm sorry. He was nice.'

Her eyes shone with tears. It had taken a while for the news about Henry to break through her hard carapace but now it had, she was truly sad.

'He took me down an old Tube station,' Kian said. Now he looked at his mother. 'January.'

Ruby looked away. She'd been working non-stop through January. She'd left the kids with her mum.

'Where?' West asked the boy.

'Up by Tower Hill,' Kian said. 'We had to go down the end of the platform and then walk along beside the rails for a bit. It was cool.'

'With trains running along beside you!' Ruby yelled. 'Fucking mad!'

West held up a hand to quieten her.

'Why was it cool?'

Kian shrugged. 'Sort of naughty? I dunno. But then we got up in this old station full of like, old posters on the wall and this like, mad little window where people used to buy tickets. It was like some sort of like old movie thing.'

Ruby had left the room and Kian could hear her crying in the kitchen.

He called out to her, 'Mum, I never did it to make you unhappy . . .'

'Did anyone know that you and Henry were going to do this?' West asked.

'Don't think so.'

'Are you sure? What did you say to your grandmother?'

'Oh, she was totally sweet on Henry!' he smiled. 'He could do anything, man!'

'Why?'

He shrugged again. 'Thought Mum was doing herself some good being with someone like him,' he said. 'With his own flat and a job and him being white . . . Not that my nana's a racist or nothing. She ain't.'

'She didn't know where you were going?'

'Nah, man.'

'So you just walked out . . .'

'I dunno what Henry told her,' he said. 'Like, going out for a bit or something . . . There was loads of kids at Nana's, always are. Her man was out and so it was mad.'

'She never knew.'

'Nah. Don't think so.'

'And when you came back?'

'We had tea with everyone.'

'You and Henry?'

'Yeah.'

'Did Henry tell anyone where you'd been?'

'I dunno,' he said. 'Maybe. One of the kids . . .'

West gave his notebook and a pen to Kian and said, 'Write down the names of everyone who was there, will you?'

'I don't want to get no one—'

'Just do it, Kian!' he heard his mother roar from the kitchen. 'Fuck's sake . . .'

Kian looked at the notebook. 'Don't you want me to put this in your phone, man?'

'No, I don't,' West said.

Kian shrugged yet again and began to write.

Renting in the twenty-first century seemed to have narrowed down to either 'premium' properties that contained things like jacuzzis and dressing rooms, or 'nice little flats' that were in fact too small for anyone over five foot four and riddled with black mould. Purporting to be looking for something in the former range, Lee Arnold cooled his heels until Zenab the letting executive showed him some properties in Langdon Hills. One was on the same street as Steve Galea's place.

'That looks nice . . .'

Zenab smiled. 'Oh, that's a lovely road,' she said. 'We've got several houses rented out down there. Bit pricey . . .'

At over two grand a month, she wasn't wrong. But, Lee noticed, it did have an indoor swimming pool.

'Happy to pay for the right place,' Lee said.

Zenab looked around the sad but sparkly office and said, 'I'll get hold of Anjam. He's closed on a couple of rent agreements out that way. I'm more Romford . . .' She called out, 'Anjam!'

A slim man in a very nice suit smiled a glittering smile back at her. She said something in a language Lee didn't speak and the man came over. As he held out his outstretched hand, Lee stood up and shook it.

'This is Anjam,' Zenab said. 'Anjam, Mr Harrison here wants a large property in Langdon Hills. You are something of an expert, I said . . .'

'Lovely area,' Anjam said and sat down in the seat Zenab had vacated.

'I'm interested in this one,' Lee said pointing at the image on Zenab's computer screen.

'Oh, number five,' Anjam said. 'Beautiful house. Swimming pool has to be seen to be believed. You can't really see it from these photos. It's actually in a large conservatory at the back of the house. It's stunning. But pricey.'

That was the second time price had been mentioned. Lee wasn't aware that he was looking particularly poor, but then what did he know? He was a divorced man of nearly fifty, practically dead in comparison with these young people.

'Money's not the problem,' he said.

Anjam smiled. 'Glad to hear it, sir,' he said. 'And if you like quality, this is the place for you.'

'Is it vacant?'

'Yes. Would you like to view it?'

'I think I would.'

If Anjam offered to take him today that might be a bit soon after meeting Steve Galea and so he added, 'Can't do today, though.'

'Ah.' Anjam took his phone out and looked at the screen. 'How's about tomorrow at midday?'

'That'll be perfect,' Lee said.

Shazia had gone out. She hadn't said where she was going but Mumtaz thought she'd probably gone to see her old friend Grace. Now working as a hairdresser with her sister on Green Street, Grace was a lively, funny girl who Mumtaz hoped would cheer Shazia up.

Being a Saturday there wasn't much point in contacting P&O about some ancient manifest and so she put the TV on and tried to relax. She'd called Lee with an update, but he hadn't picked up. He had his own work, which, since they'd effectively called time on their relationship four months before, he'd thrown himself into, as had she. Maybe he was with Vi Collins?

Mumtaz had always known about their arrangement, which had ceased during her relationship with Lee. But

147

the two of them went back a long way. The sex, or so she had gathered, was the least of it in reality. Lee and Vi were simply people who liked to be close to others. She did really, but she couldn't always show it. In fact, if Mumtaz were honest with herself, the idea that closeness was also a sign of weakness had never been far from her mind since the day she had married Ahmet. She hadn't been brought up to fear loving relationships. That she'd learnt from her husband and it was a lesson that seemingly she would never forget or recover from.

She looked at the television. More news about Trump's upcoming visit. Mumtaz wondered how the Queen felt about having to meet him again. The first time he'd come to the UK he'd made all sorts of gaffes.

'You ever thought about having a number one?'

Lee hadn't been sure whether Rosemary Galea, possibly ex-wife-of-Steve, 'did' men's hair or not when he turned up at her salon in Romford town centre. It had been a spur of the moment decision and one that might not bear fruit. But hairdressers talked . . .

'No,' Lee said.

Rosemary, a skinny bottle-blonde, probably in her forties, ran her fingers through his hair.

'I like a nice short haircut on a man,' she said.

So she favoured what Vi called 'bullet heads' – blokes who liked to look hard. Not exactly Lee's area. Also, his own hairdresser, Nick the Greek on the Barking Road was always going on about what nice thick hair he had.

'Mediterranean hair, Mr Arnold,' the old man would say whenever he saw him. 'The best. I don't cut too short, OK?'

Lee was happy with that.

Rosemary said, 'So what you want then, love?'

'Just a trim,' Lee said.

He'd not long ago been at old Nick's and so it was going to be a pretty sad little trim. He said, 'Tidy it up. Maybe a bit more off the back.'

'All right, love.'

Looking at yourself in a mirror while someone cut your hair wasn't one of life's great pleasures. Lee always found himself wondering why his eyes were at different levels and marvelled at the length of his nose. If he was going to get into conversation with this woman, he'd have to play the game a little bit.

'Actually,' he said. 'I can go a number four.'

He saw Rosemary's face light up. 'A Brad Pitt,' she said. 'Nice choice, you won't regret it.'

Lee thought that he probably would. But then she put both hands on his shoulders and fluttered her eyelashes, which was a good sign. They had, Lee hoped, quite a bit to talk about.

Vi met him at the bottom of Radland Road on the Keir Hardie Estate. Made up of blocks of flats and houses built by the council in the fifties, this area was peak old Canning Town. Vi's parents had remembered this part of London when it had been a wasteland. Bombed almost out of existence by the Luftwaffe in World War Two, the Keir Hardie was where the poor of the borough had been rehoused. It had been like a bloody miracle at the time. People who had grown up with outside toilets and standpipes now had proper bathrooms and running water. It always struck Vi as bizarre that these sturdily built old houses could now command upwards of four hundred thousand pounds in the brave new world of insane London house prices.

She got out of her car and joined West on the pavement. What was also a bit strange about the Keir Hardie these days was the lack of kids on the streets. Kids didn't play out like they used to but Vi also wondered whether parents were keeping them indoors deliberately. There had been more instances of gang-related activity, especially stabbings, all over London in recent months. Another sign, Vi felt, of how desperately investment – not in property but in people – was needed in the capital's more deprived areas. Gentrification was going full steam ahead in Newham, but the majority of the residents still got left behind. As they always had.

'Brenda Joseph's got a pile of kids,' Vi said to West as she walked along beside him. She was still smoking the fag she'd sparked up in the car and, although she could tell he disapproved, she carried on puffing. This was Newham not fucking Notting Hill. 'Think Ruby's the second or third. Her dad, Devon Henderson, was a nasty piece of work. Used to knock Brenda about. He was a puff-head . . .'

'Beg pardon?'

'He smoked a lot of skunk,' Vi said. 'And much as that can chill a person out, in some cases it had the opposite effect. Devon also did a bit of growing in his time. Anyway, Brenda saw the light sometime in the eighties and chucked him out. Enter Desmond Joseph, hard-working widower also with a bunch of kids of his own. Then he and Brenda had another kid of their own. All the kids are mixed race, most of 'em live round here but Ruby's the only one I know who's been in any bother with us. Nothing heavy – bit of possession, couple of domestics with various men. Strange to think she was going out with that Henry

150

Dubray. Mind you, she's a pretty girl, lot older than you think.'

'She's thirty-nine.'

Vi shook her head. 'Shit.'

The noise coming from the Josephs' house wasn't colossal but West knew he wouldn't want to live next door to them. Vi knocked on the door and eventually a tall, grizzled black man opened it.

Vi introduced them both and showed her ID. Desmond Joseph let them in to a hallway that was full of kids' shoes, coats and Lego.

'If I said it wasn't always like this, I'd be lying,' Desmond said. 'Me and Brenda've got seven kids between us, then there's the grandkids . . .'

Vi wasn't expecting Brenda Joseph to remember her. It had to be a good decade since she'd last called her in to the nick to pick up Ruby. But she did.

She looked up from wiping a small child's face with a flannel and said, 'Hello, DI Collins.'

Vi smiled. Brenda Joseph was very much like she was, if less successful. She'd always looked after her kids with a fierceness that did her nothing but credit, and she worked at whatever shit job she happened to have like a trooper.

'Can I have a word, Brenda?' Vi asked.

Vi and West had decided between them to keep his involvement with Ruby Henderson's wider family to a minimum. Counter Terrorism officers frightened people and, although Ruby knew there was a possible link to national security fears through Henry, it was important that Brenda and the rest of the brood be kept calm.

Brenda gave the little kid to her husband and took Vi and West into a room that was probably meant to be for dining but was actually a dumping ground for washing. As they went, Desmond said, 'You wanna talk to me too?'

'No, love,' Vi smiled. 'Just Brenda.'

He shrugged.

Brenda took piles of washing off chairs so they could sit down.

'I've had Ruby on the phone about it,' Brenda said before either of the officers could get a word in. 'So I know what it's about. I'm sure you're wrong about Henry. He was a nice boy. Bit young for her, but . . .'

'He took your grandson Kian on what could've been a dangerous journey to an old Tube station,' Vi said.

Brenda shook her head. 'Never knew he done that until Ruby told me. Mind you, our Kian can be a little shit. Don't get took in by that butter-wouldn't-melt look he gives people.'

Vi didn't want to get into the rights and wrongs of Kian's character. She said, 'Brenda, we want to know who, if anyone, Kian might have told about his adventure with Henry.'

'Never told me or his mum!'

'But maybe he told someone else. One of the other kids, an uncle.' Vi leant forward so she could get closer to Brenda and lower her voice. 'Listen, Kian's done nothing wrong – but look, Henry's body was found in a place where things are tense at the moment . . .'

'This is about national security,' West cut in.

Vi saw Brenda's eyes widen. 'Fuck!'

'Not that we think that Henry—'

'This to do with that fucker Trump?'

'No . . .'

'It . . .'

'Fuck me!' Brenda leant towards Vi so that their noses almost touched. 'That was the only thing I didn't like about Henry,

152

all that grubbing about in places people shouldn't go,' Brenda said. 'I mean, who'd want to do that? I can't see him being dangerous, though. I mean, I know he didn't like Trump, but then who does?'

'Brenda, we don't think that Henry has anything to do with any sort of plot against the President of the USA,' Vi said. 'It's simply the circumstances of where he was found are sensitive. We suspect he was with another person, who may well also be innocent of any sort of plot against Trump.'

'How'd ya know that?'

Vi looked at West, who said, 'We just know.'

'Oh.'

'Brenda, to be honest,' Vi said, 'we're struggling to find who Henry did these urban exploring trips with. We know he used to hang about with some people in Walthamstow but when he moved to Canning Town it seems he lost touch with them or kicked 'em into touch or whatever. We know he used to take people to these old asylums and whatever, and earned some money for doing it. But we don't know who.'

'Ain't it on his phone?'

West shook his head. 'Seems not.'

Henry's phone had been, as far as the technical officers could tell, used exclusively for work. But then it was important to remember that 'urban exploration' was also trespass. A lot of the venues explored were dangerous and, in some cases, contentious.

Eventually Brenda said, 'I'll see what I can find out. Course, I'll have to tell Des.'

'We imagined you would.'

She shrugged. 'Can't think that any of the kids would know anything, except for Kian. Here, you don't think . . .'

'No.' West smiled, but not Vi noted, with his eyes. 'He has an alibi for when we believe the offence took place. If indeed Dubray's death was unnatural.'

Rosemary Galea, hairdresser, was indeed the ex-wife of Steven Galea, loan shark.

'Maltese, my ex,' she told Lee as more of his hair hit the deck than he'd bargained for. God, was the woman going to sculpt him into her ideal man? She was a bit touchy-feely, to be fair. 'Come from one of them massive families they have. Eight brothers, can you imagine it! No girls. Dead jealous he was, I couldn't stand it.'

'My missus too,' Lee replied. She hadn't been but that wasn't the point. It was all about rapport when you were trying to get someone to open up.

'All that Mediterranean temper they all have. Awful! Then when I did get out, he's off with some rich tart with a massive gaff up Langdon Hills!'

Lee knew nothing about Steve's girlfriend except that she, like Steve, didn't own that house they both used. That apparently, was Barzan Rajput.

'My wife just buggered off,' Lee said. 'There wasn't no one else.'

'Well, no,' Rosemary said. 'Good-looking man like you, she would've been mad to go off with someone else. To be honest, Steve wasn't no great catch, looks-wise. But he did know how to show a girl a good time.'

'What did he do?'

She sighed. 'Oh, he was in business,' she said. 'He had worked up the City, but when I met him he had a nightclub down Southend.'

'Which one?'

154

'Oh, it's gone now,' Rosemary said. 'Called Rebels. Another thing, I discovered later, undermined by his family. Not intentionally, you understand. Just cos of how they are.'

'What do you mean?'

'Oh, they're a funny lot. In one way like really moral and all that. Couldn't stand the idea of us living together, and when I did marry him I had to become a Catholic. But then there's this other side,' she said. 'Him and his brothers. I never really understood it, to be fair. But they'd gang up on people. Like *The Godfather* it was sometimes, people disrespecting them and that. Godfather without the money I should say. All finance stuff. I never understood. But I do know there was a big fight between Steven and his brothers and some other blokes at the club and then after that it closed down. One of the reasons I started this place. Do you want product on your hair, love?'

Lee hadn't been looking at himself in the mirror with anything near the attention he should have been. Now he did he could see that his haircut wasn't so much Brad Pitt as Skinhead circa 1975. Christ! What was product when it was at home?

'Er, no,' he said.

Rosemary ruffled his very sparse hair through her fingers and said, 'Pleased?'

'Yes. Yes, I am actually.'

'Glad you followed my advice?'

'Yeah.'

If Jodie, his daughter came to visit she'd probably refuse to be seen with him. God alone knew what Mumtaz would think.

He paid and tipped Rosemary who, he felt, had been waiting for him to ask her for a date. But he didn't. There was just so much a bloke would do for his job and she had made him look like a member of the BNP.

As he started to put his jacket back on, Rosemary said, 'Course, now he's with her, my Steve's like a pig in shit.' She half whispered, 'I've heard she keeps him now. Well, more fool her, I say!'

TWELVE

'You know they won't let you get nowhere near him, don't you?' Grace said as she watched Shazia slowly get up off the bed.

Still sodden with sleep, Shazia said, 'Who?'

'Trump. They won't let you get anywhere near him.'

'Oh.'

She'd spent the night at the flat Grace shared with her sister in Silvertown. At the top of an old council block the tower was about half owned by the local authority and half under private ownership. Grace and Primrose's flat was one of the latter. Owned by a private landlord, they paid just over double the rent that the council tenants paid.

Shazia went to the toilet and, when she came back, she said, 'It's not about getting close to Trump, it's about making sure he can't say that he's popular here.'

'He will, though,' Grace said. 'Man lies about everything.'

Shazia got back into the Z bed. 'Can't control what he does,' she said. 'But we do what we can. It's important to me to be there to register my disgust.'

'And this white boy you taking with you?'

'Dex is probably even more into protesting against Trump than I am.'

'And your mum?'

Shazia rolled her eyes. 'She says that if I get arrested, I won't be able to join the police.'

'Which'd be a good thing!'

'No, it wouldn't! You know it's what I want to do and although I know you think I'm crazy, it's just what I want to do, you know?'

Grace shook her head. 'Anyway, forget all that now,' she said. 'Come up Camden with your home-girls.'

Primrose's salon always shut on Sundays and the sisters were planning to go clothes and possibly tattoo shopping up by Camden Lock.

'You can get inked, man!'

Shazia shook her head. 'Amma would go mad. Muslims don't get tats.'

'Christians neither,' Grace said. 'Why you think I got Prince inked on my ass?'

'I know, so your mum won't see.'

'Damn right! You can get tattooed on anywhere your mum won't see. Have anything you like – skulls, roses, butterflies, snake . . .'

'Grace, I don't want a tattoo,' Shazia said. 'I'd like a new pair of boots but . . .'

'So come!'

She shrugged. She had no money to just fritter away in Camden but she had nothing better to do either. And it would be a laugh.

She said, 'OK.'

Jason Pritchard was the sort of bloke who got up early. Sundays meant nothing to him and so when he called Lee Arnold at 9 a.m., Lee wasn't surprised, even if he was pissed off. He'd only just got up and he felt like shit.

'So where we at with the old slapper?' he asked as soon as Lee picked up.

'Could be that the man of the house in Langdon Hills isn't the one Lorraine is in hock to,' Lee said. 'Could be his missus.'

'You think?'

'Could be.' He caught sight of himself in the mirror in the hall and rolled his eyes. 'Could be complicated, Jase.'

'In what way?'

'I've a notion the pair of them may be cuckooing a bloke called Barzan Rajput. Seems the house belongs to him and I'm not sure whether he lives there or not. Hopefully, I'll find that out later on today. As you know, prosecuting loan sharks is a tricky business and even if I do have to call the Old Bill in, there's no guarantee we'll be able to do anything about Lorraine's debts.'

'Mmm. Don't really want the Old Bill involved . . .'

Although Jason purported to have no feelings left for his ex-wife, and in fact the coldness he'd exhibited when she'd got roughed up seemed to imply he didn't care, he did. She was still the mother of his children and, if she was getting leant on to pay ever more of his money over to these characters, he wanted them dealt with.

'Do you want me to carry on?' Lee asked.

'Oh yeah. Yeah.'

159

He was glad about that. If Jason had said no, then the haircut that Chronus was now squawking at in horror would have all been for nothing.

There was a knock at the door. Brenda heaved herself into a sitting position and nudged Des in the ribs.

'Door.'

He grunted. Brenda looked at the clock, it was only nine-thirty. God almighty what had one of those bloody kids done now?

She swung her legs out of bed, put on a dressing gown and stomped downstairs. Whoever it was had absolutely no idea about Sundays and sleep.

'John.'

And there he was, fresh as a daisy, large as life, standing on her doorstep holding onto a copy of the *Sunday Times*.

'I'm not too early, am I?' he asked.

Christ, he was so far down the spectrum he was almost fucking Rain Man!

'Well, yeah you—' Brenda began but he pushed past her and walked into the living room. There were cups and plates everywhere. Brenda, Des and the grandchildren had had a film night on the sofa and she'd been too tired to clear up. She could see that her brother was horrified, but she didn't much care.

'Sit down and I'll make you a cuppa,' she said.

'Sit down where?'

Rather than state the bleeding obvious, Brenda walked into the living room and threw a load of throws and cushions on the floor.

'All right?'

John sat down and opened his paper. Brenda could remember a time when there wasn't a copy of *The Times* to be had in Canning Town. But then that was before a load of dickheads had bought their council houses and decided they were middle-class.

She made to go into the kitchen to put the kettle on and then she stopped.

'What the hell you doing round here so early, John?'

'Early? Is it?'

'I was still in bed,' she said. 'Clue's in the dressing gown.'

'Oh.'

But then he just went straight back to his paper. It being Sunday, wasn't he supposed to be at church or something?

'Think!'

'I have thought,' Kian told Ruby. 'I don't remember saying nothing to no one.'

'You could've passed on information to someone who knows what happened to Henry!' Ruby said. 'It's fucking important!'

'What do you care!' he shot back at her. 'Moved on to the next one now, innit!'

His eyes began to tear up.

'Oh, don't bloody cry!' Ruby said. 'That does no one any good!'

But she put her arm around him.

'I know you liked Henry, he was good to us. But we can't bring him back and so the best we can do is try to help find out who killed him.'

'I don't know why you think it was me who—'

'Because you like to boast about what you've done,' she said.

The boy looked at the floor. He'd had a lot of trouble with bullying when he was at school. Now at college it seemed to have stopped. But Ruby couldn't forget all the times the school had got her in because Kian had done something stupid to prove he was 'a man' to the other boys. All the lies he'd told to big himself up. Going down into a disused Underground station, actually walking along beside the tracks while trains thundered past was something, Ruby felt, had to be too good a story for Kian to keep to himself.

Eventually, wearied by his silence, she said, 'Look, just think about it OK?'

He nodded. Years of bitter experience had taught Ruby that Kian was the sort of boy who had to come round to things in his own sweet time. In the meantime, she had a date to prepare for.

Anjam Rajput drove a new Range Rover with blacked-out windows. Of course he did. Like his shiny suit, which was beautifully cut but a tad too short in the leg, it was part of an image that didn't quite work. Not a 'young executive' nor a wide boy, Anjam was something in his own mind but Lee wondered whether even he really knew what that was.

Langdon Hills was a fair way from Romford. Anjam, who didn't know that Lee had been there before, kept apologising.

'You'd think the traffic wouldn't be so bad on a Sunday, wouldn't you?' he said as they queued for the flyover at Gallows Corner. 'Gonna be a bit of a change for you after Newham, living out here.'

'I'm going to be working in Basildon,' Lee said, sticking to the story he'd told Zenab.

'Whereabouts?'

Never one to neglect his homework, Lee said, 'First Data.'

They had large offices in Basildon, beside the A127.

'Oh. You a techie?'

'Mmm.'

The Range Rover mounted the flyover and came to a halt at the top.

'Man!'

Anjam wasn't the most patient person.

'You got lots of appointments today?' Lee asked.

'A few. Although if you don't like The Willows I can show you some other very nice houses nearer to First Data. I mean, Langdon Hills is premium isn't it? Pricey . . .'

'I don't mind,' Lee said. 'It's worth paying good money for something clean and comfortable. I've a wife and two kids to consider.'

'Right.'

Once past the flyover the traffic thinned. Of the two major roads that led out of East London into Essex, the A127 was probably the better bet at the weekend. The other artery, the A13 led to both the vast Lakeside Shopping Centre at Thurrock and the QE2 Bridge over to Kent and more shopping opportunities at Bluewater Shopping Centre.

'If you're driving you turn off at Dunton,' Anjam said. 'Nearest station's Laindon. Takes you in to Fenchurch Street one way, Southend the other.'

'Handy.'

'Yeah, although I do also have some very nice four beds closer, as I say. I've a very nice barn conversion in Pitsea.'

Lee didn't answer and the car became silent. Eventually Anjam asked if Lee would mind listening to some music. Lee said go ahead. It would be interesting to hear what kind of tunes Anjam liked. What came on was surprising. Abba?

In general, the kids didn't like John much. Some of the grandkids ran away from him. And who could blame them? A stern figure to say the least, he wasn't what anyone would call friendly in spite of the soft, almost cuddly American accent. The exception to this rule was the five-year-old whirlwind that was Mickey Jay. Son of Tina, one of Des's kids, Mickey Jay was a bright boy, always asking questions. In his own way he was as irritating as John. But somehow the little kid and the man from America got on – sort of.

'What you reading, Uncle John?'

Brenda heard the boy's gruff little voice from the kitchen. John hated it when the kids called him 'uncle', which was probably why Mickey Jay did it. Bright he may be, but he was an annoying little bugger and he knew it and used it.

'Oi!' Brenda called out. 'Mickey Jay, leave John alone to read his paper!'

There was a moment of silence, then some giggling, then she heard the child, in a stage whisper, say, 'Do you want me to bugger off, Uncle John?'

Little shit!

But then she heard John say, 'No. No it's all right. But you just sit down quietly next to me.'

Mickey Jay liked being close to adults. If Brenda had a moment to herself on the sofa and he was about he always came and joined her. He'd sat with John, curled into his side, thumb in his mouth, a few times now. It probably came, Brenda sometimes thought, of all the times his mum had brought men home and asked that her son instantly take to, if not love, them.

Unlike Ruby who could play and use men, Tina was very needy. She'd got pregnant with Mickey Jay when she was fifteen as a way, in part, to keep hold of the boy she was going out with at the time. Of course, he'd buggered off almost immediately. But he'd been followed by a succession of 'daddies' who had always started spoiling the kid when they wanted to get in with his mother and then ignored him when they wanted to move on to some other girl. Brenda had to remind herself that Tina was still only twenty on a daily basis – because that was how often she had to look after Mickey Jay sometimes. The girl had gone out with her mates on Saturday night, dropping the kid off at Brenda's on her way. Now Mickey Jay was hanging around John of all people, while his mother was, no doubt, in bed somewhere with some other loser.

Brenda heard the child say, 'Who's that?'

She heard John's paper rustle. Then he said, 'That's the president of America.'

Obviously looking at the many, many photos of Donald Trump that would be all over papers like *The Times*.

'That's where you come from, ain't it?' Mickey Jay said.

'No. I come from here originally, Britain,' John said. 'I just lived in America a very long time. And it isn't "ain't" it's isn't.'

'What is?'

'It's "That's where you come from isn't it" not ain't . . .'

'Oh.'

Thinking back to how he'd been as a kid, Brenda wasn't surprised that John had become a 'grammar Nazi' once he got an education. When he'd been Mickey Jay's age, she remembered how he'd once spent a whole day colour-coding his toy cars. Did this mean that Mickey Jay would grow up to be a weird bastard too?

'What's his name?' she heard the child ask.

'The President of the United States? Donald Trump.'

There was a long pause then, and then she heard Mickey Jay ask another question.

'Why's he all orange?'

Brenda smiled. Out of the mouths of babes . . . Everyone wondered why an old git like Trump seemed to be hung up on fake tan.

She heard John say, 'I don't know.'

She smiled.

But then she heard or thought she heard, John whisper something else to the kid.

'He's a very silly man,' John said.

There wasn't a willow tree to be seen outside The Willows. This wasn't surprising. People just named their houses after anything they liked. There was one gaff in Forest Gate that had a plate on the wall saying 'The Bollocks'. What was surprising was that The Willows was directly opposite the place where Steven Galea lived. Lee had looked it up on Google Earth but it hadn't done it justice. The Willows' front door was opposite that of Galea's place which Lee now noticed was called The Glen.

Anjam drove his car onto the drive and both men got out.

'So, as you can see,' the agent said, 'you've got an in-out drive although no gates, which may or may not be something you'd like.'

'Don't bother me.'

Anjam smiled. 'Well, it's a relatively new build, as you can see – 1990s . . .'

Keen to get inside, not wanting to meet Galea, Lee said, 'Can we go in?'

'Of course.'

They walked up to a stylish black wooden door, which Anjam opened with a flourish. A gleamingly white central entrance hall greeted them, complete with spotlights that made the ceiling look like it was studded with diamonds. On the floor there was matt black laminate flooring – and some chairs, huge and red and smelling strongly of new leather. It was a bit like being inside a Premier League footballer's wish list.

'It's very . . .'

'Oh, it looks great,' Anjam said. 'But it does have a few issues. Probably why it's been on the books for so long.'

'How long?'

'Six months.'

'Oh.'

'Usually round here they just fly out the door,' he said. 'But . . .'

Lee looked around. A small-scale 'grand' staircase rose out of the central hall, above which was a gallery leading off, no doubt, to bedrooms, bathrooms etc. It didn't smell damp and he couldn't see any cracks in the walls . . .

Anjam took him through to the kitchen, which was at the back of the house. All brushed steel and sparkling glass plus more spotlights, this then led on to the conservatory and that swimming pool. It was all wonderful – if you liked that sort of thing. And of course, Lee would eventually have to 'decide' that he didn't. Not that Anjam was making that difficult. From the pristine conservatory they went into the pristine garden where the agent pointed to the back of the house next door.

'That's your problem,' he said.

Beyond a few planks of wood stacked up against the back wall and a pair of quad bikes on the patio, Lee couldn't see anything wrong with the neighbouring house.

'What?'

Anjam leant across and whispered, 'Pikeys.'

This wasn't an easy one for Lee. Having grown up in Custom House, on the edge of what were then, the Beckton Marshes, he'd known a lot of 'Pikeys' or Romanies as he preferred to call them. They'd had horses over there when he'd been a kid, some of them had given ad hoc riding lessons. But they could be insular and Lee knew that they were often disliked, especially now and especially in Essex where a sort of 'moral' panic had taken hold about 'Gypsies' during the last decade. Right-wing local politicians had done more than their bit to fan the flames about illegal stopping places and 'outsiders' colonising the county.

'I'd be lying if I said they weren't noisy,' Anjam said. 'Trouble is, the sort of people who can afford this property aren't the type who are prepared to put up with it, quite rightly. I mean, I have to be honest with you . . .'

Lee wondered whether he did. He also wondered whether it was true. A couple of planks of wood and some quad bikes did not a Romany encampment make. Why was he really trying to put people off this place? Was it because he lived across the road? But if he had nothing to hide, he had nothing to fear. And, anyway, did he even actually live in that house with Galea and his woman?

He had hoped that Anjam would mention this. Even more so now because if he did live opposite that might just put a prospective client off. A letting agent living opposite could make one feel watched. They walked back inside the house.

'So,' Lee said, 'where would you live if you found yourself having to live in Basildon? I was led to believe this was probably about the best area.'

'It is a very nice area,' Anjam said. 'And this is a very nice house, but . . . I suppose if I were to live in or around

Basildon, I'd probably go the other side of the A127 to Billericay. Your prices go up, of course, but there's more premium property there. Here, you can really get anyone living next door. They just have to have a bit of money. Do you want me to show you that barn conversion in Pitsea?'

THIRTEEN

Was Shazia coming home for lunch or not? Mumtaz phoned her.

'I'm going over to Dexter's place,' she said. 'I'll be back tonight.'

Mumtaz didn't want to say anything about how Shazia had come home and only spent a few hours with her. Even then she'd harangued her about Lee. So she didn't.

'All right,' she said. 'I'll see you later.'

She looked out of the living room window and into the street. And it was raining. Maybe the inclement weather had set in to welcome Trump to the UK. She was just about to go back to lay down on the sofa from sheer lack of interest when she heard the entry buzzer.

'Hello?'

'It's Vi,' a familiar voice said. 'Can I come up?'

'Of course.'

Mumtaz buzzed Vi Collins in. When she got to the top of the stairs the two women embraced.

'I hope you don't mind,' Vi said. 'There are some Sundays when doing the washing and watching the telly just ain't enough for a girl!'

Mumtaz took her coat. 'I agree entirely,' she said. 'Shazia is back to go on this anti-Trump demo but she's off round her boyfriend's place in Notting Hill. I may as well be invisible.'

'Kids!'

Vi sat down.

'And I'm just not up to Mum and Dad today,' Mumtaz said. 'Amma will feel she has to cook everything in sight and then I'll be force-fed and I just don't feel like eating.'

They both laughed. Even though she wasn't Asian, Vi knew a lot about Indian and Pakistani mummies and aunties.

'It's a pity you don't drink,' Vi said as she took a can of premixed gin and tonic out of her bag.

'Oh, you go ahead, I'll get you a glass,' Mumtaz said. 'And smoke if you want to. Lee does and really I am past caring these days.'

She went into the kitchen picked up a glass and returned. As Vi poured her G and T into the glass and lit a fag she said, 'You seem down, love.'

Mumtaz shrugged. 'Just fed up, to be honest,' she said. 'Shazia has always been headstrong, but these days I sometimes feel as if I'm just in her life for the odd piece of advice. And if that goes wrong . . .'

Vi laughed. 'The wonderful world of parenthood.'

'Like this march she's going on tomorrow,' Mumtaz said. 'I've told her I'm worried in case she gets arrested and I know she has similar fears. But I also know she'll go and, should she get arrested, she will blame me.'

Vi shook her head.

'It seems to be what I'm for these days. Vi, I don't suppose you know anything about this demo or march or whatever it is tomorrow, do you?'

'Actually, I do,' Vi said. 'Not much . . .'

'Bren!'

Des didn't often call Brenda into their bedroom in the daytime, especially with so many kids up and about. She went inside and closed the door behind her.

'Can I tell you something?' he said.

'You wanna blow job?'

'No, well yes, but . . .'

They both laughed. Brenda sat down on their bed beside him. 'So what is it?' she asked. 'Not like you to come over all serious.'

'Those coppers who came round yesterday, about Ruby's bloke . . .'

'What about them? We don't know nothing.'

'You don't,' Des said.

'You mean you do? How?'

He took a deep breath. Then he said, 'Dylan.'

Brenda very rarely saw Des's son Dylan, who lived in a bedsit in south London.

'What about him?'

'He's a flusher,' Des said.

'Oh, a . . .'

'Works down the sewers cleaning them. He found a body underneath Regent's Park day before yesterday.'

172

'Henry?'

'He never knew him but, yeah, I think so,' Des said. 'Why he was so upset and wanted to talk. Frightened the life out of the poor kid.'

'Blimey!' Brenda put a hand up to her head.

'I didn't twig until you told me after the coppers had gone,' Des said. 'Then I couldn't stop thinking about it. I mean, Dylan don't really know Ruby or Kian. But then I thought . . .'

'What?'

He shrugged. 'I dunno. That Dylan maybe got talking to Ruby or . . . I mean I don't know that Dylan knew anything about Henry. I tried to think whether I ever told him what Henry used to get up to. I'm not even sure I twigged that Henry went down sewers. I know he got into old hospitals and that . . .'

'You'll have to talk to Dylan,' Brenda said.

'Yeah, but what do I say?'

She thought for a moment and then she said, 'I dunno. Why was Dylan down there? I mean, I know it's his job, but why was he there?'

'He says they was checking it over because Trump's gonna be staying at the Ambassador's house in the park. Security.'

'So why wasn't the coppers doing it?'

'Couldn't tell you. Maybe them coppers who was here know?'

'I'll need to give Vi Collins a call,' Brenda said.

'Dylan won't thank us for getting him involved with the Babylon, or whatever young black men call the police these days,' Des said.

'Well, if he found Henry, then he's already been interviewed by them.' Brenda playfully punched his shoulder. 'Doughnut.'

They both smiled but then their faces became grave again.

*   *   *

Luckily for Lee, he was inside Anjam's car when Steve Galea came out of the house opposite. When he saw him, Anjam popped his head inside the car and said, 'Sorry, just got to speak to this man for a minute.'

Lee said, 'All right.'

Behind the safety of the blacked-out windows, slightly open so that he could hear what was going on, Lee watched and listened. Or tried to.

Galea looked angry, which seemed to be his default. But he wasn't shouting and so it was difficult to hear what he was saying. Anjam, by contrast, looked browbeaten, ashamed even. Head lowered, he was nodding in agreement with whatever Steve was saying. But then a woman came out of the house. Slim, dark-haired and made up like a dog's dinner, she stood behind Steve with her arm on his shoulder. Much taller than him, she had legs that seemed to go on forever. Lee could see the attraction. But then something very unexpected happened.

'He's coming in to Stansted Airport,' Vi said. 'Dunno what time he's due to land, but maybe that's some sort of state secret. There's a state banquet at the palace in the evening. God knows what the Queen makes of it all.'

'But not a protest tomorrow?' Mumtaz asked.

'Oh, there'll be people out shouting and hanging up anti-Trump banners,' Vi said. 'But Tuesday's the big day. Course we're all on high alert but I don't think somehow that Trump's gonna go down the Boleyn for a pint.'

'Shazia told me she's protesting tomorrow.'

'She may well be. People are coming from all over the country.'

'I'm not happy about it,' Mumtaz said. 'I mean, I'm happy

that people are protesting, but if Shazia is still intent on joining the police . . .'

'It wouldn't work in her favour if she got arrested,' Vi said.

'That's what I think.'

Vi's phone rang and she looked at the screen to see who was calling.

'Oh, bollocks!' she said. 'I'll have to take this.'

'Do you want me to . . .'

Vi waved a hand. 'No, it's all right.' Then she spoke into the phone. 'Hello, love.'

'Oh, DI Collins, it's Brenda Joseph.'

She sounded breathless.

'What is it, love?'

'I need to see you,' she said, 'about . . .'

'Okey-dokey.'

'I know it's probably your day off, but can you pop round to ours?'

'Course.' Canning Town was only ten minutes away. Thank God she'd only had one G and T. 'I'll come now. Give me about ten or fifteen minutes?'

She heard Brenda sigh with what sounded like relief. 'That'd be great.'

'See ya then.'

Vi ended the call. She stood up.

'Sorry, girl, I've gotta go,' she said to Mumtaz. 'Duty calls.'

They'd kissed, Anjam and the woman – and not in a friendly way. That had been a snog.

When he got back into the car, Lee said, 'Very attractive lady.'

Anjam blushed. A very rare thing to see in young or youngish men these days, Lee was surprised.

'Oh, that's my girlfriend,' he said.

'Oh. So if I did come to live here we'd be neighbours?'

Anjam smiled. 'Why I know so much about the Pikeys,' he said. 'Maria's always complaining about the rubbish they leave on the street.'

'I'm surprised you took it on your books,' Lee said as Anjam began to drive off.

'Business is business.'

'But you're not exactly selling it, are you?' Lee said. 'Leastways, not to me. Bit too close to your own gaff?'

He laughed, nervously. 'Not at all,' he said. 'Be lovely to have some nice neighbours. But I do also feel that I have to be honest with you. I mean, if you moved in there and next door started kicking off you'd want, quite rightly, to have words with me, wouldn't you?'

Lee shrugged. 'Guess so.'

'I mean, I might live here but I don't live next door to the Pikeys and so I can sort of put up with it. I'll be honest, I wouldn't like to live next door.'

'So, how're you going to get rid of the place?' Lee asked. As they turned out of the street, he could see that Maria was still looking at the back of the car.

'Honestly? Wait for some people like them to come along,' Anjam said.

'Like the neighbours?'

'Yeah. Or maybe wait until the owner wants to sell. I've no doubt the neighbours would have someone lined up they want to live next door to. Pikeys are like that, always trying to get their own people in.'

It always amazed Lee, the way people who obviously came from immigrant backgrounds themselves, as well as the white British, always doubled down on Travellers. And so openly too. Prejudice against these people was still very acceptable.

Lee changed the subject, partly because he didn't want to rant at this man but also because he wanted to know more about Maria.

'Lovely girlfriend you have,' he said.

'Maria? Oh yes, I'm *so* lucky!' Anjam enthused. 'She's so beautiful. Of course, Mum and Dad would rather I had a Muslim girlfriend, but I told them, "That's not the way people do things here." I mean, they know that, but it's like, a different generation, yeah?'

'Yeah.'

They joined the A127 again and began to head for Pitsea and this famous barn conversion.

After a little puddle of silence, Lee said, 'So who was the bloke with your lady? Looked like he was getting a bit aerated . . .'

Anjam laughed, if a little tightly. 'Oh, that's Maria's brother,' he said. 'Her family are Maltese and their men are a bit protective. He's a funny little man.'

And Lee could only agree with that. Steven Galea was indeed both funny, but not ha-ha, rather more along the lines of odd. And he was little. What he wasn't, however, was – if his ex-wife was to be believed – this 'Maria's' brother.

Camden was heaving. In spite of the fact that everything was expensive, it always was. But was there an extra frisson in the air because of Trump's visit? There were certainly more Trump products on show. From T-shirts featuring the president saying, 'Grab them by the pussy!' to knitted pink 'pussy' hats to books and calendars featuring Trump's most famous dumb sayings.

Grace's sister had decided not to come along and so it was just the two of them. Grace had an appointment at a tattooist's on the High Street at midday, but in the meantime they looked for boots.

They stopped at some gothy-looking shop and went inside. Grace picked up a boot, covered with studs, with a platform sole about six inches high and said, 'How about this, Shazia?'

Shazia considered it for a moment and then said, 'Nah. Couldn't walk in those.'

'Yeah, you could,' Grace said. 'You have to suffer for your style, man.'

'Yeah, but there's suffering and suffering. If I fell over and broke a leg that wouldn't be a good look.'

Grace shrugged and then carried on looking.

The owner of the shop, a middle-aged Asian man gave Shazia a look she knew of old. Contemptuous it seemed to say, *What's someone like you doing looking at immoral clothes for Westerners?*

Like her late father, she knew he wouldn't see the irony in peddling his 'immoral' wares. She picked up a shoe that had a heel that was at least five inches high, an ankle strap and a pointed toe, in red. It virtually screamed 'fuck me'.

'I'd like to try these,' she said to the man. 'In a size six.'

He took the shoe from her wordlessly and went out to the storeroom at the back of the shop.

Grace, who had seen this said, 'If you can't walk in those boots, how you gonna manage with them shoes?'

Shazia shrugged. How could she explain it? She couldn't. Eventually she said, 'I'll manage.'

Grace, now shuffling through a load of vampire coats said, 'Up to you.'

* * *

Brenda took Vi straight through to her kitchen where Des was sitting at the table.

'You wanna cuppa?' she asked.

Vi was by no means drunk from one G and T but a cuppa wasn't a bad idea.

'Thanks, love,' she said as she sat down. 'Strong, two sugars.'

Brenda put the kettle on and threw a tea bag into a cup followed by two large teaspoons of sugar.

'I'm sorry to bother you,' Brenda said, 'but me and Des thought you ought to know something.'

'What?'

Des said, 'One of my sons, Dylan. He's from my first marriage. We don't see that much of him. He's got his own place . . . But he comes sometimes, especially if he's worried about something. His mother died before me and Brenda got together and like all her kids, he misses her.'

'Why Des is so grateful his kids still feel they can talk to him,' Brenda said. She poured hot water into the cup.

'So me and Dylan spoke on Friday,' Des said. 'He'd had a horrible day at work. Him and his mates found a dead body.'

'I know that one,' Vi said. 'Never good. Poor kid.'

'Thing is, DI Collins,' Des said, 'my boy's a flusher. He was one of them as found poor Henry's body underneath Regent's Park. Course, we didn't know that.'

Brenda gave Vi her tea.

'They didn't know each other?'

'We tried to think, and we could only come up with one time they met, which was here,' Brenda said. 'Not all my kids by Devon and Des's from Clarice know each other well. Far as we know, Henry's name meant nothing to Dylan.'

'He didn't recognise him,' Des said. 'It was me as put two and two together.'

'Problem with having such a big family,' Brenda said. 'Kids and grandkids come in and out like ships in the night.'

'Dylan will have been interviewed by Counter Terrorism already,' Vi said. 'But I'll let West know about this connection. Thanks for letting me know.'

'I'm sure Dylan's got nothing to do with it,' Des said.

Vi didn't know Dylan but she said, 'Did your lad like the idea of working down the sewers or did he just take the job because it was a job? I mean, flushing isn't for everybody.'

'He never talked to me about it before he got the job,' Des said. 'But I know he finds it interesting. They find some strange things down there. I don't mean bodies . . .'

'Like what?'

'All sorts. Money, jewellery, make-up. It's amazing what does slip down the bog or the sink. I s'pose they're in a hurry . . .'

'Dylan and Henry will have had a lot to talk about,' Vi said.

'I s'pose one or other of the kids could've told Dylan about Henry or Henry about Dylan,' Brenda said. 'It's difficult to know what goes on between them all.'

'I understand that. But I hope you'll understand that we'll have to speak to Dylan again,' Vi said. 'Not saying I suspect him of anything, but it is a connection so we'll have to follow it up.'

Brenda sighed.

Des said, 'I thought you'd have to. He's due over here for tea later this afternoon if you want to hang on.'

Ever since they'd started working together back in 2012, Lee and Mumtaz had always shared information about their cases. But ever since their relationship had broken down that had all but stopped. It wasn't good and it was becoming a habit. If one of them didn't stop it soon, they'd drift apart professionally as well as personally. Last time she'd stayed over in his spare room they could have talked, but somehow they hadn't. Lee decided that now was as good a time as ever to put that right. Hoping to God that Shazia wasn't with her mum, he rang Mumtaz's bell.

'Hello?'

'It's me,' Lee said. 'You got a cuppa up there with my name on it?'

He heard her laugh. 'Always.'

She buzzed him in.

'I was just about to surrender to the *Politics Show* on the TV,' Mumtaz said when he got to the top of the stairs. 'You've saved me from myself. God! What's happened to your hair?'

Lee put his hand protectively up to his all but bald head and said, 'Ah, well thereby hangs a tale . . .'

She switched the TV off and went into the kitchen. 'Sit down and I'll bring tea.'

Lee could see that Shazia was in residence somewhere as there was a big rucksack in the corner of the living room.

'Where's Shazia?' he called out to the kitchen.

'Off to see her boyfriend in Notting Hill,' Mumtaz replied. 'She's back this evening.'

Lee knew the girl was down for the march against Trump. Like most of the adults in Shazia's life, he agreed with her stance although he was afraid she might get hurt if things turned ugly, or screw up her career if she got arrested. But there was no point saying anything.

Mumtaz came back into the living room carrying two mugs of tea.

'So to what do I owe the pleasure on a Sunday?' Mumtaz asked as she sat down opposite her guest. 'I've just had Vi round here.'

'Oh?'

'Just for a chat, but then she was called away.'

He laughed. 'I remember it well.'

She put an ashtray on the coffee table.

'Smoke if you like,' she said. 'The landlord never comes these days and quite honestly I don't care if he does. The place is riddled with damp and he won't answer any of my calls. Mr Brooks downstairs told me he's not paying any more rent until he deals with his bathroom, and I don't blame him. It stinks in there. Even the shower curtain is mouldy.' She shook her head. 'I never thought I'd have to rent. It's a minefield.'

Lee wanted to say that she needn't. That she could move in with him whenever she wanted to, but he didn't. They'd talked and talked about the way they felt about each other and the difficulties they faced because of that and they had come to a 'rational' decision. Now was not the time to rake all that up again.

Lee sipped his tea. 'Thought it'd be a good idea to review what we're doing,' he said.

She nodded.

'I've actually been working this morning,' he continued. 'Out in Basildon following up on this domestic. Seems that the woman I've been investigating owes money to some people who might be cuckooing.'

'Really?'

He told her about Lorraine Pritchard and her dealings with Steven Galea, about Anjam Rajput and his supposed girlfriend.

'So do all three of them live in that house?' Mumtaz asked.

'I'm not sure. Anjam said that the house was his and the

land registry bears that out inasmuch as it's registered to his mum and dad. He told me he lived there with Maria, but he didn't mention Steve. He's a funny bloke, Anjam. Late thirties, sharp-looking, but he's kinda soft too. I can imagine him being pushed around with not much effort. Apparently, his parents wouldn't approve of Maria. So they don't know.'

'That would figure.'

'But what I'm pretty sure he doesn't know is that Maria isn't Steve's sister.'

'How do you know that?' Mumtaz asked.

Lee told her about his encounter with Rosemary Galea – and that haircut.

Laughing he said, 'I really felt that if I didn't have at least a number four she'd get the hump and then it would have been for nothing. As it was, as the hair fell away, she seemed to start to fancy me. Opened up like an oyster.'

Mumtaz shook her head. 'I wish I could say that I like it, but I don't.'

'I knew *you* wouldn't,' he said. 'I don't like it meself! But what can you do? Anyway, the point is that Rosemary told me Steve only has brothers. All very macho from the sound of it. Once owned a nightclub down Southend, but the "boys" screwed it up by getting into brawls with local hard nuts.'

Mumtaz frowned. 'So what does it mean? For your client?'

Lee sighed. 'He knows his wife's spending's out of control. What appears to be happening is that she's involved with loan sharks.'

'Galea.'

'I think so, yeah. And normally I'd just present my evidence to Jason, Lorraine's husband, and leave it to him. But Galea is violent. He's smacked Lorraine around, presumably when she didn't pay up on time. God knows how much debt she's in.'

Mumtaz shook her head. She knew all about how debt to certain people could be life-threatening. Her husband's creditors had all but wrecked her finances. There was a reason she was in a damp, rented flat. She also knew that there wasn't always anything that could be done about it.

'They seem to be using the house as a centre for their loan shark business,' Lee continued. 'And if I'm right, they're using Maria as the hook that means they can do that with Anjam's blessing. I wouldn't say he was afraid when I saw him together with Steve today, but I think that it's affecting his life, and if Steve is as violent as I think he is, Anjam could be in danger. Gave me some load of old pony about not being able to rent out the house he took me to look at because there are Travellers living next door.'

'Were there?'

'I dunno,' Lee said. 'He pointed at a couple of quad bikes and some planks of wood in the back garden and said the word "Pikey". He was trying to put me off.'

'Why?'

'Don't want one of his tenants living opposite his girlfriend's little loan operation. Steve for one was angry after I'd been in to view. And who knows what else they're running from a great big gaff in Langdon Hills, eh? Drugs? Girls?'

'So time for the police?'

'Dunno,' he lit a cigarette. 'Jason, the client, don't want to call Old Bill but I think that I may have to. I think I'm gonna have to put someone apart from me on it.'

'We're a bit stretched at the moment,' Mumtaz said.

'I know. How you getting on with John Saunders?'

'Well . . .'

* * *

184

'What time's he due there?' West asked.

'About four, for tea.'

'What? Afternoon tea in Canning Town? Cucumber sandwiches and scones?'

Vi had never seen Counter Terrorism in the same light as MI5, but now she wondered. Five were all posh and almost all male, but Counter Terrorism were generally a tough bunch who grew up playing football in the street and had a good grasp of shit TV. But then West did speak 'nicely' and where didn't his type get in? She resolved to 'educate' the sod.

'Brenda and Des are old-fashioned East Enders,' she said, 'Sunday tea here's all about seafood. Mussels, whelks, cockles, a few prawns if you're lucky, white bread and Mr Kipling cake. My mum done it every Sunday all her life. It's part of our culture. Sir.'

'Oh. Oh,' West said. 'Well, er . . . I've learnt something today, then . . .'

'Always happy to oblige, sir.'

Vi didn't dislike West but anyone who 'punched down' was fair game as far as she was concerned.

'Assuming he's still at home, we could pick him up now,' West said.

Vi had an address for Dylan but she wanted to keep this low-key, for the sake of the family.

'We know he'll be here at four, sir. Why send in the troops?'

There was a pause and then he said, 'What if he fails to show up?'

'And what if he's not at his gaff? What if he's shagging someone he met in the pub last night?'

And yet even while she was saying it, Vi wondered whether that even happened any more. Didn't young people all meet online these days? One of her nieces had told her about 'hook-ups' on something called Tinder. In principle it sounded like a good idea for mature single people like Vi herself, but for twenty-year-old girls? Really?

'Sir, we know he'll probably come here,' Vi said. 'So my instinct is to go with that.'

She heard him sigh. Was he busy with something or someone himself? Or did he just resent having to schlep out to the Keir Hardie Estate on a wet Sunday afternoon?

He said, 'All right, DI Collins. I'll see you there at three.'

'Thank you, sir.'

'Will you stay with the family until then?'

'Yeah.'

What else was she going to do? She'd even offered to peel shrimps for tea.

'He's a strange man,' Mumtaz said. 'At the risk of putting people in boxes, I'd say he was autistic. Or at least on the autistic spectrum. But then there's an argument we're all on the spectrum somewhere . . .'

'I think you're at risk of getting your psychological knickers in a twist,' Lee said. But he smiled when he spoke and so she smiled back.

'Oh, you know what I mean, closed off,' she said. 'But also quite passive aggressive . . .'

'Do you think that DNA test they did can be relied upon?'

She shrugged. 'Unless you take a test controlled by an academic institution, who can know? I'm sure Brenda could get hold of material from him easily, but I get the feeling she doesn't want to go down that route.'

'Maybe the expense?'

'Possibly. Although John's "new" family are fantastically wealthy,' she said. 'The Gustavssons endow mainly Christian-rooted charities all over the world.'

'Never heard of 'em.'

'Few people have,' she said. 'They're very secretive. To give you an example, they don't actively support any political organisations and yet John, at least, is openly a supporter of Trump.'

'P'raps he's here to see him.'

'He can see him any time he likes in the States. There's not much on the Gustavssons, but what I have managed to pick up online points to at least the possibility that they help to fund Trump. A lot of people believe that.'

'But no one knows?'

'No, and anyway it's irrelevant,' Mumtaz said.

'Maybe John has just come to see his sister and her family?' Lee said.

'Maybe.' She shook her head. 'But if that's the case, why not stay with her?'

'Doesn't like kids?'

She smiled. 'Maybe not, although Brenda says he spends hours and hours at her place. Not necessarily talking to her kids, admittedly . . . He's in a Travelodge in Marylebone, which, were he at meetings or had business in the City I could understand, but all he does is just wander about. He goes into bookshops and spends time alone in his room.'

'Maybe he meets someone there?'

'What? In his room?'

'Maybe. We could wire it up . . .'

'I'd have to talk to Brenda. She doesn't have much money. She's already spending out on what is, in effect, a feeling.'

'Do you believe in it, this feeling?'

187

She thought for a moment. It wasn't a simple yes/no proposition as far as Mumtaz could tell. And yet if she was to continue with this in good conscience it had to be.

She said, 'I think I do . . .'

'There's a "but" coming?'

'Yes, but . . . It's not about Brenda. I totally believe her. She's using her savings to fund this and she is not minted. I wonder, although I've not asked her about this, whether he has some ill intent towards her.'

'Why?'

'Well both his parents are dead. Only Brenda remains from that time.'

'But she had nothing to do with selling him to some weirdos in the States. Rich weirdos who've given him a bloody good life, as far as I can see. What's he got to complain about?'

'Lee, his dad sold him. Probably for the price of some booze,' Mumtaz said. 'He didn't sell Brenda.'

'She was an adult.'

'But Reg was a drunk for decades. He could've monetised Brenda years before . . .'

'Maybe he wasn't desperate then.'

'Maybe.'

'Anyway, he got his,' Lee said. 'Old Reg died destitute, didn't he?'

'Yes.'

'So divine justice has been done.'

'You think?'

She looked at him and Lee turned away.

'The other way of looking at it,' Mumtaz said, 'is that Reg got away with it. He sold his own child, he got pissed out of his mind for a few years and then he died. And his end, as far as I can tell, was comfortable. Being cared for by nuns in one of the holiest places in the country. I tell you, if that were my dad, I'd still have a bitter taste in my mouth.'

'Who's that woman?'

Brenda had all but forgotten about John. Vi was out of the way, in the garden smoking, but John could see her and she could see him. Mickey Jay was playing with his cars on the floor, completely absorbed in a fantasy world of talking Range Rovers.

'Here to see Dylan when he gets here,' Brenda said.

'What for?'

'Oh, he was one of the flushers who found that dead body underneath Regent's Park on Friday,' Brenda said. 'I never knew because Des never told me until this morning. That woman's Vi Collins, she's with the police.'

'Dylan's Des's son?'

'Yeah.' She sat down beside him. 'The bloke who died was my Ruby's ex. Me and Des don't think they ever met, but the coppers want to check it with Dylan.'

'So why don't they go to wherever he lives?'

'Oh, he's young!' Brenda said. 'Always out and about, and at his work's difficult. We know he's going to be here for fishy tea this afternoon.'

'But that's hours away . . .'

Brenda shrugged. 'I've offered Vi a bit of food. She's already peeled a load of shrimps.'

FOURTEEN

Shazia pressed the cling film covering the dressing on her wrist down hard. It hurt.

She hadn't meant to get a tattoo. But when she found that Grace was going to be in the studio for upwards of two hours *and* the artist who wasn't inking her mate was at a loose end . . .

She hadn't had a clue what she'd like. Grace was having a map of Africa on her back. This first session had just been to do the outline. Shazia's artist, Xavi, had presented her with all sorts of options, from tiny butterflies on her ankles to 'sleeves' featuring Spiderman, Superman and the Black Widow. Eventually, she'd settled on a small copperplate written word. Survivor.

That, she felt, summed her up. It was only when she left the studio and got on the Tube to go to Dexter's place that she began to question what she'd just done. The word invited questions. Survivor of what? A road accident? A terror attack?

Much as people said otherwise, there wasn't really any appetite for tales about incest unless they were told about celebrities. Or if those listening to such stories were prurient ghouls. And who wanted them digging around in your life?

Shazia had thought that the only thing she had to worry about with this tattoo was how Mumtaz was going to be about it. But she was the least of her worries. As she peered underneath the dressing she felt her heart sink. There were going to be no end to the questions about this for a very long time.

Everyone in Canning Town seemed to have at least two cars. When he'd been little, one of those would have been permanently in the front garden held up by bricks. But that was less common now the rich people and the students had moved in. That was the upside. The downside was that people like Dylan couldn't afford to live there unless they stayed with their parents. And while he had nothing against Brenda, she wasn't his mum and so he didn't want to live with her.

Of course, the types of cars had changed. Where once there were Mondeos and Fiestas now there were Range Rovers, hybrids, and of course loads and loads of bikes. Dylan had a bike when he was a kid, but he hadn't had knee pads and a high-vis jacket. He'd thrown the helmet Des had bought him into the Victoria Dock.

Jogging along from Victoria Dock Light Railway Station, Dylan listened to Thelonious Monk on his oversized cans and half closed his eyes to let the sounds seep into his soul. After finding that dead dude in the sewer he felt that, more than ever, his soul needed cleansing. Things like that were bad for your head and he knew he'd need to screw up all his courage to get back down below the ground again on Monday. It was part of the reason why he'd taken his dad up on the invite to fish tea. If being around Des, Brenda and all the assorted kids didn't take your mind off things, then nothing would. He just hoped that his stepmother's weird brother John wasn't about. Not that he knew him very much. Then there was that weird kid of Tina's – Mickey Jay. Lived in a world of his own mostly, and who could blame him? Tina left him with old people – his dad and Brenda – for most of the time. Although he'd never say it to anyone outside the family, he considered Tina a bit of a bike, if he were honest.

He turned the corner and, although he was aware of the fact there was a big, sleek Merc outside his parents' house, he didn't think anything of it. With so many big cars on the estate, people parked wherever they could.

The only time he became aware of the owner of the vehicle was when his dad showed him into the living room.

Lee went home before he did something stupid. He'd had the best, easiest conversation he'd had with Mumtaz for months. It had almost been like the old days when they'd been an item. She'd even, albeit unknowingly, flirted with him with her eyes. He'd got an erection.

When he arrived home to the sound of Chronus listing West Ham first-team players from the 1975/6 season, Lee determined to put his energies into his work.

'So what's the score?' Jason Pritchard said when he picked up the phone and saw the caller was Lee.

'I don't know whether Lorraine found these Langdon Hills people through her Uncle Terry or vice versa,' Lee said. 'But the set-up feels like a cuckooing.'

'Fuck.'

'Seems like the owner of the place is in a relationship with the woman who's telling him the other bloke is her brother.'

'So they're both shagging her you mean?'

'Could be. Now Jase, I'm not saying these people are big players, but there's a Maltese family of brothers involved. Bit on the lairy side. I don't know them . . .'

'What's the name?'

'Galea.'

Jason didn't answer right away. 'What? Steve Galea?'

'You know him?'

'Everyone in Essex under fifty knows Steven Galea,' he said. 'Oh fuck.'

'What?'

'Well you're right about him and his brothers being second rate,' Jason said. 'But I think you might've underestimated how "lairy" they can get. The eldest one, Giovanni, once owed money to Steve and so they had a ruck and Steve bit the top of his ear off. Four of 'em have done time. Not Steve, but I don't know how. What's the bloke you think they're cuckooing, like?'

'Nice. Helps his dad run a letting company. Dad's a villain, it is said, but the boy seems kosher. He's clearly besotted with this Maria who's told him she's Steve's sister.'

'Ain't got no sister.'

'So I gather.'

Jason sighed. 'How could Lorraine let herself get involved with that bunch of bastards?'

'Desperation?'

'I give her money! She's got the bleedin' house!'

'She's starting her life again,' Lee said. 'Unexpectedly on the market. I know what that feels like. But at least for blokes we don't have to make ourselves look beautiful. Which is a good thing because most of us are ugly.'

Jason laughed.

'Normally I'd say it's up to you now and you'll have to have it out with her,' Lee said. 'But because of the situation, I'd like to speak to a few faces.'

'I told you, I don't want plod involved!'

'I know, but if Steve Galea's got his hooks into this other bloke . . .'

'If his dad's a villain, then he can sort it out!'

'Jase, they're sharking,' Lee said. 'And if I'm right, then Lorraine's Uncle Terry's involved too. Nobody gets other people involved in loans like this if they're doing all right. He's a victim too. You know how these things work! I buy a car off Terry for a price I can't afford, he fixes me up with a loan from Steve and gets a bit off his own debt for his pains.'

'If you put Terry out of business, my name'll be mud with her family! Even if they do all hate him!'

'And if someone doesn't stop it soon, Terry'll go bankrupt *and* get his legs broken.'

'I never met the bloke,' Dylan told DI West. 'I've not met Ruby that often. How was I to know he was her boyfriend?'

'Ex,' West said.

'Ex.'

Dylan looked at his dad and Brenda resentfully. 'Why didn't you talk to me about it?' he said. 'Why get the police down here?'

'We know you've got nothing to do with it, son,' Des said. 'Just gotta make sure you never said nothing about Henry to anyone else.'

'I didn't know him!' Dylan said. 'Fuck sake! And if I had I would've steered clear 'cause of what he done. Those people are mad!'

'What people?'

'People who go urban exploring! Going into places they shouldn't, calling out ambulances when they get hurt! They're a fucking liability!'

'Have you ever met any?' West asked.

'What, down the sewers? No. But I've come across them in pubs and the blokes I work with have seen them.'

'When?'

'I dunno. But everyone hates them. Bloody rich boys doing it because they're bored and they got too much time to kill! How'd someone like Ruby meet one of them?'

'I dunno,' Brenda said. 'Brought him home about six months ago.'

'What? And he come round here?'

'Sometimes.'

'Why?'

Brenda shrugged. 'He was always very nice. Helped out with the food and the kids. I'll be honest, Dylan, I thought she'd landed on her feet for once.'

Dylan rolled his eyes.

Vi said, 'Love, we know you didn't do anything wrong. But we do need to find out whether there's a connection between you and Henry.'

'There isn't! Wasn't!'

'On the face of it, no,' she said. 'But it is a bit of a coincidence that you found your stepsister's bloke dead.'

'Well, yeah, but I never knew . . .'

'If we could ask Henry, we would,' Vi said. 'But we can't. So we have to ask you whether you can remember whether you knew of Henry, even if you never met him, and if so whether you told anyone else about his exploring? Not to get him into trouble but just in passing.'

When he thought about it, Dylan could see that what they were asking him wasn't so outlandish. A lot of people talked almost without thinking about all sorts of things. All he had to do to prove that was go on a tea break with his colleagues.

He nodded and then he said, 'I honest to God never even knew about the bloke. One of the kids may've told me that Ruby had a new boyfriend, but I never really took no notice. The blokes I work with talk about these explorers from time to time, but I've never seen one down the sewers. I was out of work for bloody ages and so I'm just grateful for the job. Keep my head down and get on with it. If anyone here told people they shouldn't about this Henry then it's probably one of the kids. They love all that tunnelling business, don't they?'

Brenda snorted. 'Oh, Dylan, who would the kids tell, eh? All they do is go to school and come home. Might play out but . . .'

But Vi's mind was working on what Dylan had said. Henry was known to take people into dangerous or derelict buildings if asked. And so many kids were almost always hanging around Brenda and Des's place . . .

That tattoo did something to Dexter's libido. On the pretext of showing Shazia around their massive great house on the corner of Farmer Street, he took her up to his bedroom and shagged her behind the door. It wasn't the most sensual sex Shazia had ever had, but it was a little bit exciting with the family's au pair ensconced in the room next door.

Later they went up onto the roof garden from which they could see amazing views over West London. Shazia thought it must be a great place from which to view the Notting Hill Carnival, although Dex had already told her that his parents were usually away at their place in France in August.

'But you can see it, can't you?' she said, assuming that Dexter and his brother didn't go to Provence with their mum and dad.

But he said, 'Oh no, we always go away with the old folk. It's really cool in Gordes. It's one of the hilltop towns, got caves and everything. Jonny and I go down to Marseille . . .'

He wanged on for a bit about scoring dope down by Marseille Harbour, sailing off to the Chateau d'If off their nuts on ketamine and various mishaps in the Camargue. But Shazia was too taken with the view to listen. What, however, did get her attention was when Dexter's mother (call me Alice) came out into the roof garden and said, 'Dexter, dear, will your friend be staying for dinner?'

Why Shazia got the feeling that 'Alice' knew her name and deliberately wasn't using it, she didn't know. But that was how she felt.

'Well, yes . . .'

'Oh, I er . . .' She'd promised Mumtaz she'd be home for dinner. As it was, she was hardly spending any time at all with her. 'I'd love to, but I did say I'd go home . . .'

'Oh.'

It was difficult to know whether her refusal had caused offence or not. Alice was clearly riled about something. When they'd first met she'd been fine. Had she heard them shagging? Shazia felt her face glow hot.

'All right,' Alice said eventually. 'Well, Dexter, dinner will be in thirty minutes and so if you'd like to get ready . . .'

'Yes, Mama.'

And then she left.

When she'd gone, Shazia said, 'Oh God, I hope I haven't upset your mum!'

Dexter smiled. 'No,' he said. 'Forget it.'

Shazia whispered, 'I thought she might've heard . . .'

'Oh, she probably did,' he said.

'What!'

'Just glad I'm getting some from someone who isn't called Pippa, knowing her.'

What? For a moment Shazia had to think before she replied. Was he implying that his mother . . .

'Jonny's been going out with this girl called Lucy who's the spit of Kate Middleton. Total WASP, you know.'

'Kate Middleton's very attractive,' Shazia said.

'Yeah, but a bit safe, you know. I mean . . .' He took a joint out of his pocket and lit up. 'Don't worry about it.'

But suddenly Shazia did. She didn't want to be some 'trophy Asian', if that was indeed what she was! She'd never felt that she was before they came here. Dex was behaving like a bit of a dick with his stories about being 'off his face' at his mum and dad's pad in France. Were his family what some people called the 'chattering classes'? As she understood it, left-wing intellectuals who liked, so some said, to increase their 'cool' capital by doing things like sponsoring orphanages, adopting children from war zones and publicly and loudly, espousing causes in order to big themselves up. Her amma and Lee couldn't stand people like that. They said the way some of these people behaved was both racist and snobbish.

She followed him downstairs to the large first floor hallway and put on her coat. He carried on smoking the joint in spite of being inside his parents' house. But then they probably smoked dope too.

He kissed her goodbye just as a tall blonde girl came down the stairs. Dex glanced at her and smiled.

'Oh, Briggite,' he said, 'this is Shazia, my girlfriend.'

The girl and Shazia shook hands.

'She's our au pair from Sweden,' Dexter told Shazia.

'Oh.'

'And you're from Pakistan, via Forest Gate, aren't you?'

How could he be so bloody crass? He hadn't even got the country her parents had come from right!

But she didn't want to embarrass Brigitte and so she said, 'Actually Bangladesh.'

The Swede smiled. 'Two very different places, Dexter,' she said. 'You know there was a war between Pakistan and Bangladesh back in the nineteen seventies.'

'Oh . . .'

Shazia could have kissed her.

'That's right,' she said. 'Nice to meet you, Brigitte.'

And then she left.

Dexter watched her go without, it seemed, a clue as to how stupid the two girls had made him look. When she got to the bottom of the road he called out after Shazia, 'See you tomorrow!'

Terry was on his own in the shed at the back of the forecourt. Staring down at his phone, he looked miserable. When he saw Lee, however, he smiled.

'Hello, mate,' he said. 'I didn't think I was gonna see you till Monday. You thought about that motor again, have you? Too good to miss. I knew it was right for you and your missus . . .'

Was it the expression on Lee's face that brought Terry's wall of car dealer words to an end?

Lee sat down and offered Terry a cigarette, which he took.

'Terry, I know you're in trouble,' Lee said.

He protested loudly. 'Who says?'

But his face flushed a deep shade of puce.

Lee said, 'All right, let me lay it out for you.'

'Lay what out?'

'Tel, let me speak,' Lee said. 'When I've spoken I'll help you.'

'Help me?'

'Yeah.' He raised a finger. 'Now let's have a word about Steve Galea, shall we?'

The main thing was not to overreact. After all, as tattoos went, it was discreet. Unfortunately, it wasn't inoffensive because it invited questions. But Mumtaz knew better than to try to reason with a teenager. And also, she could see that Shazia regretted it.

'Grace is having this map of Africa on her back,' Shazia said. 'The artist just did the outline today and that took ages. It's going to be beautiful. Like a statement, you know?'

'Yes,' Mumtaz said. She put a mug of tea down in front of the girl and sat down. 'I'm not against tattoos per se, I just think they should be beautiful if possible and not raise questions you don't want to answer.'

'Amma, you know what my dad did to me, I need to own it.'

'Own it? What does that even mean?'

There were a lot of expressions in common use that made very little sense as far as Mumtaz was concerned. 'Owning' something was one of them. Just because a person acknowledged – owned – what had happened to them did not, to her way of thinking, necessarily precipitate healing. Like a physical wound, psychological cuts and bruises healed at their own pace and, although balm could be applied to them and sometimes even helped, it was not a cure-all.

Shazia shrugged.

'I thought if I had it on my wrist and so I had to talk about it . . .'

'But you don't really want to, after all?' Mumtaz asked.

'What do I say?' she said. 'People who didn't know Dad could think I'm making it up to get attention. I didn't think it through.'

Mumtaz nodded. She'd never wanted to get a tattoo but she knew people who had. And while some of her friends had been delighted with their inkings, a fair few spent all their time covering them up. Or having them removed.

She took Shazia's hands. 'I tell you what,' she said. 'Why don't you have that changed to something else when it's healed?'

'Like what?'

Her eyes looked hurt and Mumtaz wondered what else had upset her.

'I don't know. Maybe a flower? Like a sprig of something? Speak to your artist. What he's done is well done and so I'm sure he'll be able to change it,' Mumtaz said. 'I doubt very much whether you'll be the first to go back to him wanting to change a tattoo.'

'Yeah, well . . .'

'And so what else is the matter?' she asked the girl.

Shazia seemed to shrink down in her seat. She said, 'Dex is a dick.'

'Really? Why?'

Dexter had seemed like a nice enough young man but he was also a bit posh and that, Mumtaz knew from her own

201

experiences at university, could be a problem. For a start, people like that had so much more money than anyone else, it made keeping up with them difficult.

But Shazia just waved the question away. 'I think I'll go and have a lie down for a bit,' she said as she picked up her cup of tea. 'Unless dinner's ready?'

'No, not really,' Mumtaz said.

'What is it?'

'Just a dhal, rice, the usual.'

Shazia stopped and doubled back. Then she put her arms around Mumtaz's neck and kissed her.

'I can't tell you how great it is to be home!' she said.

When she'd gone Mumtaz shook her head. Teenagers. Then, just for a moment she frowned. She hoped that Dexter wasn't being a 'dick' in any way that could hurt Shazia . . .

Terry Gilbert put the fag that Lee had given him, out and then lit up one of his own.

'I s'pose if I'm honest it all really started donkey's years ago, way before Steve Galea was on the scene,' he said. 'It's hard being your own guv'nor, as I'm sure you know.'

Lee had come clean to Terry about who he was and what he did. It was the only way to progress this now without everything coming as a shock to the old geezer. He had, Lee was learning, a lot of troubles of his own.

'Jason's getting bled dry by Lorraine,' Lee said. 'He had to do something.'

'I know. I know.' He shook his head. 'It was the bloody bankers as done for me. 2008. I nearly lost the lot in 2016 and then the year after it all got really serious and that was when Steve happened.'

'How'd you meet him?'

'At an auction in Hertfordshire. He outbid me on a Porsche and we got chatting. Reckoned he had a few bob and offered to help me out. Now I'm not a bleedin' idiot and so I knew it had to be hooky, but I pushed that to one side in me head. For a while it was sweet, you know? He was local, he never put the screws on. Then one day he wanted his money back. All of it.'

'What are we talking?'

'Twenty grand. Course I couldn't do it. So up went the interest rate. I don't have to tell you where this is going.'

He didn't. Lee had seen it all before.

'I borrowed from the wife's old man, so we ended up falling out. Then it was friends . . . I sold all sorts . . .' He shrugged. 'So course, when Lorraine come to see me with her own problems I was fucking useless. The mistake I made was telling Steve about her. I think I was moaning, to be true. Something about my silly niece getting herself into bother having her face and her tits done to get herself a new husband. I wouldn't have done nothing about it if Steve hadn't dangled a carrot at me.'

'What carrot?'

'An interest holiday. If I managed to rope her in I could have six months off paying interest. Course, silly arse here thinks that'll give me enough time to get meself sorted. I never and so I got Lorraine roped in and I'm back to square one. Me and Lorraine been helping each other out when we can, but it's all going in the same direction and it'll end badly.'

Lee knew that he was probably right. However, if Galea and his sister/girlfriend were beating people up that could be a different matter.

'You seen Lorraine in the last couple of days?' Lee asked.

'No.'

'Well when you do, ask her about her bruises,' Lee said.

'Did he beat her up? Steve?'

'Oh yes,' Lee said. 'Now, Terry, I want you to listen to me now and do exactly what I say. Because if you don't you, Lorraine, Jason and a – to you – unnamed Asian bloke could be in a world of shit.'

Vi and DI West left the Joseph family to their fishy supper and stood beside her car down the road.

'We have to accept that Dylan's involvement could be mere coincidence,' West said as he watched Vi light up a fag.

'Yeah, but you lot are encouraged to pursue the coincidence line, aren't you?' Vi said. 'Given what's at stake.'

West said nothing.

Vi leant against her car.

'You know,' she said, 'this area round here is one of the last sort of traditional East End manors left. Most of 'em've been co-opted by the Henrys of this world. People more like you, DI West.' She smiled. 'Families like the Josephs may look as if they're all over the place, but they're actually very tight. If any of them kids know anything about Henry, Brenda'll get it out of 'em.'

'The president arrives tomorrow morning,' West said. 'He's due at the Embassy residence in Regent's Park after the banquet at Buckingham Palace.'

'Oh, if she's anything to tell ya, she'll tell ya, or rather me,' Vi said. 'I bet Brenda's holding them kids' feet to the fire, figuratively, right now. Because honest and upright as I know that family is, I also know that Des has a couple of plants in his attic.'

'Plants?'

'Blow,' she said, 'For personal use only. You can take the stoner out of Brixton but you can't take the Brixton out of the stoner, know what I mean? He's a good lad, Des, but I'm pretty sure he don't want us stomping about in his well-heated attic. So let's give Brenda a bit of time and see what turns up, shall we?'

FIFTEEN

Donald Trump and First Lady Melania arrived at Stansted Airport in the morning. They then continued their journey to central London by helicopter. Most Londoners, Lee Arnold included, knew when the Commander-in-Chief was nearing the end of his journey because of all the activity over their heads in the sky. Police helicopters, military jets. No one, least of all Britain's benighted prime minister Theresa May, wanted anything negative to happen.

'Do you think they'd bomb us if Trump was assassinated?' Mumtaz asked Lee.

He looked at the iPhone on his dashboard and shook his head. She was taking this visit of Trump's far too seriously. It was almost as if the American president meant her, personally, harm.

'We'll moan about Trump later,' he'd replied. 'Just to let

you know, I'm gonna be out and about in Romford and its suburbs this morning.'

After witnessing Steve Galea and his 'sister' see off Anjam Rajput in Langdon Hills the previous day, and after his discussion with Terry Gilbert, Lee had contacted an old friend. Sajid Iqbal had been one of the few Asian boys at Lee's old school on Shipman Road, Custom House. Back in the seventies that area had been almost a hundred per cent white. And although he'd come from a religious family, Sajid had rebelled big time. Probably in an attempt to fit in with those around him Saj had, for a while, been the only Asian punk for a three-mile radius. Now the imam of a tiny mosque, once a wool shop, in Gidea Park, Saj as Lee had hoped, knew of Barzan Rajput and his family.

'I wish I could get our people out of his properties, but I can't,' he'd told Lee when they'd spoken on the phone. 'But they're poor and Rajput's the cheapest landlord in the area.'

Lee pulled up in front of Saj's 1930s semi and walked up to the front door. His old mate's gaff had to be worth at least half a million quid. But then before he re-got religion, Saj had been a senior partner in a local firm of solicitors.

When he opened the front door, his old mate looked just the same as he always had – after his punk phase had ended. Smart black suit, crisp shirt, no tie and just the vaguest hint of a beard. He put his arms out to Lee who walked into his embrace a trifle awkwardly.

'Lee, m'dear old bloke,' he said in an accent that was half-cockney, half-Oxbridge. 'Come in.'

Lee took his shoes off at the door, noticing how neat and tasteful Saj's large entrance hall was. Things changed a bit, however, when Saj took him to what he called 'the family room'. Dominated by a huge, sagging, leather sofa, the family room was sprinkled with recognisably girls' toys, pink jumpers and a large poster of Harry Styles on the wall.

'I know,' Saj said as he stood in the doorway, shaking his head. 'You'd think we had ten kids, but we've still only got Shamima and Layla. Clearing up isn't their thing.'

Saj had met his wife, Benazir, when he'd been with Stuart and Ram Solicitors and she still practised full-time. No wonder the house wasn't perfect. These were busy people.

Saj made tea and then the two men sat down.

Saj said, 'So Barzan Rajput. Not one of mine, as I told you, but he's shall we say big around here, in certain circles.'

'What circles?'

'To be blunt, the poor. I'm talking a lot of refugees – from Syria, Iraq. Some Albanians. They see him standing there looking like a hafiz with his regulation beard, his shalwar kameez and kufi and they think here's a nice pious man who will not jeopardise his soul by ripping people off. Total con, of course. The man's a crook. Anyone who puts a family of seven in a room with a broken sink, no curtains and rats is a crook.'

'Do you know anything about his son? Anjam?'

'Who runs the letting agency? Not much,' Saj said. 'Seems quite personable. I know daddy bought him a nice house in Langdon Hills. There's a sister too, but she's in Dubai. The family owns property all over the Romford area and beyond. They don't come to my little mosque.'

'Do you know where they do go?'

'Harold Hill. My colleague over there has more experience with them than I do. Although we've talked of the family. Barzan's slum dwellings sadden all of us.'

'But you don't report him or . . .'

Saj shrugged. 'And how would that help the people he houses? Who else will house them? I don't need to tell you how hard these times are for the poor.'

He was right. So much of Britain's social welfare system had crumbled in recent years, those at the bottom of the pile were grateful just for a roof, any roof.

'What about violence?' Lee asked.

'Oh, Barzan has got his heavies,' Saj said. 'That's how he operates, through fear. You don't pay your rent, he takes it personally. His boys go around and beat you up to teach you some respect. It's all very much based upon loyalty to the family. You know people talk about the Italian Mafia, but the Pakistani, the Albanian, the Romanian Mafias, they are all the same. It's tribal.'

'And so if Barzan found out someone was taking advantage of his son . . .'

'In what way?'

Lee told him about his suspicions regarding Anjam, 'Maria' and Steve, plus his fear the younger man was being cuckooed.

Saj frowned. 'If that is what's happening, that won't go down well with the father,' he said.

'So there's no way Barzan knows?'

'If he did, the people doing this wouldn't be doing it any more.'

'So what if I told him?' Lee asked.

Brenda hadn't got much sleep the previous night and had gone to work in a zombie-like state. A visit from her eldest boy David, with his four-year-old twins, Ronan and Ava, in tow hadn't helped. Those two were like a travelling explosion, especially when they got together with other kids. David, a single parent, wanted to take some woman out and so the twins had to be with Brenda and Des – and Mickey Jay, who for some reason, they didn't like.

For the first hour it had been like World War Three. John, unable to cope with Mickey Jay, let alone the Twins of Evil, had left while Des, the only other adult in the house, had got stoned out of his gourd in the shed. Brenda reckoned she'd finally got to sleep at about three, which meant that when she'd got up at five she'd been shattered.

Now returning home after work she was disconcerted to see that Mickey Jay was still at home.

'What you doing here?' she said when she saw him running up and down the hall.

'I've got a cold!' he said jubilantly as he sneezed and snotted all over the wallpaper.

'Oh, Christ! Stop doing that!'

She went into the kitchen and put her handbag down on the table. Des looked up from his copy of the *Racing Post* and said, 'Cuppa?'

'No.'

'No?'

Brenda always liked a cup of tea when she got in from work. But not when she was howling mad.

'What you thinking keeping Mickey Jay off school?' she asked her husband.

'He's got a streaming cold.'

'He's snotty is all,' Brenda said. 'Could've gone to school! And what about the Twins of Evil?'

'Oh, I took them to school,' Des said. 'Much more of them and I'd've lost me mind.'

Brenda sat down and put a hand up to her head. 'I had the little shits all night long.'

210

'You should've woken me up, I'd've helped.'

'You were stoned and snoring,' Brenda said.

Mickey Jay ran in from the hallway and said, 'What's stoned, Nana?'

Brenda shook her head. 'Oh, great.'

Something was happening at Brenda Joseph's place. She wasn't telling Mumtaz about it and so she had to assume that it didn't have anything to do with John. She did, after all, have a really huge family. However, when she'd phoned Brenda she'd got short shrift and that wasn't normal. Whatever was happening, she generally made time for any requests for information or news about John. She would certainly like to know what Mumtaz had found out about his current net wealth.

The Gustavsson family as a whole were worth twenty billion dollars. Alone, John was worth three. It was a shock. Even though Mumtaz had known the family were rich, she hadn't realised quite how rich. It also begged the question, yet again, about what he was doing in the UK. He didn't need Brenda and her family. There could of course be something in his psyche about 'belonging' somewhere, but . . . He'd been given away. Who in their right mind would want to relive that? Especially if the person concerned, like John, was unable or unwilling to express emotion effectively. From the short time she'd spent with him, Mumtaz had been easily able to discern how awkward, unconfident and nervous he was around others. Why put himself through it?

He didn't need money, he was fanatical about his religion and he seemed to have very little need for people. So what was he about? Really?

'I'm off into town.'

211

Mumtaz looked up and saw Shazia about to leave.

'I said I'd meet Dex,' she said.

She didn't look happy about it. Yet again Mumtaz wondered how Dexter's being 'a dick' was manifesting. She didn't think that the girl would let a man abuse her, not again. But she couldn't be sure.

She said, 'I thought Dex was a . . .'

'He is a dick, but maybe I should give him a chance,' Shazia said. 'He was home yesterday and . . .' She put her head down.

Had he made her feel small because he lived in Notting Hill? Had his family been horrible to her?

'Anyway,' Shazia continued, 'it's the protest that's important.'

'I thought the big demo was tomorrow?'

'It is. But we have to hassle him wherever he goes.'

She left.

It was difficult to argue with young people who felt as if the world was changing to their detriment. Trump was just a symptom, but if he went unopposed where would it end? How would people feel about themselves if they just accepted something they found unacceptable?

She thought about John Saunders again. How did people like him do that double-think thing? How could anyone deify someone who lied, cheated and exhibited such awful cruelty to those who opposed him? How could they believe his stance on an issue like abortion? From what she had read, it would seem that the man was a sexual pest, he clearly had no regard for women in any scenario except the bedroom. How could someone like that be said to hold Christian values? John had been very upfront about his beliefs and appeared to think that Donald Trump was at least a price worth paying to propagate those. It was connected to a theoretical phenomenon called 'the Rapture', which as Mumtaz understood it, was the end of the world. John's branch of Christianity wanted this to happen. She thought about some of the Muslims she'd met who had almost the exact same goal.

She had a nasty creeping feeling that other people did too, for reasons she didn't even know about.

Barzan Rajput had the look of a man who'd never seen the funny side of anything. Dressed entirely in white, his feet barely contained by a pair of broken Dr Scholl sandals, he gave the impression of a frail, helpless old man down on his luck. Only the sharply dressed heavy who had let them in and the top-of-the-range iPhone on the old man's desk made this first impression a lie.

With Saj's words about how, if he'd come alone, the old git would have made him wait for an hour for this 'audience', Lee sat down. He let Saj talk, which, in the first instance seemed to involve some rapid fire Urdu preceded by some bowing. But eventually, after some really quite disconcerting tooth sucking and beard stroking, the old man turned to Lee.

'Imam Sajid tells me you are concerned about my son Anjam, Mr Arnold.'

'Yes,' Lee said. It was hot inside Rajput's office, which was a Portakabin on some sort of building site. God knew what the connection was! And it smelt of old, poorly maintained electric fire.

'You say he live in my house with other people?'

'I think they may be taking advantage of him,' Lee said.

'In what way?'

'I believe the man, at least, is running an unlicensed moneylending operation from your son's house.'

His face showed no emotion.

'I also think your son is being played by the woman.'

'How?'

'He seems to be in love with her. She's told him she's the man's sister, but I know that man and he doesn't have a sister.'

Barzan Rajput put a hand up to his mouth and licked his lips. 'And this is to you . . .'

'I'm a private investigator . . .'

'I know this from Imam Sajid.'

'I've been working for a man who wanted me to find out what his ex-wife is spending all his money on,' Lee said. 'She borrowed from this couple, they whacked the interest up. I'm sure you know how it operates, Mr Rajput.'

He shook his head. 'In Islam, sir, we do not charge interest. It is a pernicious system, forbidden to us.'

'I know. Which is why I thought you'd like to clean it off your premises, so to speak.'

He looked down at the floor. 'Mmm.'

'I mean, I could get the police involved . . .'

The old man held up a hand to silence him. Lee shut up. He looked at Saj who flashed him a very small smile. Did that mean he'd said or done the right thing or what?

For a very long time, nothing was said. Lee pondered yet again whether he'd done the right thing. After all, if the Rajputs attacked the Galeas, would that mean all-out gang warfare on the leafy streets of Langdon Hills? Or would some sort of accommodation be made between the two parties in order to save face. Saj had said he thought it would definitely be the latter. But what, really, did he know? Lee knew of old that when it came to trouble between small-scale organised crime families it was sometimes better to let them do their own housekeeping. But . . .

The old man cleared his throat. 'Mr Arnold,' he said, 'I must thank you for bringing this to my attention. I will watch my son and, if I observe that what you tell me is so, I will act.'

'I hope with restraint . . .'

'Imam Sajid has told me you were once in the police force, Mr Arnold, so that I would say is a given,' he said.

'I have to have your word . . .'

Saj's face did some weird, alarmed gyrations.

Barzan Rajput smiled. 'I do not even know the name of these people, nor will I ask you, Mr Arnold,' he said. 'And so, if anything untoward may occur, your name will be kept well away from the proceedings. But what will be, will be. I will deal with it and I will further make sure that the lady you have been observing pays not one penny more to these people.'

Lee wondered whether he should tell the old man that Steven Galea had beaten Lorraine up. But then he decided against it. If Barzan Rajput was the intelligent operator he thought he was, he'd know that such things happened. Not that this alone made him feel any better about the situation. Galea should have been reported to the police. Vi would go spare if she ever got to know. But by allowing Rajput and Galea to settle their differences without police involvement, perhaps victims like Lorraine and Terry might just see some light at the end of the tunnel. Maybe.

Saj, in an act that was completely in line with his role as a minister of religion and entirely at odds, possibly, with his own personal security said, 'And remember, Mr Rajput, that violence too is prohibited by the Koran. Mr Arnold comes here in good faith to end this abuse.'

Rajput nodded. 'Believe me,' he said, 'the only casualty I envisage is my stupid son's broken heart.' Then he sighed. 'I suppose I will have to bend my mind towards getting the ridiculous boy married as soon as possible.'

Kian turned up.

When Brenda asked him why he wasn't at school he told her he had a study day.

'So, shouldn't you be at home or in a library or something?' Brenda said.

'Mum's got a new bloke, innit,' Kian said as he flopped down onto her sofa and switched on the TV.

Brenda whipped the remote out of his hands and switched the TV off.

'What new bloke?'

'I dunno,' he said. 'Some drug dealer.'

Kian was a good kid, but he did tend to overdramatise.

'What do you mean?'

'Albanian, innit,' he said. 'Lives down the Gascoigne.'

The Gascoigne Estate in nearby Barking was well known as the haunt of several well-organised gangs of Albanian cocaine dealers.

Brenda sat next to her grandson. 'Your mum on the Charlie again?' she asked. 'Don't lie to me Kian.'

He put his head down. It told Brenda all she needed to know. As a teenager Ruby had been addicted to coke. Then she had Kian and, latterly, her relationship with Henry had given Brenda some hope that her daughter might be making some good choices, at last.

'He good-looking this geezer?' she asked.

Kian said, 'If you like that sort of thing. Got tattoos all up his arms and his neck and that.'

'How long's this thing been going on?'

'I dunno. Six months?'

'I thought you said this was a new bloke! So while she was seeing Henry?'

'Guess so.'

'Right.' Brenda stood up.

Kian said, 'What you gonna do?'

'Making up the Z bed for you,' she said. 'I've heard about them gangs down Barking and I'm not having you living round that.'

'Nan!'

'No, Kian! You ain't going back there until I've spoken to your mother!'

He hung his head again.

Mickey Jay put his cheeky face around the door and said, 'Where's Uncle John?'

'Oi, you get back to bed if you're supposed to have a cold!' Brenda said.

'Yeah, but where's . . .'

'I don't bleedin' know!' Brenda yelled. 'Probably up west somewhere with fucking Donald Trump!'

As if she hadn't had enough aggravation in her life! And then her long-lost brother turns up and turns out to be a bloody born-again nutcase! Coming and going as he pleased . . .

Vi Collins put her phone back on her desk. Of course she remembered when Brenda Joseph's brother went missing. She'd told Mumtaz that. What she hadn't told her was that she too was working on something that involved the Joseph family right now.

That John, the ten-year-old who'd gone AWOL in '76 had

suddenly turned up out of the blue was a shocker. Vi could understand why Brenda might not quite believe he was who he said he was and have a bit of investigation work done. According to Mumtaz, John Saunders had been adopted by some American billionaires she'd never heard of. Now, allegedly, he was a Trump-supporting Republican. But like Mumtaz, Vi was intrigued to find out what had happened to the British police investigation into John's disappearance. His father, Reg, had apparently left the country with the boy, although whether he'd travelled under his own name or not wasn't known. The kid ditto. And what did he want now? That was, according to Mumtaz, what puzzled Brenda.

There'd been a middle-aged bloke in the house when Vi had been with the Josephs on Sunday. Had that been John? No one had bothered to introduce her but then, to be fair, there were always so many bodies in that house it was almost impossible to remember who they all were. Maybe he had been introduced? If he had, then it must have passed her by.

It was strange to think that someone who had once been a bit of a dreamy kid from Canning Town was now a Trump-supporting born-again Christian. It was also not a little bothersome that, casting her mind back, her memory of John's disappearance included the notion that the coppers hadn't spent a lot of time looking for him. Some poor kid of an alcoholic, what did he matter? And things hadn't changed that much. The seventies were now just a memory, but it was a memory that some glamorised and even sought to revive. John Saunders' idol, Trump, for one. Vi remembered men like him back when she was a young WPC. Middle-aged coppers who put their hands up your skirt and called you 'darling'. They'd had all sorts of offensive names for the female plods

218

back then. Hers had been 'Teflon knickers' because she'd never let them grope her with a smile on her face.

Brenda knew that Ruby was in. There was a window open upstairs and there was a posh car on that patch of old mud she used as a driveway out front. Brenda yelled up to what she knew was Ruby's bedroom.

'Oi! Rube! I know you're up there! Get down here! Now!'

For a good five minutes nothing happened and so Brenda shouted again. 'Ruby! Get down here!'

She heard a rustling sound and some muffled voices and then the front door opened. Ruby, fag in hand, dressed in a very short man's dressing gown stood in the doorway and said, 'What?'

Brenda pushed past her and went into a hallway littered with toys, shoes and an engine block. Ruby had always been a messy mare.

'Mum!'

'What you want me to do Ruby, eh?' Brenda said. 'Yell at you in the fucking street? That's what people round here expect and I'm not in the business of giving them bastards a free *Jeremy Kyle Show*!'

'What do you want?' She put her hand up to her tangled hair.

'I've got Kian round at mine,' Brenda said. 'Telling me you've got some fucking gangster round here.'

'What?'

'Some Albanian off the Gascoigne. Got you doing Charlie . . .'

'Mum, I'm not doing Charlie and Rifat isn't a gangster he's got his own garage down Thamesview . . .'

Brenda kicked the engine block. 'Looks like he's got one here,' she said.

'That's from a mate's car . . .'

'I don't care! So how long you been seeing this one?' Brenda crossed her arms over her chest. Would Ruby lie to her about this too? She'd lied to her about being on Charlie again. 'Well?'

'Oh, I dunno . . .'

'You are Ruby's mother?'

A man considerably younger than Ruby, dressed only in a pair of tight-fitting jeans, bounded down the stairs and took Brenda's hand. Kian was right, he was good-looking.

'Rifat Peja,' he said as he shook her hand and smiled.

Brenda didn't crack her face. 'Are you,' she said.

'I am. And I can assure you that I have not given Ruby anything that may harm her.'

She had to hand it to him, he was charming and his English was good.

'So how long you been going out?' Brenda asked.

She saw that Ruby was about to speak but Rifat got in first. 'Only a week, Mrs . . .'

'Joseph,' Brenda said. She looked at Ruby. 'This right? Cos Kian tells it different. Says you been seeing each other for six months.'

'Oh yeah, but I was going out with Henry . . .'

'Yeah, well that's what I thought.' She looked at Rifat who smiled while his eyes shifted everywhere but her face.

'No, no,' Ruby said, 'I wouldn't . . .'

'I should hope not.'

'No . . .' Ruby looked down at the floor. The little tart had been shagging both of them.

Rifat said, 'I can assure you, Mrs Joseph, that I would never have begun a relationship with Ruby had I known she was with another man. It is dishonourable.'

'Really?' Brenda put her hands on her hips. 'Not dishonourable to be shagging her out of marriage though, is it?' she said. 'Bet you wouldn't do that to one of your own women?'

He said nothing.

Brenda turned to Ruby. 'And you,' she said, 'think about your kids more and your fucking sex life less. I've got Kian round mine and he ain't coming back until you tell me that this' – she looked at Rifat – 'ain't gonna be here. You hear me?'

SIXTEEN

Trump, it was said, was in Buckingham Palace. Outside, opposing groups of protesters waved banners, sometimes shouted and kept watch. Those opposing the president particularly wanted to be sure to be in a position to harangue him should he make an appearance at the front of the building.

Dex leant down to Shazia and whispered, 'I think this woman next to me is a Trump supporter.'

Shazia looked round her boyfriend and saw a large woman with bright red hair wearing a dress made out of a Stars and Stripes flag. She carried a banner saying 'We Love You Mr President!'

Shazia, holding her own banner, which said 'American Psycho', rolled her eyes.

'Ya think?'

He laughed. But the woman had picked up on their exchange and said, 'I s'pose you think it's funny and kinda edgy to mock our president. You'll learn, when you grow up, that Mr Trump is the only thing between you Brits and the Muslims!'

'I—'

Shazia didn't even let Dexter stand next to the woman. Sweeping him away with one strong, furious hand she said, 'I don't know who you are, missus, but you take that back!'

The woman shook her head arrogantly. 'No, ma'am,' she said. 'I support our president a hundred and ten per cent . . .'

'That isn't even a thing!' Shazia hissed. One thing she had inherited from her father was an absolute hatred of meaningless platitudes.

'Well, girl, you wanna end up wearing a burka . . .'

'I won't!'

She felt Dexter's hand on her arm, as he attempted to cool her down.

'Fuck off!' she snapped at him.

'Oh my!' the woman said.

'Shaz . . .'

'As if it's any of your business,' Shazia said to the woman, 'I'm a Muslim and I don't wear a burka. I don't even cover my head. Because that's a choice!'

'Won't be when the Taliban get here.'

'Oh—'

'Oi you, keep it down!'

A copper, a tall, slim Asian example wearing a heavy stab vest, pushed his way through the crowd and stood between the two women.

'What's this?' he asked.

Dexter, in what to Shazia was his 'usual middle-class style' said, 'Oh, Officer, it's nothing, it's—'

'This bloody woman just insulted my religion!' Shazia broke in.

'I did not!' the woman said. 'I simply told the truth. If you can't take it, honey . . .'

The copper looked at the American woman and said, 'You a tourist, madam?'

'I am,' she said. 'From Baton Rouge, Louisiana.'

'Well, I hope you have a wonderful time here in London,' the copper said.

Shazia squeaked. 'What?'

The officer looked at her. 'And you,' he said, 'if you want to make a complaint . . .'

'She said that Trump was the only thing that stands between the UK and what she just referred to as "the Muslims"!' she said.

A white bloke carrying a banner, which showed a picture of Trump yelling behind the caption 'Fuck Off, Trump' said, 'The young lady's right.'

'Thank you!'

Dexter, she noticed, put his hands over his ears and sort of half-smiled. He was bloody useless.

'After what Trump said this morning about Mayor Khan . . .' Shazia continued.

Even before his plane had landed, Donald Trump had tweeted some very offensive opinions about London Mayor Sadiq Khan who, needless to say, was not a fan.

The policeman moved both hands downwards in a calming gesture. 'I'm sure Mr Khan can look after himself,' he said. 'But we can't have people yelling at each other out here. You want to do that, you'll have to go.'

'Oh, and what about freedom of speech and expression?' Shazia said. 'Ring any bells with you, Officer?'

'Miss . . .'

'We're here to protest,' Shazia said. 'That is our right. We're British, we can do this!'

'Yes, but miss, you can't breach the peace.'

'I'm not breaching the peace!'

She felt Dexter try to put his arms around her, but she shook him off.

'If I may suggest,' the copper continued, 'you move away from this lady or she moves away from you . . .'

'Oh, so insulting my religion . . .'

He put his hand on his hips. 'Do you want to make a complaint, formally?' he said.

Shazia suddenly felt very alone.

Everything was perfect except for the fact that Barzan Rajput was really too old and tired for it all. Luckily, he had 'people' who would help him. Having a key to his son's house had always been a good idea, even though this was the first time he'd used it. When he got inside he was appalled to see the state of the place. Dust all over the floors and windowsills, clothes scattered across the threshold into the living room. But he kept his peace and put his fingers to his lips to instruct his men to keep theirs. Then it was up the sweeping central staircase, which he noted had lost a few struts from its bannister rail, and onto the landing.

The door to the master bedroom was open. Barzan heard the bed spring squeaking even before he crossed the threshold. Anjam, he knew, was at work, and so this was indeed, perfect. The naked back of a man kneeling on the bed between a pair of obviously female knees was the first thing he saw. Both participants were white and the man, clearly thrusting himself into the woman, gasped, 'Oh, fuck it, I'm coming!'

Barzan who, although a religious man, was not without humour said, 'Really? So soon?'

And then yet more amusement was to be had when the couple realised there was someone else with them.

'What the fuck . . .'

The man fumbled some duvet in front of himself while the woman, a stunning brunette, her fine figure marred, in Barzan's opinion, by tattoos across her breasts, sat up.

The old man pointed at her. 'I take it,' he said, 'you are the object of my son's affections.'

She didn't reply. The man with her, who Barzan recognised, started to move towards the edge of the bed until he saw Rajput's men walk into the bedroom. Barzan turned to one of them and said, 'Could you find me a chair, please? My feet hurt.'

The young man went to another room and retrieved a chair. The old man sat down and smiled.

'Now,' he said, 'Mr Galea . . .'

He watched as Steven Galea's eyes widened. It hadn't taken him long to work out just who the idiot boy Anjam had become involved with. A few phone calls to some men he knew who traded information for hard cash was all it had taken. Plus a quick call to a friend . . .

'I am, I think, correct in my assumption that this lady isn't your sister?' he said. 'Unless your taste in women runs to what I suppose could be called "niche". . .'

'No, no . . .'

'I am glad to hear it,' the old man said. 'But I feel my son, Anjam, would not be so happy.' He looked at the woman. 'I must confess, I can see what he finds attractive in you, my dear. I think we all can.'

226

She pulled some duvet away from Steve and covered her breasts.

'And if you had not also been using this house as a cuckoo's nest, then maybe I would have let you carry on deluding my son,' Barzan said. 'He is, after all, probably one of the most stupid people to ever walk the earth.'

'How did—'

'How I found out about your scam isn't important.' Barzan waved a hand. 'What is important is that this ends now.'

Steve Galea just looked at him.

'Because I have to say, Mr Galea, that I am insulted. You must know who I am. I certainly know who you are. And so it is a matter of honour.'

'I never—'

'Ah, but you did,' the old man said. 'You did exactly want to humiliate me. I know how your family operate. Preying on my son, no doubt collecting compromising material on him with which to hurt me . . . And this lady?' He shrugged. 'Anjam has always been very keen on Western women. I don't see the attraction myself, but there it is. Anyway, I'm assuming you are Mr Galea's wife or girlfriend or . . .'

'I'm his girlfriend,' she said. 'And this is business. So do what you're going to do and let's get it over with.'

The old man saw Steve Galea's eyes widen and he could understand why. This woman was either bluffing for all she was worth, or she had absolute balls of steel.

'Well . . .'

'Go on,' the woman said. She let her arms drop to her sides, the duvet that had been covering her breasts, falling away. They were very nice tits, but that wasn't the point . . .

'And if I decided to kill you?'

'You won't,' she said.

'Why not?'

'Because that's not what you do,' she said. 'Steve may think you're some big shot whose son he can use and then make money out of you. But that was never my plan. For me it's always just been about the loans. That Anjam, God bless him, fell for me when he became a client . . .'

'Anjam owes you money?'

'Oh yes,' she said. 'He's paying off his debt by letting us stay here. Anyway, that makes us good cash. I am content with that.'

'I am not, young lady.'

'No,' she said. 'You feel abused, as you should. But at bottom, Mr Rajput, you're just a slum landlord and so I know you won't kill us.'

'Do you?'

'You might get your boys to beat us up a bit . . .'

'A bit?'

'Well . . .'

He smiled.

Lee didn't want to implicate her in anything, but he still felt he had to tell Mumtaz what he'd done.

She said, 'I can't criticise what you've done because I don't have your experience with organised crime, but . . .'

'Think the Sheikhs but nicer,' Lee said.

The Sheikh family – people involved in slum landlording, people trafficking and prostitution – had been involved with Mumtaz's husband. He had been in debt to them and they had finally orchestrated a fatal hit on him when he didn't pay up. They had then come after Mumtaz – although in the last year, having made her almost penniless – they had not appeared.

'But they may hurt these people, this Steve and the woman,' Mumtaz said.

'They may,' Lee said. 'But the Rajputs aren't murderers. They're not very nice and if you don't pay the rent you owe them they're downright unpleasant, but they're not the Sheikhs.'

'And what about this Maltese family? Couldn't what you've done start some sort of war?'

She'd made them both tea. She placed his cup on his desk.

'No,' he said. 'Don't think so.'

'You don't think so?'

'The Galeas are opportunists,' he said. 'They start businesses, rip people off, go onto the next thing. They're not rooted anywhere. The Rajputs, however, are rooted in Romford. That is their turf. They run slum houses, they lend money to vulnerable people and old Barzan will send the boys round if you don't pay up. He's pissed off that Anjam has been used but he won't start a war.'

'What about the Galeas?'

Lee sighed. 'Well, if Barzan gives Steve as big a kicking as I hope he will, I think that's the last we'll hear of them for a bit.'

'I thought you said you asked Barzan Rajput not to resort to violence?'

'I did,' he said. 'But he will. He can't not. Steve had it coming. Cuckooing another businessman is well out of order.'

'And if Steve or this woman get hurt?'

He shrugged. 'I just hope old Barzan doesn't go back on his promise to cancel all of the debts owed to Steve. That would make my client very happy and that is my main concern.'

'That's a bit harsh,' she said.

'That's real,' he replied. 'You're in Upton Park, Dorothy. Kansas this ain't.'

'Anyway, why did your client's ex-wife borrow the money in the first place?' Mumtaz asked.

'For beauty treatments, Botox, clothes that sort of thing.'

'Really?'

'Going back on the dating market when you're past your sell-by date ain't for the faint-hearted.'

'That's sexist.'

'It's true,' he said. 'Blokes are simple-minded. They want young girls.'

'You don't.'

'No . . .'

'I mean I assume you and DI Collins . . .'

She knew they were seeing each other, and he knew she knew.

'Vi's a laugh,' he said. 'She's a mate. Anyway, I can't live like a monk . . .'

That stung. Sex with Lee had been good and Mumtaz had enjoyed it. But then guilt had got in the way. She knew that was her fault and hers alone. But there wasn't any sort of way back. Not now, not even when he came over and put his hand on her shoulder.

Vi picked up her phone. It was the front desk.

'There's a Mrs Joseph here wants to talk to you,' the desk sergeant told her.

Brenda? Again? What this time?

'Tell her I'll be down in five,' Vi said. 'Put her in an interview room.'

She finished the smoked salmon sandwich she'd bought from Boots and sauntered down. When she got inside the interview room she was confronted by a pale-faced Brenda.

Before Vi could even ask her what was up, Brenda launched.

'My Ruby's having it off with one of them gangsters down the Gascoigne,' she said. 'She's back on the Charlie, although she'd swear she ain't. I know the signs.'

Vi sat down opposite the woman and sighed. 'Yes? And?'

'And what?' Brenda said. 'I'm giving you information, DI Collins. My eldest girl's having it off with one of them Albanians on the Gascoigne and he's giving her coke.'

'Ruby's an adult, Brenda, she makes her own choices. What do you want me to do about it?'

Suddenly deflated, Brenda threw her arms in the air. 'Oh, I don't bloody know! Just seems at the moment that everything's overwhelming me.'

'Like what?'

Of course Vi knew about Brenda's brother from Mumtaz but she didn't want to let on about that.

'I know you've all been upset about Henry's death and like a lot of women, you care for far too many people than is good for you . . .'

'Me brother's back,' Brenda said.

'Your brother?'

'John. He went missing back in 1976. Went into the Woolwich Foot Tunnel and never come out. Don't know . . .'

'Oh, I remember it,' Vi said. 'Disappeared into thin air. Didn't your mum get a psychic down there or something?'

'Amongst others. Not that the coppers done much, present company excepted.'

'Do you know why not?'

She shrugged.

'You sure this bloke is your brother, Brenda?'

'DNA says he is. I've had some private investigator woman checking him out. Our dad took him to America and sold him to these rich people. He's had a nice life. What he wants with us, which is why I hired this woman, I don't know.'

'So he . . .'

'He comes round,' she said. 'Sits about. I don't get it. He's staying in a Travelodge and he's got millions. Them people who had him are really loaded. I thought maybe he'd come to see Trump and all that but he's American, he can see him any old time.' She shook her head. 'I don't get him, and I want him to go.'

'So tell him,' Vi said.

But Brenda shook her head again. 'I can't do that,' she said. 'He might be a weirdo and all that, but he's lived without a family almost all his life. We're all he's got, God help us.'

'Then tell him to back off a bit. Give you some space.'

Brenda didn't say anything. Vi didn't really need to be with this woman when she had so much paperwork to be getting on with. Also, with Trump in town even the outer London boroughs were on high alert. But what could she do? Brenda Joseph was a good woman, overwhelmed with family responsibility, always bright she nevertheless had few skills, mainly because she'd had no encouragement from her parents and she'd got pregnant at sixteen.

But then Brenda said something that made Vi's ears prick up.

'She won't say so, but I think that Ruby was having it off with this Albanian while she was still seeing Henry,' Brenda said. 'Poor Henry. Such a nice boy. I had hoped Ruby'd settle down with him and do herself a bit of good.'

Shazia walked to Green Park Tube Station on her own. Now they were down in London Dexter was behaving like a total knob. First, he and his mum had treated her like some sort of alien species, and then he'd just come on so middle-class about that American woman it had made her want to scream. How could what she had said be OK?

She put her hands in the pockets of her jacket and hunched into herself. There were people wearing those MAGA baseball caps all over Green Park. And some of them were English! God! Why did anyone think that following a racist, sexist, old, half-crazy moron like Trump was a good idea? Were those people also crazy old sexist racists too?

She was so lost in her own anger that Shazia didn't see the young police officer who had almost arrested her earlier until he was right in front of her. When she did see him, she said, 'Oh, it's you.'

'Yes.' He smiled. He was probably only in his early twenties. Not that Shazia gave a shit or anything.

'What do you want?' she said. 'I've stopped yelling and I'm going home.'

'Without your boyfriend?'

'It's none of your business,' she said.

'I'm sorry. I just saw that you were—'

'So you thought you'd get after me when I left the white boy and pick up the pieces with some sensible advice about being a nice Asian girl . . .'

He half laughed. 'No . . .'

'Not gonna tell me I should cover up and shut up?'

'Why would I? No,' he said. 'I just wanted to make sure you were all right. What that American lady said was out of order and you could have complained, but I really got the feeling that neither your boyfriend or you really wanted to do that.'

Shazia felt her shoulders slump. He was right. she hadn't wanted to do anything formally, she'd just wanted the woman and all the other MAGA people to go away. She just wanted all the Islamophobia, either overt or covert to go away.

Eventually she said, 'You're right. Just get so fed up with it all.'

'You must.'

'Well don't you?' she said.

He smiled. 'Islamophobia is unacceptable,' he said. 'Like every other kind of racism. Personally, I do get tired of people who insult me as if I were a Muslim.'

'Oh. Aren't you?' she said.

'No. I'm a Hindu,' he said. 'Not that it makes any difference. Racism is racism and just because the abuse isn't really directed at me, it doesn't make it any better. Are you really going home now?'

'Don't know what else to do to be honest,' Shazia said.

'Well . . .'

'You're going to chat me up, aren't you?' Shazia said, laughing as she did so. 'Oh my God!'

She saw him blush and laughed even harder.

He visibly cringed. 'Have I made a complete fool of myself?'

'No,' she said. 'But . . . Look I just need to get home now. I'm sorry, I've had a rough few days. I know you mean well . . .'

'It's OK,' he said. Then he put his hand in one of the pockets in his stab vest and took out a card. 'Look, I'll give you my card . . .'

'What for?'

'Because I like you, maybe?'

She took the card. 'Why?'

He shrugged. 'Girls with spirit do it for me,' he said. 'So sue me . . .'

She laughed again. He was funny. Dexter was rarely funny.

'No pressure,' he said. Then he put on a cod Asian accent and added, 'I'm not your auntie or anything, is it.'

Then he walked away. Shazia watched him go and then looked down at the card, which informed her that the man she'd just been speaking to was Sergeant Krishnan Mukhergee.

Steve wasn't able to drive and so Maria took the wheel. It was her car anyway. As she backed out of the drive and into the street, she heard her boyfriend groan. Rajput's goons had stamped on his stomach a couple of times and so a visit to the hospital had to be on the cards. But Steve was dead against it.

'Just drive to Mario's!' he said when she tried to make him agree with her.

'Yeah, but—'

'Just fucking drive will ya!'

Steve's eldest brother Mario lived at Wickford, which Maria reckoned was about half an hour away.

Once they hit the A127 going towards Southend-on-Sea, Steve began to speak without gasping again.

'Fucking mad bastards!' he said. 'I'll fucking firebomb that fucking shop of theirs! I'll fucking knock down that fucking house!'

'No, you won't.'

'I fucking will! You wait till I tell our Mario what's been going on!'

'Mario'll just be grateful we got away with it for so long,' Maria said. 'God, Steve, we were all but skint when we began all this and now the old Paki's let us keep almost all the money . . .'

'There was still a sports bag in the conservatory.'

'Oh, let Anjam have that,' she said. 'Only a coupla grand in there, anyway.'

He slid his eyes sideways to watch her. 'You fancy him, did ya?' he asked.

'No.'

But she didn't look at him. Poor Anjam. He'd been so overwhelmed by the attention lavished upon him by Steve's 'sister' he'd hardly ever been able to get it up with her. He'd been too nervous.

Maria squeezed Steve's knee. 'Only got eyes for you, babe,' she said.

Steve winced in pain again. 'Gotta get that money back off them punters who still owe,' he said.

'You told the old man you wouldn't.'

'I told him what he wanted to hear.'

'Steve,' she said, 'you mustn't start a war with these people. I know what you and your brothers are like, but Anjam's dad won't have it. I'm telling you. And you know that you and your brothers, much as you might be hard nuts, don't stand a chance against that lot.'

'Why?'

'Why? Look at the fucking state of you!' she said. 'They jumped up and down on you like you was a mattress or something! I still think we should go to the hospital.'

'No!'

She said nothing. It was pointless arguing with him when he was like this.

Eventually he said, 'Anyway, once I've given back the start-up money we got from me dad, we can start again somewhere else.'

'Where?'

'Dunno. Somewhere I can have a bit of time to find out how that old cunt found out about us and do something about it.'

'Well, Anjam—'

'Not that dickhead!' Steve said. 'Must've been one of the punters – or someone connected to one of them. But I'll have him. No one does this to me and gets away with it!'

So no talk of her too? Maria wasn't surprised. The old man had told her that because she'd not just screamed the place down and behaved with some dignity, he'd save her the beating they gave to Steve. One of his blokes had taken her to another room while it all went on. The old bloke's nephew or something. Whether the old man had told him to fuck her or not she didn't know. But he had. After all that fumbling about with Anjam and Steve's less than tender caresses, it had been a nice change. And he'd been fit.

SEVENTEEN

The Gascoigne Estate in Barking was outside of Vi's jurisdiction. So she spoke to a colleague over there on the phone. The name that Brenda had given for Ruby's boyfriend, Rifat Peja, was familiar to DI Marion Roberts.

'Oh, Rifat's right in the middle of things on the Gascoigne,' she said. 'We've picked his older brother up twice for pimping, but we can't get any of his girls to shop him. They're all shit scared and so they should be. Even the old mother's handy with a knife, so I've been led to believe. But course every time we turn up there, we come up empty.'

'Do you know why?' Vi asked.

'Not know, no,' she said. 'But I strongly suspect that Aslan Peja, that's the older brother, has friends in high places. Everyone takes Charlie these days.'

'Don't worry, I won't ask . . .'

'You'd better not!' Marion laughed, a harsh, half-cough. 'So what's Rifat been up to round your manor?'

Vi told her about Rifat's connection to Ruby Joseph and the notion she had that maybe Rifat, with his apparently enhanced sense of 'honour', had killed his rival for Ruby's affections.

'I heard about that urban explorer,' Marion said. 'Under Regent's Park, wasn't it?'

'Yeah. Difficult to gather evidence in a sewer,' Vi said. 'Mind you, not really my remit. We had Counter Terrorism Command all over it cos of Trump's visit.'

'Oh.'

'Far as I was concerned I'd given them everyone connected to Ruby Joseph at the time but now, it seems, we have this Rifat.'

'You told CTC yet?'

'No. Wanted to see if I could get any more intel for them from you first,' Vi said.

'Can't tell you a lot. Lives on the Gascoigne with his old mum, his brother and a sister. From Kosovo originally, so they've been here a long time. But they still hold to the old ways.'

'Meaning?'

'Blood feuds,' she said. 'They've got beefs with other Albanian families and although not yet lethal in their case, these things can be. We suspect they've managed to mop up most of the other dealers on the estate, but as I say, when we turn up they're always clean. They're no fools. In fact, I'd call them imaginative. They have to be to keep ahead with where to secrete their goods so we don't get them and neither do their competitors.'

'So what do you think about Rifat being involved in the death of a love rival?'

'I think it's possible, and I don't think it's got anything to do with Trump,' Marion said. 'Drug dealers tend to be apolitical in my experience. And you can quote me. Up to CTC what to do then, innit?'

Mumtaz put down her phone and looked at the ceiling. What was John Saunders doing and why? She knew that Brenda Joseph wasn't the sort of woman who was easily intimidated but she had been when she'd finally seen her brother that afternoon. She'd asked him straight what his plans were, and he'd said he didn't have any. Didn't he have to get back to doing whatever his parents' charities and foundations were? Didn't he have to go back to the US to see them? But he'd just said, 'I've no plans right now.'

And when Brenda had asked him where he was going to live and what he was going to do his answer had been, 'I'll stay in my hotel. I like my hotel.'

A Travelodge from which he wandered out to bookshops, to parks, to that hideous old foot tunnel across to Woolwich? Mumtaz wondered whether he was having some sort of breakdown.

Lee was involved in catching up on his emails, arranging meetups with clients regarding the possible resolution of the cuckooing situation in Langdon Hills, amongst other things. But now she was off the phone, he looked up.

'Anything I can help with?' he asked her.

He knew something, if not everything about the John Saunders case and so she used him as a sounding board for her latest theories.

'In a way John's behaviour can, I think, be interpreted as a form of cuckooing,' she said. 'Although what the advantages are to him, apart from some free meals, I don't know.'

Lee got up, walked over to her desk and sat on the edge. 'Given he's a rich bloke, that's irrelevant . . .'

'A rich bloke who comes from a family of born-again Christians. I don't know much about them, but I gather they like to at least project an air of frugality . . .'

'What, like the preachers on the US God TV who rock up dressed in Savile Row suits and ask for ten million dollars for "the Lord's work" from poor people who live in trailer parks?'

Mumtaz smiled. 'I'm led to believe the Gustavssons are not like that. As the surname implies, I think they're more about Scandinavian minimalism in all things. They quietly fund what to them are good causes around the world.'

'They're tight.'

She laughed. 'I don't think so, Lee. They fund all sorts of Christian foundations around the world.'

'And yet they bought a kid. How do they square that with their faith?'

'Maybe they felt they rescued John,' she said. 'Maybe he is, in a way, part of their work?'

Lee shook his head. 'That's fucked up.'

'To us, yes, but then we're not born-again Christians. And, anyway, there are a lot of people who claim a religious mission who really aren't, to our way of thinking, "good" at all. Look at Osama bin Laden. Millions followed him and millions still do believe in his mission.'

Lee put his head down. Religion wasn't something he understood. It had been one of the main issues between them when they'd been a couple. Agitated ever since he'd got in, Mumtaz thought that she discerned a need in Lee to talk about that again. The trouble was, she didn't want to. She feared where it might lead.

Eventually he said, 'Mumtaz . . .'

'Yes?'

He swung his legs over her desk so that he was sitting beside and facing her. Mumtaz felt her chest tighten.

'Yes?' she repeated.

He shrugged, then he said, 'Come back with me tonight. No strings. Just company . . .'

'Lee, I've got Shazia at home,' she said.

'She's a big girl, she'll understand. She'll approve, you know she will.'

Mumtaz shook her head. 'Lee, there's no mileage in this.'

'No mileage in the fact I'm still in love with you?'

She didn't dare look into his eyes, fearing what she might do or say if she did.

'And Vi . . .'

'Vi knows the score,' he said. 'We're mates. I've told you.'

'Friends with benefits.'

He didn't say anything for a moment. But in that pause, she said, 'I'm sorry. That wasn't nice.'

'But it was true,' he said. 'And I'd be lying if I said that I don't care for Vi. But that's all it is and she knows it. I love you. And if you'd be with me, then Vi and me'd be over and she knows that an' all.'

Finally, she screwed up her courage and looked at him. Lee was a rough diamond but he had a good heart, a clever brain and she knew she desired him. Tall and dark with full lips and a prominent Roman nose, he was hardly a pretty boy, but he was handsome and she was turned on by him. She felt him place a hand underneath her chin. He leant down towards her.

'Come home with me,' he whispered.

'I can't!'

'You can,' he said.

And then suddenly she didn't have a thought in her head because the kiss she instigated with him caught her entirely by surprise. As it went on, as he lowered himself off the desk, raised her to her feet and took her in his arms, she was caught by a fierce desire as if they only had this moment. As if the world was coming to an end and there was only now.

When he managed to disengage from her, Lee ran to the door and locked it. Mumtaz removed her headscarf and then her shirt.

Mr Lee Arnold was, according to his mobile answering service, unavailable. Barzan Rajput gave his name and number and left it to the PI to call him back. Then he sat back in his favourite chair and drank a pint of lassi. After such exertions in Anjam's house, he was dehydrated and not a little bit sore in the joints.

He closed his eyes and riffled through his thoughts. Had Mr Arnold known about his relationship with Mario Galea when he had told him about his brother Steven? Maybe, maybe not. Certainly, Steven hadn't known, but then what he also didn't know was that Mario was and had been, for the past few months, on the point of taking over all the Galea businesses. The boys' old father was a silly, senile old fool who still thought small and so of course he had supported Steven's pathetic little cuckooing operation.

If Barzan was correct, then Steven was probably on his way to Mario's now. Begging for sympathy, he'd get rather more than he bargained for. But then so would Mario when Barzan caught up with him. He had to have known what his brother was doing? Maybe Mario had planned to grab a larger slice of their joint venture in Malta by using compromising footage of Anjam in

243

action with the girl? If he had, then he had overestimated Barzan's ability to give a damn. Anjam was a stupid boy and when he died Barzan had made sure that his heir was not going to be his son. That honour would be conferred on his daughter, Farah, an accountant. Now there was a woman with balls of steel. In spite of himself, Barzan had little time for other men. Most of them were so stupid it hurt. Take his nephew Haydar for instance . . .

Barzan had told him to take the girl Maria away while they dealt with Steven Galea and so he'd done as he had been told. But then according to him, he'd had sex with the bloody woman. Not that he'd told Barzan about it himself. He'd boasted to his older brother, Ali Riza, who had then told his uncle about it in lurid detail. Maria had, Haydar had boasted, enjoyed it. Silly boy. She was trying to stay alive. Anyone with any sense would suck a cock in exchange for their own life.

He tried Lee Arnold's mobile again but just got the answerphone and so he allowed himself a little sleep.

Vi Collins was fun in the sack. She was dirty and irreverent and said things that made him laugh, but Mumtaz was the real deal because he loved her. As he looked up at her, still moving gently on top of him even though he'd come inside her, he reached up for her breasts. They'd become a little bigger than he remembered and he was pleased. In spite of not having taken many well-endowed lovers, he did like a decent pair of what his old dad would have called 'knockers'.

Opting to take one for the team by going on the bottom, his bare back against the carpet, Lee could now feel all the places where the coarse fibres had entered his flesh. He'd look like a porcupine when he finally stood up. Although that wasn't going to be yet.

244

She laid her head on his chest and he stroked her hair. He said, 'I'm not sorry because that was . . .'

'Neither am I,' she said. Then she raised her head and looked at him. 'Oh, Lee, how can this be wrong?'

'It isn't.' He kissed her.

'But . . .'

'Don't analyse it,' he said. 'I know that's what you've been trained to do, but I'm asking you not to. We love each other, that's it. Trust me on this, having sex with someone you love, you know about it. It's what we just did, what I did . . .'

'I love you too,' she said.

He smiled. 'So come back to the flat and let's do it all over again,' he said. 'In comfort.'

'Yes, but . . .'

He put a finger up to her lips and said, 'Ssh. Go home first, cook or get a takeaway for Shazia and then come over. She'll be delighted, I know her, she wants us to be together.'

'Yes, but . . .'

'Stop it now with the yes buts,' he laughed. 'You know she will be fine. She's come down for a few days to shout at Trump and then go back to Manchester. You're not stopping her doing that, but you are fulfilling what you know she wants for you, which is me.'

Detective Inspector West was a disconcerting sort. A bit nondescript, really, but he had a way of turning up where or when, or both, no one expected him to. To Vi Collins it seemed as if she'd just phoned him when she saw him waiting for her at the front desk.

Without preamble he said, 'Come on, DI Collins, we're off for a little ride. We can talk on the way.'

They weren't to be alone as it happened. The jeep that West was driving contained four heavily armed officers in full body armour. As they headed down the Barking Road towards somewhere as yet unspecified, West said, 'Tell me about Rifat Peja.'

'Can't, don't know him,' Vi said. 'What's going on? I was told that Peja was camped out with his latest squeeze in Canning Town.'

'He's gone home,' West said.

How he knew that Vi didn't know and she didn't ask.

'I mean, if we're going to the Gascoigne, then that's Barking and . . .'

'And this is a possible national security matter,' West said.

'We don't know whether this Peja bloke even knew that Henry Dubray existed,' Vi said. 'They shared a girlfriend. Whether he knew that at the time or not, I don't know.'

'Well, we really don't have time to gather intel or sit nicely with suspects trying to empathise and what have you,' West said. 'I don't give a shit whether Peja knew or not. Trump is here and tonight he will sleep at the US Ambassador's residence in Regent's Park. I want him to sleep soundly.'

'Bit strong,' Vi said, 'but I know what you mean.'

'That's my job,' West said.

'So you're picking this bloke up on no evidence . . .'

'I'm putting him where I can see him until the president leaves,' West said. 'Call it a way in which I can guarantee my own sanity.'

Vi didn't say anything more. What could she say? It didn't take them long to get to the Gascoigne.

Built in the sixties, it was a warren of high- and low-rise blocks between Barking town centre and the A13. Slated for redevelopment, parts of it were in the process of being demolished. But not where Rifat Peja lived. Barnes House was a typical sixties high-rise block, stained, unimaginative and dull to look at. But it was also something more than that too, it was forbidding.

As they pulled off Gascoigne Road and onto the estate, Vi said, 'I've not been down here for years. Fucking hell, look at all that steel for Christ's sake!'

She was looking at how many of the windows were covered with steel sheets, particularly on the flats lower down in the block. She'd also been a bit concerned that West was going to call attention to himself rocking up in a jeep. But there were plenty of other heavy-duty motors about to give it a run for its money. There were even a couple of Hummers, one of which had something that could have been a rocket launcher on the roof.

'Fucking hell, if I had to live here, I'd end it,' Vi said.

'Well, you're not going to end it today, DI Collins,' West said. 'I want you to stay in the car. One of my men will wait with you.'

'But won't you need him. I mean . . .'

'You don't think we're going to take Peja with just four armed officers and me, do you?' West said.

They slowed down in front of the block and came to a halt beside an industrial vehicle, which had a large metal scoop at the end of a long arm on the front. The sort of thing that was common on the estate now, a demolition vehicle.

Three of West's officers got out of the jeep and Vi saw some similarly attired men emerge from one of the Hummers.

West said to his one remaining man, 'Don't let DI Collins move. Get her out of here if things get hairy.'

'Yes, sir.'

He slipped into the driving seat next to Vi so there could be no confusion.

'Madam,' he tipped his head at her.

Vi said nothing. This lot were only a whisker and a fag paper from spooks and she didn't like it or them, especially in view of the fact that all this was only happening because of bloody Trump. Where were this lot when ordinary plods needed their help to catch drug dealers and people traffickers?

The man at her side said, 'Peja lives in the ground floor flat beside the lifts. The guv's going in from the front and the back and if all else fails we'll use the demo vehicle to knock the place down.'

'But there are people . . .' Vi began. But then she saw West and his men run into the building while other officers crouched underneath Peja's steel-covered windows. Then, from inside the building, came a sound like a bomb going off.

There was something different about her amma, but Shazia couldn't put her finger on it. Everything was quite as it had been before she left, but Mumtaz seemed, well lighter in spirit. Not that Shazia was going to dwell on that for long. Unlike Mumtaz, she was in a very low mood. On the way back to Forest Gate she'd got a text from Dexter asking her whether they were still going to meet on the Embankment for the next big march in the morning. She sent back a single word answer, which was 'Yes'. After all it wasn't just Dex who she was going to meet at the Tube station at eleven, it was a whole pile of their friends too. And maybe if she went to meet everyone, she could hit on someone else with a car who might let her cadge a lift. Unless she and Dex made up, of course. But she wasn't sure she really wanted that.

Alone in her bedroom, Shazia took out the card that copper had given her, Sergeant Krishnan Mukhergee. He'd been cute and also really open about how she'd caught his eye. For an Asian bloke. She doubted whether he'd have a snooty mum like Dex's, although she knew he was probably the darling of a dozen or so protective Hindu aunties. It had always struck her as strange the way India, Pakistan and Bangladesh were so often at odds. They might all be very different in their religious beliefs but they all had aunties who dominated their lives – even the ones who had converted to Christianity.

A knock on the door roused her. 'Yeah?'

Her amma put her head around her door.

'Dinner will be ready in five minutes,' she said. 'Then I want to talk to you about something.'

'Oh? What have I done now?' Shazia asked.

'You? Nothing,' Mumtaz said and then she laughed.

The screaming, particularly that of what Vi assumed was the old woman, was enough to chill the blood. And as if the explosion inside the block hadn't been hard enough to take, now there was the unmistakeable sound of gunfire. As she looked towards the building, she saw one of the steel sheets covering a window begin to deform as someone punched it in an attempt to get out. The Pejas she imagined were like rats trapped at the bottom of a barrel. Christ, Marion was going to lose her mind when she found out about this! She looked up at the demolition vehicle and wondered whether West was going to bring the whole fucking block down.

Vi looked at the heavily armoured man at her side and said, 'Is this really necessary?'

'I'm just doing my job,' he said.

'Do the local plod—'

'I imagine they've been informed yes, madam,' he said.

'Christ.'

'National security,' he said.

'Really?'

Even if by some truly bizarre twist of fate, Rifat Peja had been scoping out the sewers with a view to killing Trump, Vi now wished she'd kept her trap shut. Why would an Albanian Charlie merchant want to do that? Apart from anything else, it would call attention to him. But then again, of course, he was – nominally – a Muslim and so that was why they were where they were. Vi mentally kicked herself.

'Stop it! You'll kill him!'

Mario had launched himself at Steve as soon as they'd entered the house. Usually very well behaved around his wife, Mario Galea had pushed her aside in order to get to his brother.

'He's already been stamped on and God knows what else by Anjam's dad!' Maria wailed as she tried and failed, to stop Mario punching Steve in the face.

'I've got a good thing going with old Rajput and you put it in jeopardy, you wanker!'

'I didn't know—'

'No excuse!'

'Dad—'

'Dad didn't know neither,' Mario roared. 'Know why? Cause he's a wanker too! Why the fuck would I want either of you involved in what I do, eh? And if you say it's because we're family, I'll break your fucking back! What do you think this is, eh? *EastEnders*? I didn't tell you or Dad or Mikey nor any one of the family because I'm fed up being tied to you bunch of losers!'

'If I'd known I would've found someone else! Me and Maria could've found another bloke . . .'

'It's not the bit of cuckooing that offends me so much as your lack of ambition,' Mario said. 'You even had to get Dad to give you money to do that! Moneylending out of a house in fucking Langdon Hills! Fuck me!'

'Rajput made me agree to not pursue my debtors, but I ain't—'

'You'd better do as he says!' Mario grabbed his brother by the throat. 'Because if you don't you're gonna find yourself in a world of pain. Not from him, but from me! You've already fucked this up for me enough. I'm not gonna let you do no more, you hear me!'

'Yes.'

Although Maria Muscat had known the Galea family all her life, she'd never realised before just how weak Steven was. His wife, that Rosemary, had always said she thought he was weak, but Maria had never seen it herself. She'd bought into the whole glamorous Maltese gangster thing that her dad had always gravitated towards. But the Galea boys were just thugs. Even Mario with his 'big plans' whatever they were. And what was wrong with Steve using her to tempt Anjam into offering them a place to set up business? What was wrong with her in agreeing to it, for that matter?

Maria's bag, plus most of the money Steve had managed to get out of the house was in the car outside Mario's place. Of course, if she did just take off, Steve would know where to find her. But then again, once her dad heard about what had been going on and called Steve's dad to have a go at him . . . Neither of these old British-Maltese families would want a war to break out between them. Maria's old man was full of stories about how the various

251

families eventually made peace with each other when they left their clubs and bars in Soho and moved out to the country.

She excused herself to Mario's wife, Carmella, and went to use the toilet. Once in the wide, circular entrance hall of what she knew was only really a glorified Barratt Home, Maria made a dive for the front door and then ran down the path to the car.

EIGHTEEN

Lee didn't ask Mumtaz what Shazia had said about her amma spending the night away from home until after they'd made love. If this was what it felt like to get back with someone after a seemingly unreconcilable split, it was all right with him.

But when she was finally laying beside him, only their hands entwined, he remembered to ask her.

'How was Shaz about all this?' he said.

He saw her smile. 'Cheeky.'

'What she was? Or I am?'

'She was,' she said.

'What did she say?'

'I'm not sure I want to repeat it.'

He laughed. He could imagine. Shazia wasn't shy about either expressing her views or telling people when she thought she knew best. After what she'd been through with her late father, the gangsters that he had been involved with and the downsizing of her own fortune, it was a miracle that she had turned out as feisty and resilient at she had. But then a lot of that was down to Mumtaz who had both protected her and helped her deal with things way beyond her experience.

Lee squeezed Mumtaz's hand. He wanted to tell her that he never wanted to let it or her, go ever again. But he didn't. Although she didn't project that kind of image, it was possible that Mumtaz had simply wanted sex. After all, even religious people had needs. But then again, he felt that wasn't right. Sure, their lovemaking both now and back at the office had been frantic, but it had also been tender and when he'd told her he loved her she had not backed away from him.

And yet now he was no longer in her arms, he could feel his anxiety build again. He'd eventually phoned Barzan Rajput back and discovered that as far as the old man was concerned, Steven Galea was never going to be heard from again. But that didn't mean that Lee felt secure about telling Lorraine Pritchard's husband about that. Or poor old Terry of Tel's Wheels. To be suddenly free from further debt was such a wonderful thing, if that didn't prove to be correct Lee didn't want that on his conscience.

And then there was Trump. Or rather Shazia and her opposition to Trump. Mid morning the following day was when the big march against the US president was due to begin in central London. Would Shazia make what his mum called a 'display' of herself and get arrested? Although happy about Mumtaz and Lee getting back together the girl was, according to Mumtaz, upset with her own boyfriend who she'd called a 'dick'. Some hipster kid from Notting Hill, by all accounts, Lee found it hard to think she wouldn't be better off without him. From what he'd been told 'dick' sounded about right.

John had made her come. If they hadn't shared the same blood, she would have stopped him manhandling her out of the door and told Des to knock the bastard to the floor. But it had been the kids' bedtime and Des had been on story duty.

When they arrived, she said, 'What, here again! Why? It's bloody dark, John! What do I want to be down there for in the middle of the sodding night?'

John called the lift but said nothing.

'I don't see what significance this place has for you,' she continued.

He looked at her with such disgust she shut up.

But she didn't see it. Yes, the Woolwich Foot Tunnel had been where he had supposedly disappeared back in 1976, but he hadn't really disappeared at all. Their father had taken the boy away when he'd seen she hadn't been looking in the right direction. There was no mystery any more. She believed he was who he said he was, even though she didn't understand why he'd turned up when he did or to what purpose. All she could think as the lift gates clanged open was that he was mad. He was mad, she was with him and she didn't feel safe.

'Get in,' he said.

'John . . .'

'Get in!'

She did as she was told. He was deranged. Why he'd come back to England she now realised was to kill her. He blamed her. Just the look in his eyes as he stared at her, told her that. But why? What could she have done to stop her father taking him abroad all those years ago? And how had that been such a bad thing in the end, anyway? He was rich. He was rich, he had a faith that clearly gave meaning to his life. God almighty, if she had just half—

'Get out,' he said as the doors clanged open again. Before her, Brenda saw the murky off-white tiles and the dank floor of the tunnel disappear into the distance. Underneath the river.

'I'm not being funny,' Vi said, 'but why bring me along if you don't want me to tell anyone anything?'

'Because you made the call,' West said. 'You *know*.'

'Know what? We don't *know* anything,' Vi said. 'About this man, any connections he may have had to Henry Dubray . . .'

'I'm sure his girlfriend will tell us,' West said.

'Ruby? You've got hold of Ruby Joseph?'

West said nothing.

'She somewhere in the building?'

They were keeping Rifat Peja at Forest Gate nick. It looked as if they'd taken over the custody suite. Did they have Ruby too?

'We have to find out whether Peja ever met Dubray. She has to tell us.'

'Oh, and how you gonna make her?' Vi said. 'She's a tough little nut . . .' But then her words died on her lips as she remembered who West was and what he was doing.

'As soon as we're able we'll move out of here and take Peja to somewhere out of the way,' he said.

'Where?'

Again he didn't speak.

She said, 'So what now?'

'For you, nothing,' he said. 'You can go home.'

'Oh.'

'Don't want to?'

'No, it's not that, I . . .' Vi shook her head. 'All of this for some bloke who gropes women.'

'Allegedly,' West said.

'Allegedly.'

'Leader of the Free World, DI Collins. And Britain's new trading partner in a post-Brexit world.'

Vi had the feeling that West approved and so she took a fag out of her bag, shoved it in her mouth and headed towards the exit. As she left, she muttered underneath her breath, 'More's the fucking pity!'

Once outside in the car park she leant against the side of her Jag and lit up.

Fortunately, no one had actually got shot when West and his team smashed into the Pejas' flat. But Vi reckoned that was more by luck than judgement. And although Rifat had been brought to Forest Gate, the rest of the family were taken somewhere else. God knew where. As they'd left the scene, Vi saw heavily armed men securing the property, nailing yet more metal sheets across the windows and fixing a steel door over what remained of its predecessor. All to protect some terrible old bastard who hassled women and couldn't string a sentence together. It was nauseating. What Vi needed was a bloody good seeing to. And she knew just the man for that job.

He didn't speak to her at all as they walked from North Woolwich through the tunnel to south. Just a brooding presence at her side, a weird approximation of the man who had for so long sat passively in her living room. Was he going to explode in a firework display of anger? Was he just calmly going to strangle her, maybe? There was no one else about. No one.

Just in front of the southern lift, John turned and began to make his way back down the tunnel. For a moment, Brenda just watched him until he looked back at her and said, 'Coming?'

'Why?'

'What do you mean, why?'

'Why are we here? Why aren't you talking to me? Why do I feel as if you might kill me?' Brenda said.

He looked up at her from underneath craggy, untidy brows. 'I'm not going to kill you, Brenda,' he said. 'Why would I?'

'I don't know. I don't understand you.'

'You don't understand me?' He pointed at his chest. 'Well, let's unpack that, shall we, Brenda? Of course you don't because, firstly, we've not seen each other since 1976, secondly I became a different person to the one you remembered and thirdly you didn't come looking for me when our dad took me away.'

'I did look for you!' Brenda said. 'We all did!'

'Not hard enough!'

His words echoed off the tiled walls, reverberating down the tunnel, going where Brenda hoped she would be able to get without him doing something to her.

'Well . . .'

'Do you have any idea what it feels like to lose your entire personality?' he said. 'To have to become something you're not to please people you have to hope won't put you out on the street or even kill you?'

'Your new parents were rich people, known people . . .'

'They were, they are the sort of people who can do anything!' he said. 'Brenda, understand, they can do whatever they want because they're rich. Hell, they even bought a child, didn't they! From an alcoholic! A child they could make another project out of! A child they could terrify so much with their stories of heaven and hell they could make me do anything – and they did!'

'What—'

'I don't need to tell you,' he said as he pointed at her, his face twisted in rage. 'What would you care, anyway? The point is that they made me, Brenda. Someone who was once John but is God knows who now. Some God-bothering eunuch, clinging on to the only comfort I have ever known! And you know what that is, Brenda? That is money. Because money is the only thing that has never let me down. If I take money to a shop and buy something with it, I will get that thing, without a doubt. If I want someone to do something for me, then I pay them and they do it. It's the only thing in this life you can rely on, trust me. Not your family, not your adoptive family, not your friends because you don't have any of those, and not fairy tales involving pixies, fairies, saints or God! Especially not God!'

He bent double and began to cry. Brenda didn't know whether to go to him or leave him alone. In the end she did nothing. What was happening to him? And why now? She felt sick, as if the world was spinning away from her.

But then her brother stood up straight again and cleared his throat. He held his arm out to her and said, 'Come on, let's get you home.'

'John . . .'

'I'm sorry,' he said. 'Forget what I said, I sometimes get a little—'

'No, no!' she said. 'I won't forget! How can I? You think I haven't felt guilt over you going missing when I was supposed to be looking out for you? It's haunted me for decades! But what could I do, John? Eh? I had no idea you was in America! And Dad died! When he come back here, he wandered the country, ended up in Wales, for Christ's sake, and then he fucking died! Me and Mum, we knew nothing! Nothing!'

Her brother looked down at the rough, damp floor and said, 'Brenda, there is no God. There is no magic, there is no . . .'

'You've done nothing but wang on about God since you got here!'

'Playing a part! Playing a part I've played for so long and . . . But that's not me, Brenda, and I want you to know that. Me, John, I am about no God, no redemption . . . Not for me, you, none of us. And the only hope – and this is really important now – is that we tell the truth about this. The truth . . .'

She looked into his eyes and saw something that made her turn away. She didn't know what it was. She didn't want to know.

'John, why did you bring me here?'

He walked up to her and took her arm. 'Because I wanted you to see my hurt.' He kissed her on the top of her head. 'Because only you and I can come here. I have only you to share this with.'

Although still afraid, Brenda put her arms around him.

Now she began to cry.

'And because I want you to know that I'm not what the world thinks I am. I want you to know that before anyone,' he said.

It wasn't complicated, it was straightforwardly awkward. Lee hadn't needed to answer the door so late at night but, as an ex-soldier, ex-copper and PI, he had to know who was outside. It was Vi.

'Ah . . .'

'Oh, honey, did I get you up?' she said as she breezed past him and walked into the flat.

'Vi . . .'

260

He was wearing a towel, which made sense if he'd just had a shower, but then again his hair wasn't wet.

'Do you wanna talk or . . .'

She turned, leant into him and kissed his lips. 'I think I'd like "or" if you don't mind.'

She went to go straight to the bedroom, but Lee pulled her back.

'Vi,' he said. 'If you want to talk, that's fine, but well, look, I'm tired . . .'

'Oh.'

She felt crushed and also stupid. According to the Laws of Fuck Buddies you were supposed to be able to just turn up and screw, but then sometimes that didn't happen for all sorts of reasons. Not that it had happened before . . .

'Oh, sorry,' she said. Then she shook her head. 'Rough day. I should get on home . . .'

'I'm sorry,' he said. 'I just need—'

'Your kip, yes,' she said. Then she smiled and began walking back to the front door.

'I'm sorry, I—'

'Stop saying sorry, Lee,' Vi said and she walked back out into the night and shut the door behind her.

Back on the street, she lit up a fag and began sauntering towards her car. Was he going off her? Or did he really need his beauty sleep more than a fuck? He could usually be relied upon to deliver the goods, however he felt. Or was there another reason? His bedroom door had been closed, which, if he'd just rushed out of his en suite bathroom, seemed a bit odd. He never usually shut his door.

But then maybe she was reading too much into it. Maybe he really was tired. Or maybe he'd had some other woman in there?

* * *

Des had been worried.

'Where the hell have you been?' he asked Brenda when she got home.

She shook her head. 'With John.'

'I thought he buggered off hours ago!'

She sat down. 'He wanted to talk,' she said.

'So why couldn't he have done that here?'

She shrugged. She was tired, confused and upset and she didn't want to talk about it. If she told Des that John had taken her down the foot tunnel and then behaved like a lunatic he'd worry. And she didn't want that.

'Kids asleep?' she asked as she reached for her handbag and took out a fag.

'Yeah, although Mickey Jay was moaning on, asking for John.'

'Jesus!'

She'd seen Mickey Jay, albeit distractedly, talking to her brother, wanging on at him like he did to all men. Without a consistent role model in his life – Des was really too old for the job – the kid latched on to any bloke who gave him the slightest bit of attention. How could one family fuck up so many generations?

Brenda got to her feet. 'I'm going to hit the sack,' she said. 'Coming?'

'Nah.' Des sat down heavily on the sofa. 'Thought I might wind down with an old friend.'

'Who?'

'Netflix.'

She smiled. Poor old bugger didn't get a lot of time to himself, he deserved an hour or so with *The Terminator* or some super-hero bollocks he'd probably fall asleep to. Brenda walked upstairs slowly and into her bedroom.

As she lay on her bed, she thought about what John had said and how he had behaved down in the tunnel. He'd made her afraid. Of him to begin with, but later just afraid of what he may reveal next. He'd alluded to having to change who he was and what he believed for the Gustavssons. But how had they enforced that? Had they simply broken his spirit or had they abused him in some way? And all that rage he clearly felt against her for not looking hard enough for him . . .

She'd been a young girl with kids of her own at the time. And a violent husband. What more could she have done? She'd told him she thought about him every day of her life, which she had and still did. What more did he want? And had he told her about who he claimed he really was, just to punish her? Because pain in the arse as the 'old John' of Christian piety had been, he hadn't unnerved her like the man she'd been with in the foot tunnel. That man had made her blood freeze.

Brenda put her fag out in the ashtray by the bed and began to undress. It wasn't going to be difficult to go to sleep, even after the incident with John, because she was exhausted. But she worried what she might dream.

Would it just be her and John in that awful tunnel again? Her, screaming at him not to go with their father, forty-two years after the fact? Or would her unconscious simply focus on his eyes and the way they had bored into hers as he'd told her who he 'really was'.

She'd heard her phone beep a couple of times while she'd been walking home and now it beeped again. She picked it up and looked at the screen. She had a text. Oh, God almighty, not from John saying he was sorry, was it? When he'd left her he'd told her he intended to leave her alone. But then he was probably fucking bonkers and so . . .

But no, it was just from her daughter Ruby who told her she was 'out for a bit'.

Weird, she didn't usually tell her mother where she was going. But Brenda was too tired to even begin to wonder. She took her clothes off, threw them on the floor and got into bed.

Sometimes she did irrational things. She always had. After her mother's death she used to sometimes dress up in her clothes and sit at the bottom of the garden of their old house in Forest Gate. Sometimes she wondered whether she had unconsciously encouraged her father to abuse her by doing that. She knew that was ridiculous and that the abuser, not the victim, whatever he or she may have done, was always a creature without excuse or mitigation. But it was a thought that wouldn't go away and so Shazia left the flat and went out. Her amma was at Lee's flat hopefully having tender love made to her by that lovely man. But where should she go?

She did think about going to Notting Hill and staring up at Dexter's posh house, maybe pausing to break the odd window. But then she decided against it. She didn't hate him, he was just different. He wasn't right for her, but that was OK. Rather find out now than later . . .

She'd walk to the Embankment. She was going to meet the others there at eleven and it was two now. It wasn't that long to wait. Her amma wouldn't be back from Lee's. She'd taken an overnight bag, for God's sake! Planned sinning now was it? Shazia laughed. How could love be called sin, because they were in love. She'd thought they'd been in love even before they had.

When she got to Forest Gate Station, which was shut now, Shazia headed down towards the Romford Road. Turning right she'd walk to Stratford and then head across the Olympic site to the A12. Then she'd have to drop down to Poplar after which she'd be able to do much of the journey along the banks of the Thames. Limehouse, Wapping and all that – just like Charles Dickens! He'd done a lot of night walking it was said, back when London had been a lot more dangerous than it was now.

But then as if to make a foolish liar out of her, she heard a police siren noisily slicing its way through the still night air and instinctively Shazia hid herself in a shop doorway.

Detective Inspector West hadn't had much truck with Albanians before. He'd heard they rarely spoke English and resorted to insane levels of violence in pursuit of their nefarious business goals, but he'd never actually met one before. And, although Aslan, his mother Besjana and his sister Emina had all been armed when they had entered the flat, Rifat had not. Shots had been fired, but they'd only hit inanimate objects. They'd been terrified.

West looked down at the man sitting in the chair in front of him and said, 'How well did you know Henry Dubray?'

The Albanian sighed. 'I didn't know him,' he said. 'I knew of him.'

His English was extremely good, which was another surprise to West. But then the family had come to the UK during the Kosovo conflict when Rifat had not been much more than a toddler.

West sat down. 'What did you know of him?' he asked.

'I knew that Ruby had been going out with him,' he said. 'But then she met me . . .' He smirked slightly.

'Was she still sleeping with him when she became involved with you?'

'I dunno. She said she wasn't.'

265

'Weren't you suspicious?'

He shrugged.

West said, 'I don't see you as the type of man who would put up with competition. Your family certainly don't.'

'You don't understand.'

'About blood feuds? Maybe not first-hand but I know of them, to use your own expression. I know your brother claims not to have left your flat for over a year. I know what that can mean.'

Rifat lowered his head. The male members of Albanian families involved in blood feuds could be sequestered in their own homes for years. Only men were legitimate targets in these disputes and so women and children could move freely. But surely, if that were the case, Rifat, as an adult male, would have to have been sequestered too.

West said, 'But you go out. Which, if what I've been told is true, is a bit odd.'

Still Rifat said nothing.

'Well?'

'If you think I'm grassing up—'

'And if you think you're not in a world of shit, then think again,' West said. 'Let's see where we are, shall we? So far, your girlfriend has told us that when she met you six months ago she was still having sexual relations with Henry Dubray. She says you knew this but that you approved of her continued relationship with Mr Dubray because he had money. She claims he supplemented her income from out-of-work benefits to some significant degree.'

'I never—'

'Shut up! I'm speaking! Now you can call me racist or stupid or anything the fuck you like, really, but I understand that men in your culture do not take kindly to having their women shagged by other men.'

'Ruby was just a bit of fun . . .'

'Says you,' West said. 'Newsflash for you is that she thinks you're the real deal. The One. Love of her life . . .'

Rifat groaned.

'Clearly a breakdown of communication going on here. But let's park that for a moment, shall we?' West said. 'Let's get back to why you can go out and your brother can't.'

'I told you I won't—'

'And I told you you're in a world of shit! Henry Dubray was found dead in a sewer underneath Regent's Park. He was an urban explorer, as I'm sure you know, and so the nature of the place where he died shouldn't come as a great shock to anyone. However, Regent's Park, as well as being one of London's best-known open spaces, is also where the American ambassador has his residence . . .'

'Is it?'

'You know it is! And you also know that American President Donald Trump will be hosting a dinner there tonight for, amongst others, the Queen.'

'What's that got to do with me?'

'Really? You don't know? Rifat, even your girlfriend, who is by the way besotted with you for some reason, which I suspect has rather more to do with her use of Charlie, admits you met Henry Dubray on at least two occasions.'

'What?'

'As a "friend" of Ruby's you were interested in what her boyfriend did. Trying to impress her, I imagine. Urban exploring's not for wimps, it's a bit macho . . .'

'I am under a *besa*,' Rifat said.

Confused, West replied, 'A what?'

Rifat took in a deep breath and said, 'If two families are in blood, then under some circumstances a *besa* – or truce, I suppose – can be declared in the case of one family member or even the whole group. It doesn't usually last long but in my case . . . Look, another member of my family did something a long time ago. It was before I was born back in Albania . . .'

'Seriously?' West shook his head. 'You're at war but not at war?'

'Provided I do nothing to them, I can move freely . . .'

'To who?'

'The other family.'

'Who are?'

He shook his head.

'Not telling?' West said. He sighed. 'Could be a crock, then, couldn't it? Or it could be the reason why things are so lairy on the Gascoigne. Either way, you're fucked unless you tell me about Henry Dubray. The truth, I mean. Tell me the truth, Rifat, and all this shit you and your family and your rivals have caused on the Gascoigne goes away. I want to know about that sewer and I want to know about it now.'

NINETEEN

It was bloody raining. Shazia had been walking for most of the previous night and she was knackered. It had been good at the time; she'd discovered all sorts of strange nooks and crannies on her journey along the north bank of the Thames. So much of it was now covered in new developments, but she'd still managed to catch glimpses of the river, particularly at Limehouse and Wapping. She'd sat on Wapping Old Stairs, beside the silent Town of Ramsgate pub for a good hour, in the dark, watching the water lap against old river defences and wharves. As the sun had risen, she'd stood on Tower Hill and watched dawn break over the ancient fortress, her mind turning to the protest to come.

Although both her parents had come from Bangladesh, Shazia had always felt entirely European. Like her amma, she'd never known anything else but the European Union. In times past Britain had been more closely allied to America, so this new arrangement with Trump was nothing novel. Ever since the Second World War, Britain had always, to some extent, followed in America's wake. But this was different. Like a lot of people, Shazia felt that some of Mr Trump's ideas were extreme and unacceptable. Trustworthiness was a real issue and Shazia, for one, mourned the lack of freedom of movement in Europe that would follow the imposition of Brexit and the coming of Trump's America.

Tired and damp, Shazia walked into the branch of Costa Coffee opposite Embankment Tube Station and ordered a cappuccino. It was just gone ten and Dexter, Miles, Sarah and Dimpy had all arranged to meet up at the station with her, to go on to Trafalgar Square for the anti-Trump rally at eleven. If the weather continued like this, however, it was going to be a bit of a soggy march to say the least. Britain in early June did not disappoint and Shazia knew that the bad weather would put some people off.

They'd agreed to meet at Liverpool Street Station at ten. Jason had suggested they go for coffee at the Starbucks on the concourse, but Lee had wanted to go to the Hamilton Hall pub, just outside the station. Back in the day it had been called the Railway Hotel, which had boasted a bit of a reputation for, it was said, bedrooms rented by the hour. Now it had a covered outdoor terrace for smokers.

Lee arrived first and ordered a coffee. Jason Pritchard, carrying a heavy-looking sports bag, rolled up a few minutes later. Once the two men were settled with their drinks, Jason said, 'So you reckon it's all over for Lorraine, then?'

Lee had already outlined the basics about his ex-wife's debts, the Galeas' involvement and the coming of the Rajput family.

'Yeah,' he said. 'I think it's a case of one pile of bollocks hitting up against a bigger pair.'

Jason laughed. 'Not sure the Galeas would take kindly to being compared to a pair of nuts, but I know what you mean.' He shook his head. 'Cheeky sods! If I'd known she was being ripped off by Steven Galea I'd've ripped him a new one meself.'

'I think Barzan Rajput did that.'

'Cuckooing clouds what you can see,' Jason said. 'Like having cataracts. If I'd known Steve Galea was squatting in that house . . .'

'Well, I don't think Lorraine'll have to think about servicing that debt again,' Lee said. 'And yes, I know, that all depends on Barzan Rajput's goodwill. But I think he was telling me the truth when he told me there'll be no repercussions. Not that I think he does goodwill, exactly, but I think he may have another project on the go. Don't know what it is but I get the feeling this situation with his son has been more of an inconvenience than anything else.'

'Just so long as she's stopped spending my money!'

'You'll have to have words,' Lee said. 'We got it fixed this time – and without resorting to the law. But if she does it again, and she may . . .'

'I know, mate,' Jason said. 'Bleedin' clusterfuck all round. I fucked up and then she did. We're blokes – we don't see these things coming.'

'What? Oh, you mean all the expenditure on Botox and that . . .'

'Yeah.'

'The dating game's hard for women,' Lee said. 'Us, we can go on forever so long as we're not skint and we don't look

271

like a bag of spanners. Women don't get to do that.'

'Listen to the feminist!' Jason said. 'But I hear you. Anyway, look, your bill . . .'

'I'll email it,' Lee said.

'Ta.'

Then they talked about other things for a while and then, intrigued by Jason's heavy sports bag, Lee said, 'You off to the gym?'

'Nah.'

'What? Work?'

'I'm off down Trafalgar Square,' Jason said. 'Anti-Trump rally. That's me banner in there. I'd get it out to show you but then I'd never get it back in again.'

'What does it say?' Lee asked.

Jason leant over and whispered in his ear and Lee laughed.

Going to work had been a no-no. When Brenda had up and gone into the bathroom at her usual time of five, she'd thrown up. Then she'd thrown up again a few minutes later and again at just before six. She'd called in sick. Then the diarrhoea started. She'd left it to Des to get his own packed lunch and take whichever kids they were looking after to school. She finally stopped shitting through the eye of a needle at just before ten and so she walked downstairs to the living room and sat down.

Only Kian was about, which was just as well seeing as he was at least quiet. She couldn't have done with roaring six-year-olds on her case. When he saw her, he said, 'You all right, Nana?'

'No, not really, love,' she said.

'Des said you been chucking up, so I never bothered you.'

She put her hand up to her head.

''Cept Mum phoned you and couldn't get an answer and so she called me,' Kian continued.

'Yeah? What about?'

'She went out last night,' he said.

'Where?'

'Dunno. Maybe Rifat's . . .'

Brenda closed her eyes. 'Christ. Did she take Carrie with her?'

'Nah. She's with that lady next door.'

'What the Nigerian?'

'My little sister loves her,' he said. 'You wanna cup of tea, Nana?'

Now she was completely empty she did. 'Ta, darling,' she said. 'That'd be lovely.'

Kian went into the kitchen. Had her strange experience with her brother turned Brenda's stomach? She couldn't remember feeling this unwell for years. And John had really frightened her the previous night. She hoped he kept his word and didn't turn up again for a few days, although quite what he was going to do if he didn't come to hers she couldn't imagine. She was still having him followed by the Arnold Agency when he was up West and so she reckoned she'd hear if he was up to no good. Given his apparent hatred of Donald Trump, she wondered if he was going to be on the protest march in Central London. Maybe he'd come to the UK to protest freely in case his rich parents disapproved of him doing so in the US? Like all rich people, he might disapprove of the Gustavssons, but there was no way he was going to break with or upset them. Because of course he wanted their money.

John, she had decided, wanted everything. He wanted to blame her for what his father had done, his 'new' parents for attempting to indoctrinate him and for other unnamed crimes, he wanted to 'be himself' but he clearly wasn't prepared to

273

beggar himself in order to do that. Christ, he was a middle-aged man, if he hadn't rebelled by this time he was never going to! It was all so adolescent! But then he'd never married or had kids, never really grown up!

And yet . . . And yet he had scared her. That, if nothing else, had been real and it had frightened her. Sometimes down in that awful, awful tunnel he had sounded like someone who was planning to kill himself. The things he'd said about not wanting her to think badly of him. Think badly of him when? And why, exactly? Brenda hadn't got any sort of feeling from him that he had any insight into what he'd said. He hadn't even stopped when some bloke had passed them in the tunnel. He'd raved at her, blamed her, retracted the blame, scared and horrified her and yet he hadn't seemed to have any idea about the harm he had caused.

If John did end up killing himself, would she feel guilty that she kind of knew but did nothing?

'Why should I believe you?'

It wasn't the first time Detective Inspector Conor West had asked him that question and Rifat Peja knew it wouldn't be the last. He got it. The safety of the American president was in the hands of West and people like him and so if he messed up the consequences could be dire.

Rifat had finally 'cracked' in the early hours of the morning. Sick and tired of being disbelieved about everything from his *besa* with the Hoti family to his relationship with Henry Dubray, he finally resorted to the truth. Except it seemed that West didn't like his truth. Or rather his version of it.

'Because it is true,' Rifat said. 'Yes, I did get to know Mr Henry Dubray. I met him at Ruby's house and I can say with my hand on my heart that he never knew about me and Ruby.'

'Oh, so that makes it all right then, does it?' West said. 'Poor dead man never knew you were shagging his girlfriend.'

'It wasn't like that.'

It was and Rifat knew it, but he was too tired to argue.

'I found what Henry did interesting,' Rifat said.

'The urban exploring.'

'Yes! I've told you!'

'Did you tell Ruby?'

'No!' he said. 'Why would I? If she'd known she might have tried to stop me. Women always wonder what their men are talking about when they get together. It didn't concern her.'

'So that's why Henry's number was on your phone?'

'Yes! I told you this!'

'Oh, so . . .'

'I wanted to look at a sewer. I don't know why, I've always been fascinated . . .'

'Really?' West crossed his arms.

'Yes, really, I . . . I left it to Henry to decide where we go, and he chose that one. What am I to do? What? We go down, we have safety equipment – he was really professional . . .'

'And how did you find it down there with all the turds?'

'It was awful!' he said. 'It stank . . .'

'What did you expect?'

'It was more than just smell, it got into your head. There is no other way I can put it. It was mingin', man!'

'Yes, it was horrible, you've said. What happened then?'

'We walked about,' he said. 'He, Henry, he told me about slime on the walls. Showed me condoms floating about, rats.'

'How far did you walk?'

'I dunno.'

'A mile? More? Less?'

'I said, I dunno. Then we come to this place, not far from one of them entrance things . . .'

'Manholes.'

'Yeah.' He breathed in deeply, preparing to tell his interrogator what he'd already told him. 'And that was when Henry fell over. He took off his helmet to get rid of the sweat and he fell over.'

'How?'

'I dunno, I've said, he just fell. It's really slippery down there.'

'Henry was an experienced urban explorer,' West said. 'And he was wearing what I am told were very suitable boots . . .'

'He fell, OK!' Rifat yelled. How many more times did he have to say it? How long before this bastard let him have a cigarette? 'I've told you! I was a bit busy making sure I didn't fall at the time, so I didn't see him go!'

'And you did . . .'

'I told you, man! I tried to get him up, but I couldn't hold onto him because of all the slime! He fell on his face!'

'He had a wound to the back of his head, consistent with being attacked . . .'

'Well, maybe something fell on his head!' Rifat said. 'I don't know! I tried to get him up but I couldn't – he was a dead weight. I've told you this! He fell, I couldn't get him up and then he died and I just left. OK? I ran away, I should've told somebody what happened, but I didn't.'

'Why not?'

'I've told you! I didn't because I didn't want to have any contact with the police! You see how my family lives!'

'You deal arms and drugs according—'

'No! We are at war! With the Hoti! Coppers come on the

276

Gascoigne to see us, they think we're grassing them! Now you come to our flat and make such a noise the whole world knows you're there, we can't never go back there again!'

'Not my problem. Now tell me again, about how Henry Dubray died. Tell me why you were so interested in sewers. Convince me. Start again.'

Lee wouldn't be back in the office for the rest of the day and, in a way, Mumtaz was quite relieved about it. They'd made love almost all night long and she was, to be honest, really tired. But it had been wonderful, except of course when Vi Collins had turned up. That had been awful. And although Mumtaz knew that Vi hadn't seen her in Lee's bed, she felt instinctively that she somehow knew. If – and it was still a big 'if' – Mumtaz and Lee did get back together, Vi would have to be told and sooner rather than later. Knowing, as a woman herself, how women even in their thirties were made to feel old and ugly in patriarchal societies, she knew how hard it would hit Vi's sense of herself. And anyway, she had things to do.

She called the operative covering John Saunders and enquired about his movements.

The PI in question, Ralph, said, 'Been out of his hotel once this morning to go to Daunt's bookshop. That's it.'

'What did he buy?'

'Today? Copy of *Little Women* by Louisa M. Alcott.'

'Really?'

'Really. Goes in, buys a book – one – leaves. Have a look at my emails.'

Mumtaz knew he had but she'd not really paid a lot of attention to what John Saunders liked to read, until now. *Little Women* was way off his usual history and biography fodder.

Mumtaz had a conversation with Brenda earlier that morning. She'd had a notion that maybe John was going to go on the anti-Trump protest. She told her about a frightening encounter with her brother the previous evening and how she felt he might be about to harm himself.

Brenda had said she was ill with some sort of vomiting thing, but she felt she really needed to go over what that conversation with John had actually been about. Brenda had been a bit garbled. So she rang her up and asked to go round. Probably not a good idea from a health point of view, but Brenda was up for it and agreed to see her at midday. Then she looked at Ralph's emails . . .

'The business is fucked anyway,' Terry Gilbert told Lee as they walked around his yard at Gallows Corner. 'But I appreciate what you done for me and for Lorraine. I feel like a right doughnut now, getting her involved.'

'It's all too easy to drag other people in if there's a chance you can reduce your own debt,' Lee said.

'I know, but I should've seen the writing on the wall. I mean, Steve never did make good on his threats to send his boys round even when I couldn't pay. But he had this way about him . . .'

'Yes, I know. I met him, remember?'

'Yeah. Tried to get you in too, didn't I?' Terry said. 'I s'pose it was the name an' all as done it. Galea. Mad bastards. Maybe now we're leaving the EU we won't have to put up with all that foreign filth coming over here . . .'

Lee wanted to say something to contradict him, but he didn't. People like Terry had their own ideas about what was wrong with Britain and they didn't chime with his. They never would.

'And not getting the Old Bill involved, well that was good,' Terry continued. 'I know you was plod years ago, but I ain't got no love for 'em. I was born in Stepney and us East Enders, we always sort our own business.'

'So what will you do now, then?' Lee asked.

'Dunno, really.' He put his hands in his pockets and shivered a little. It was bloody parky for June! 'Get out of this fucking trade, for sure!'

'Then what?'

'Sell up,' he said. 'Wife's been banging on about going out to Spain for years on end, so I s'pose we'll do that.'

And again, Lee bit his tongue. Britain's exit from the European Union was less than a year away, if politicians were to be believed, and once that was done and dusted there'd be precious few retirees heading down to Spain or anywhere else for that matter. Unless, of course, they were rich.

Dexter wasn't talking to her, but that was cool. Shazia didn't mind even if Dimpy thought it was a bit weird that she'd asked her for a lift back to uni. When her friends had pressed her on the subject, all Shazia had said was, 'We're just on a bit of a break.'

But she knew that wasn't true. It was over and, although she'd had some fun times with Dexter in the past, she was glad. If she was going to become a top player in the police, she wasn't going to have time for relationships. Anyway, she'd had enough of all that. Unlike her stepmother. Just the thought of Mumtaz and Lee back together again made her smile. He always treated her amma so well and he was so much in love with her. If they'd not got back together it would have been a waste.

When they arrived at Trafalgar Square, Shazia and her friends found themselves part of a large, if not vast group of people. Many were holding banners, including one middle-aged man who had by far the rudest, it said, 'Oi! Trump! Take your bigly arse and your tiny hands back to America! Cunt!'

Shazia reckoned the police would remove that if they could. She also reckoned that the banner's owner was probably, by the look of him, the widest, wide boy ever and was probably from the East End. Other banners said things like 'An American Dickhead in London' and 'Trump Go Home'. Lots of Black Lives Matter shirts were in evidence and over the whole panoply floated the twenty-foot-high Trump Baby blimp. However, against all that was the relentlessness of the rain, which was having a negative effect no matter what anyone said. People worked hard to keep their spirits up, but it was only when the whole crowd marched along the Embankment, accompanied by bands of climate change activists playing drums, that the demo really got into its stride. Even then the rain didn't give up and it had been disappointing that they hadn't been allowed to march past Downing Street. Trump, according to his schedule, was supposed to be in there having a meeting with the Prime Minister Theresa May.

In spite of the fact she knew she'd personally done her best, Shazia was disappointed. She'd really wanted something dramatic to happen – like the whole city, everyone, turning out to bring London to a standstill and preventing Trump from moving around. But it seemed it wasn't to be. In fact, a lot of people she found herself looking at had distinctly glum expressions on their faces. In spite of the drummers' best efforts.

Suddenly enraged by what she saw as a let-down by her fellow citizens, she said to Dimpy, 'Do you know what? I think the only way to oppose people like Trump is to use violence.'

Her friend looked dismayed. 'Shaz!'

But Shazia ignored her. Unlike Dimpy, who had been brought up in a big loving family in Hounslow, Shazia had been exposed to gangsters at an early age. She knew what they looked like, how they behaved and how, with them, it was dog eat dog – always. And some of the new crop of world leaders coming up now, Mr Trump included, to Shazia fitted that profile.

Brenda visibly trembled as she spoke. Her face was so white it was almost green. Mumtaz appalled at her appearance, said, 'Brenda, seriously, I think you may need to see a doctor.'

But Brenda shook her head. 'No, I'm not chucking up any more and the shitting's stopped. No, look I think this has happened because I've been wound up about John for so long. And now I can't shift the idea he's about to do something to himself.'

'It sounds as if he's a far more troubled man than maybe people think.'

'Troubled don't cover it!' Brenda said.

Kian appeared from the kitchen with tea for them both.

'Tea, ladies.'

'Oh, thank you,' Mumtaz said.

Brenda smiled. 'You're a good boy.'

Kian winced a bit and then said, 'You talking about John, Nana?'

'Yes, love. Nothing for you to worry about.'

'I know, but if he made you feel bad, we need to know, yeah? Me and Des'll sort him out.'

Still smiling, Brenda said, 'You'd better go and do your homework, love.'

'OK.'

He disappeared upstairs. Mumtaz could only imagine how crowded the three bedrooms in this house got when Brenda's family of kids and grandkids were all in residence.

She said, 'Brenda, do you think that John needs help? I mean maybe psychiatric . . .'

'Yeah,' she said. 'But then he's a foreigner, ain't he. How'd ya do that?'

'Just because he's a foreign national doesn't mean he can't be detained for his own safety.'

'What, sectioned?'

'If it's as serious as you think, yes.'

Brenda shifted awkwardly on the sofa. 'I dunno,' she said. 'Des reckons he could be on "the spectrum", like he's Asperger's or something.'

'Possibly,' Mumtaz said. 'That did occur to me when I met him. But that doesn't mean he can't also be a danger to himself too. Have you tried contacting him today?'

'No,' she said. Then she sighed. 'I know I should but after last night I'm sore, like not physically but inside. After his outburst I was left with all these questions about what I should've done to find him all them years ago.'

'You did what you could.'

'Did I?'

'You were a young mother in an abusive relationship, you had enough on your plate,' Mumtaz said. 'Believe me, I know.'

Brenda looked at her and frowned.

Mumtaz took her hand. 'I don't normally talk about myself, but I was in an abusive marriage for a number of years,' she said. 'I know how it dominates your life. Things happened when I was married to my husband that make me feel absolute shame now. And all because I simply didn't have the resources to deal with anything but my husband's violence.'

'You survive.'

'That's it. And that is all you can do, because that is all you have the energy to do.' She smiled. 'Try ringing John now, while I'm here. Maybe what happened last night was just a one-off.'

TWENTY

He had to see two new clients that afternoon. One was a firm of solicitors who wanted to use the agency for process serving and the other was a man in Stratford who wanted to talk about his neighbours who, he reckoned, were spying on him. Of course, the latter case could be one that involved mental illness and so Lee wished he had Mumtaz with him. Her psychological expertise had come in really handy over the years. That was apart from the fact that he just wanted to see her – all the time.

But she was pursuing her own projects and had sent him a text saying that she was going out to visit her client in Canning Town. Brenda Joseph and her strange brother. As he'd told Mumtaz, Lee vaguely remembered the case of the missing Saunders boy. All the local kids were accustomed to using the Woolwich Foot Tunnel to go over to south London but mainly to muck about and tell each other scary stories about how the tunnel was actually a time machine or full of ghosts or just about to disappear under a deluge of water from the river up above. But after John Saunders all of that stopped for Lee. His mum, Rose, forbade him to go down there.

'There's something wrong with that tunnel,' she'd said. 'Always made me shudder, it did. Don't you go down there, you little tyke! You hear me?'

But of course he had. Usually when his dad was at home and his mum was out. The old man hadn't given a shit and was just happy his kids wanted to go out when he came home drunk. A lot like John Saunders' old man, really . . .

Lee switched on the car radio in time for the news. Trump apparently was at Downing Street while the protesters were gathering on Parliament Square to do a lot of shouting, listen to more speeches and . . . Lee shook his head. What bloody good did marching against someone like Donald Trump do? He didn't care what a load of British climate activists, leftie kids and the Labour Party thought about him! In spite of his notoriously thin skin, these groups were just off his radar and so he didn't give a toss. But then Lee chastised himself for his negativity. It was brilliant that kids like Shazia were prepared to stand up and be counted in their opposition to someone who was openly sexist and who, many believed, was using his power to pursue a racist agenda. Lee was just disappointed, although not surprised that his own daughter wasn't taking part. But then Jodie Arnold was the kind of teenager who only really cared about having a good time. The only way she'd ever wake up and smell the coffee was if someone took her iPhone off her and they stopped making hair extensions.

Still, he was anxious about Shazia's safety. Sometimes demonstrations could get out of hand and, when they did, things could escalate quickly. He wasn't overly worried, but he was aware of a general low-level anxiety. Later he'd phone Mumtaz and find out if she'd heard anything.

'The problem with your accident story is that our pathologist reckons that Henry Dubray was hit on the back of the head – which implies an action by someone with intent.'

All Rifat wanted to do was lay down. But West just kept on coming.

Where was he anyway? And how long were they going to keep him here? Where were his mother and siblings? He said, 'As I told you, I wasn't looking at Henry when he fell down. Maybe something did hit him on the head? A loose brick or something . . . I dunno. Maybe someone else was in there with us?'

'But you'd've seen someone else . . .'

'Maybe.' He shook his head.

'Certainly,' West said. 'And also, when Henry fell over why didn't you just hold his head out of the shit and piss and call for help on your phone?'

'I don't know! It all happened so fast! One minute he was in front of me, upright, and then he was on his face in the water. I couldn't get hold of him. As I've told you before, he was slippery . . .'

'Didn't occur to you to pull his head up . . .'

'I couldn't get a fucking grip on it!' Rifat screamed. 'Or him! How many times do I have to tell you this shit?'

'As many times as it takes to convince me you're telling the truth,' West said.

But he knew that even in the unlikely event that should happen, he was keeping this young man where he could see him until Trump was safely on his way back to the US. Other potential threats to the president were other people's problems, this Albanian was his and he was going to make sure he kept him safe.

Brenda threw her phone onto the sofa beside her and said, 'Not picking up. Probably sees it's me and can't bring himself to talk to me. Or . . .'

'As far as we know he is in his hotel room,' Mumtaz said.

'Laying there dead . . .'

Mumtaz took her phone out of her pocket and said, 'Well, let's see, shall we?'

'What you doing?'

'Phoning my man on the spot,' Mumtaz said. 'We have a very quick and easy way of testing whether someone is in a hotel room or not, especially if they are alone.'

She then went into the kitchen to make her call. When she returned she said, 'Shouldn't be long.'

When he'd been a child, Ralph Heinemann had spent a lot of his time daydreaming about being James Bond. When he'd grown up, in part, as he thought, to fulfil this ambition he'd become a police officer. His parents hadn't told him that in order to join the actual security services you had to be posh, while being in the police meant that you were just another oik. But then Ralph's parents hadn't known that. He'd been brought up in the rough end of Rochester in Kent where no one had the slightest idea about class consciousness. Now a PI in his early sixties, Ralph liked the job because he could play tricks on his own mind when he was on a case, like conning himself he was actually observing a foreign spy. He particularly liked 'letter dropping' because it looked so innocent and yet could be so subversive.

He put the letter down on the counter in front of the hotel receptionist and said, 'Delivering this for one of your guests.'

He didn't say the name, but it was written on the envelope, J. Gustavsson.

The receptionist, a man, said, 'Oh, right. Can I say who it's from?'

'I was just told to deliver it,' Ralph said.

The receptionist said nothing. Most of them were told to neither confirm nor deny the presence of a guest at their premises.

Then Ralph said, 'Can I use your toilet, please?'

The receptionist pointed to a door behind him, just beyond his desk. Perfect.

'In there,' he said.

'Ta.'

Communal hotel toilets were rarely occupied and even if they were, it would be easy to hear whether the receptionist called anyone on his phone. Luckily, however, Ralph had no toilet buddies with whom to contend and so he positioned himself behind the flimsy door while he waited for the receptionist to call up to Gustavsson. It didn't take long.

'Ah, Mr Gustavsson,' he said. 'Letter for you down here.' Then he heard him say. 'Don't know, no. Hand-delivered. OK.'

Then he put the handset down.

Ralph left it one more minute and then he quit the toilet with a cheery, 'Thank you,' to the receptionist and then he was gone.

John Gustavsson would have to make up his own mind about how his favourite bookshop in London got hold of his location in order to make sure he knew that politician, writer and traveller, Rory Stewart, was going to be giving a talk at the Marylebone shop the following week. Ralph smiled to himself. It amused him that picking up fliers from shops, places of worship and takeaways could be so useful in his business. Some people, if asked what PIs used in their everyday work, would never believe it. Some people thought they used guns.

Ralph felt that was wishful thinking. He'd never progressed to gun handling when he was in the police, which, he felt, was a shame. As he walked into the graveyard of St Mary's Church and called Mumtaz, he mentally shot at least three people.

Dexter's laughter got on Shazia's nerves. In fact, the way the lot of them, Dimpy included, responded to the news that some Trump-supporting Brit had been hit with a milkshake by protesters in Whitehall, made her feel a bit sick. She didn't know any of the details, but it seemed that some white bloke had been shouting his mouth off about how Donald Trump was some sort of 'people's president' when someone had thrown a milkshake at him. In the past week several right-wing politicians had been 'milkshaked'. Shazia felt it was silly and pointless and distanced herself a little from her group of laughing friends.

While people were concerning themselves with individuals deluded enough to think that anyone with Trump's record as a billionaire could be anyone's 'people's president', nothing was being done to expose that and other really obvious deceptions. Well, that was what Shazia thought. Action of a considered and possibly legalistic type was what was needed now, surely, not somebody – probably called Pippa or Sebastian – chucking a strawberry milkshake at someone she'd now just picked up had been drunk. That was just pointless.

It was still raining and she was now bone-tired and depressed. She could always call Dimpy and talk about where she'd like to pick her up from, later. All she'd had to eat all day was an almond croissant and she felt rough. She thought about saying goodbye to her mates, but then she looked around and found that they had gone. Still laughing, off to shout and rave and achieve nothing and then, probably, get drunk.

Shazia began to make her way towards Westminster Tube Station. As well as the protesters, the area around the Houses of Parliament was packed with tourists taking photos, mainly on their phones, of the buildings and of course the inevitable selfies. She was just about to enter the station when she felt a hand on her arm. Oh, surely not Dex running after her! God!

But when she turned around to see who it was, she found herself looking at someone she didn't recognise.

'Hiya,' the young man said. 'I thought that was you.' He smiled.

Asian, tall, wearing very tight jeans she noticed. She said, 'Um . . .'

He laughed. 'I know,' he said, 'you don't recognise me out of uniform. Krishnan Mukhergee.'

'Oh.'

In spite of still feeling pissed off about just about everything, Shazia smiled. She still had his business card in her pocket.

'You on the march?' he asked.

'Yes, but I'm off home now.'

'Again?' he laughed. 'I always see you when you're off home.'

'So what are you doing here?' she asked. 'Undercover this time?'

'No. Day off,' he said. 'Hey, do you want to come for a coffee?'

He was good-looking and clearly had a sense of humour.

'OK,' she said. 'Although I'd prefer something stronger.'

'Oh, suits me,' he said. 'I only suggest coffee . . .'

'Some bad Muslims drink,' she said. 'I'm afraid I'm one of them.'

Vi Collins was surprised she hadn't heard from Brenda Joseph. She knew that West, or more likely, one of his subordinates, had brought Ruby Henderson in for questioning. Vi wondered whether Brenda knew. She also wondered about DI West. To bring Rifat Peja in on such a tenuous link seemed to Vi to be fraught with risk. But then, maybe in West's world to not bring the Albanian in posed an even greater risk. It was, after all, just possible he'd been in the sewer under Regent's Park with Henry Dubray.

Quite a few Albanians spoke Italian. Vi knew this because her Italian heritage DS, Tony Bracci, was sometimes called in to translate. She twirled her chair around to face him and said, 'You know a bit about Albanians, don't you, Tone?'

He looked up. Fair-haired and with a ruddy complexion, Tony looked about as Italian as Gary Barlow.

'I've met a few, yeah,' he said. 'Lot of 'em back in my old manor.'

Tony came from Barking where his Italian forebears had been ice merchants.

'Why?'

He didn't know what had happened the previous night and Vi wasn't able to tell him.

Eventually she said, 'Asking for a friend.'

'Oh.' He smiled. Vi knew what he thought. Probably wondering which one of her 'old girl' mates had agreed to marry a thirty-year-old Albanian.

He leant towards her and said, 'There's a lot of them on the old Gascoigne Estate. Fucking coke central, guv. Course, this is all hearsay, but it seems the Albanians are the biggest dealers. Lives revolve around it. If they put as much thought into getting proper jobs as they do in finding places to conceal Charlie, then they'd all be at the tops of their respective games.'

'What places?' Vi asked.

'What, for concealing Charlie?'

'Yeah.'

'Oh, you know, under floorboards, in breast implants, the old condom boogie . . . Word is a lot of dealers, Albanians included I imagine, are needing to find places these days outside their gaffs. The amounts are too big now. They buy in bulk cos it's cheaper that way . . . Starting to see a move towards putting stuff on derelict sites, putting some sort of guard at the site . . .' He was shocked that Vi was using her phone while talking to him, she never usually did that. 'Guv?'

Vi held up a finger.

'You,' she said, 'have just given me some intel someone way above my pay grade may well find useful.'

'So we know John's in his hotel room,' Mumtaz said.

The hotel receptionist had spoken to Mr Gustavsson on the phone.

'Are you sure he wasn't just blowing off some steam to you prior to returning to the States?' Mumtaz asked. 'I mean, totally inappropriate . . .'

Brenda shook her head. 'I've not been able to find out when he's going back,' she said.

Kian, who had been in the room playing a video game said, 'Some of his stuff's here, in't it, Nan?'

'Oh yes,' Brenda said. 'A coat, from when it was colder a while ago, and a book, I think.'

'That's up in the bog,' Kian said.

'The toilet,' Brenda corrected. 'Is it?'

He looked round. 'Yeah. Want me to go and get it for you?'

'If you would,' Brenda said.

While he ran upstairs, Mumtaz said, 'My daughter's at the demonstration in Whitehall this afternoon. She's nineteen but I still worry.'

'Blimey, you must've been about ten when you had her!' Brenda said.

'Actually, she's my stepdaughter, but I am old enough to be her mother – just.'

Brenda said, 'Had my eldest at sixteen. All full of it I was, until I found meself alone in a flat in south London with a sink full of nappies and a bloke who only came home to knock me about.'

Kian returned holding a book. He handed it to Brenda and said, 'Dunno what it's about.'

She looked at it.

'Oh, I remember him reading this,' she said. 'Brought it with him first time he come. I think it's a . . . a like an action story, by the look of it.'

She handed it to Mumtaz. It was a hardback and didn't have the look of a novel to her. With its plain maroon cover, it was more like an academic book. An old one.

Mumtaz opened it and came to the title page. That made her a little uneasy she would later claim. But it wasn't until she got to some upfront reviews of the book that she felt a little tension build in her chest.

* * *

293

He came to her.

'I'm knackered and could do with a break,' West said as he joined Vi in her office.

She'd sent Tony Bracci off on a mission to Greggs for coffee and sausage rolls and so he'd be some time. Whoever else saw them, saw them.

'Where you based?' Vi said as she offered him a chair.

He didn't say anything. She knew it had to be nearby because he'd got there so quickly.

She said, 'All right. Now look, I've been chatting to my DS who sometimes acts as translator for Albanians. A lot of 'em speak Italian and that's his second language.'

'OK. And your point is?'

'My point is that, as my DS puts it, some of the drug dealers are buying in bulk these days. It's cheaper for them but it does require finding places to stash large amounts that won't be easily found. Now obviously this, ideally, necessitates finding places outside their own gaffs.'

'Yes.'

'Now,' she said, 'while not naming anywhere specific, my DS alluded to an idea that some of them might use derelict buildings. He gave me no examples, but if you think like a dealer, you can see the advantages.'

'Unless someone comes across your gear.'

'They post guards, I believe,' Vi said. 'But look, whatever the whys and wherefores, I'm telling you this because of Rifat Peja. Course, I don't know what he's told you but maybe, only maybe, he got Henry Dubray to take him down that sewer so he could scope out a new place to stash his gear. Whether Dubray knew this or not . . .'

'In a sewer?' West frowned. 'Strikes me as a bit, I don't know . . . How would you do that?'

'I dunno,' Vi said. 'Seems fucking desperate to me.'

'And a long way from Barking . . .'

'I'm not saying this happened, what I'm saying is there could be more to this than meets the eye,' Vi said.

'My only concern is the president . . .'

'I know,' she said. 'But this could be another explanation.'

'He knows he's in a lot of trouble,' West said, 'he could've come out with this, if it's true, and cleared the whole thing up.'

'Oh, for God's sake, you know it don't work like that!' Vi said. 'Blimey I know you're a youngster compared to me, but when did you last have dealings with a drug dealer who gave you the gen on his MO without you having to prise him open like a tin can?'

She saw West smile. 'You're not—'

'West, put it to him,' Vi said. 'He won't put it to you, however much bother he may be facing over Trump. If he's got gear in that sewer, then that's family property and he'd rather die than give it up to you.'

'So what's the point?' he said.

'Point is, if you've put the fear of Christ in him over Trump, you may be able to corner him about this,' Vi said. 'And if you haven't put the fear of Christ up him, then do so!'

He sighed. 'Nothing was found with the body . . .'

'Well, excuse me,' Vi said. 'But if Peja was just scoping the place out there wouldn't be. I mean, I know that Dubray's dead, but maybe he had a nice little sideline going helping drug dealers hide their gear. I think we need to investigate that possibility, don't you? President or no president.'

Mumtaz put the book on the passenger seat and got into the car. There was no point calling ahead, she'd just take it straight to Forest Gate Police Station. Vi or Tony or someone else they knew was bound to be in. Someone who wouldn't instantly think she'd gone mad.

She'd never read *American Brutus* by Michael W. Kauffman. But she knew about the subject of his book. Although she'd never had a great interest in American history, Mumtaz knew that one of their greatest presidents of the nineteenth century, Lincoln, had been assassinated. In the short time she'd had to read the introductory blurb, however, she learnt that he'd been shot, from behind at close range, while at the theatre by a man called John Wilkes Booth. That was all she'd managed to take in before her brain began putting this well-thumbed book together with what Brenda had told her about her brother. And about how she had felt in his presence.

God knew she had no reason to like anything about the current president of the USA, but if John Saunders meant him harm in some way she had to alert people to that. But did he? Maybe he was just simply interested in Lincoln? But he wasn't, according to Brenda, who he projected himself to be. And if what he'd told her was the truth, then he would hate Trump. And yet his public persona was that of a fairly typical Trump supporter.

Mumtaz drove up Prince Regent's Lane. How did a person deal with being actually sold as a child? How could a ten-year-old ever actually forget his past and become someone else? And how would that child feel about those who had done that to him as an adult? Whatever 'normal' might be, John Saunders didn't stand a hope in hell of ever becoming that whatever benefits the Gustavssons' money may have brought him. What if they had sexually or physically abused him? Or both?

Mumtaz knew she shouldn't make calls while she was driving, but she tried to call Lee. If he could meet her up at Forest Gate maybe he'd be able to calm her down, make her appear less deranged. But he wasn't picking up. She left him a message to call her back when he could.

It seemed to take bloody forever to get to Forest Gate nick but in reality it was just normal traffic for Newham. Was there someone she could call who would accelerate this? And anyway, what was 'this'? She didn't know anything about the assassination of Lincoln except that it had been done by this Wilkes Booth man in a theatre. Had Wilkes Booth even been American? She didn't know. Ditto his motive was unknown to her. And anyway, why had John left this book at Brenda's house if he meant the president harm? Why had he revealed himself in his true colours to his sister if this was what he intended to do?

Unless Brenda was correct, and he wanted to die . . .

What was missing of course, in all of this, was how John might achieve this. As far as she knew, and in spite of his wealth, John didn't know Trump. Did his parents? It was possible and there was a reception for the Queen hosted by Trump that was due to take place at the US Ambassador's residence in Regent's Park at 8 p.m. It had been reported that as well as UK government ministers and royalty, some American business leaders were to attend.

Could this mean the Gustavssons?

'You look like shit, mate.'

Rifat Peja looked up at the tall, skinny woman wearing a suit that looked as if it had come from the nineteen eighties – he'd seen the movie *Nine to Five* – and wondered whether he was hallucinating.

'What?'

She knelt down beside him. 'No sleep, darlin'?'

Rifat looked at West. 'He won't let me.'

Vi Collins smiled. 'Yeah, he's a bit of a bastard like that,' she said. 'But see, he's got a job to do, which is to make sure nobody hurts the American president and so he gets a bit lairy, if you know what I mean.'

He didn't but he said nothing.

'But I'm a bit different meself,' she continued. 'Me and my DS we're just ordinary plods and so we thought that if we could talk to you then maybe we could get somewhere. Us not having the responsibility of looking after the president on our minds.'

She was a copper but he felt she was different. How, he didn't know. He said, 'Him . . .'

'DI West . . . ?'

'He thinks that because we're Muslims we want to kill Trump,' he said. 'That's racism, innit?'

She took his hand. 'Depends on your point of view I suppose, darlin',' she said. 'Now look, you come with me and meet Tone, who's waiting for us in the next room, and we'll get you a cup of coffee and we'll have a chat.'

'Can I go to the toilet too?' he asked. 'I've only been once since I got here.'

The woman flashed a scowl at West and then said, 'Course you can, love.'

And then she raised him to his feet and took him to another room where a fair-haired fat man was waiting for them.

Mumtaz just abandoned her car. On double yellow lines outside Forest Gate nick at the top of Green Street. If she didn't get a ticket, then that would count as an official miracle. She ran up to the front desk where she saw a familiar face.

'Sergeant Baqri,' she said to the spare, middle-aged man at the desk, 'can I see DI Collins or DS Bracci?'

'Both out I'm afraid.'

'Oh, bloody shit!' Then she chastised herself. 'Sorry! Sorry!'

'Can anyone else help you, Mrs Hakim?' Baqri asked.

'I don't know . . . I don't know whether it's important or . . . I don't know!' She flung her arms in the air. She was coming over properly mad. Why on earth had Lee been unavailable? 'Who . . .'

'I know that Detective Inspector Archer's in the building,' Baqri said.

'Archer? Don't know him, I don't think . . .'

'DI Collins does,' Baqri said. 'He's young but he's on her wavelength . . .'

Mumtaz knew that Sergeant Baqri knew Vi reasonably well and so she opted to be guided by him.

'All right, all right if he can see me . . .'

Baqri picked up his phone.

'So what's it about Mrs Hakim?' he asked.

And it was then that Mumtaz knew she had nothing.

TWENTY-ONE

He dressed with care. Such occasions necessitated it. He'd lost count long ago of the number of times he'd had to do this. Tuxedo, bow tie, shiny shoes. Occasionally he'd wondered what his dad might have made of it. One of his few memories was of his old man watching Bruce Forsyth dressed in a dinner suit on some show on TV and saying, 'Look at him poncing about in a penguin suit!'

That had been Reg all over. Drunk as usual, and offensive. How he'd ever got to actually talk to Etta and Michael was something he'd never asked them. Why would anyone, much less American billionaires, want to talk to someone like Reg? But they must've found some common ground. Maybe the old git had reeled them in with sob stories. He'd certainly spun them a good line on that cruise. Going on about how 'poor Johnny' couldn't get a good education in Britain, about how they had to use an outside bog and the story about how his mother was too drugged up to take care of him.

Of course, there'd been some truth in all of that. Their house still had an outside toilet, but it also had an inside one too. The council had put it in. Sheila, his mum had been doing Valium for years, but John was only not getting a good education because he didn't want one. School had been boring. He wasn't interested in geography or how plants grow. The only subject he'd ever really liked was maths.

It had been no better in the States. He'd only graduated high school because of who his parents were. They'd force-fed him lies not just about God and Jesus but also just straight lies from people's heads. Wasting his time on fiction. Books set in a country, the US, he didn't understand. *Little Women* had been the worst. A romance about a family of silly girls. He always enjoyed buying copies and then tearing them to shreds. It provided a release. Why destroy something of merit when you became frustrated? John had always chosen his victims carefully.

Detective Inspector Archer had gone away to 'make some calls'. Alone in the interview room, Mumtaz thought that he was probably not requesting information about the president's banquet guest list at all. He was phoning two psychiatrists with a view to getting her sectioned. That's certainly what she would have done had she heard her own story for the first time.

But then Archer hadn't seemed shocked and he hadn't said he disbelieved her. However, if he was a friend of Vi's then he was probably taking a punt. Like she did. Mumtaz looked at her phone and wondered whether Lee would call her back soon. She knew she would have felt so much more confident speaking to Archer had he been beside her. He could at least pretend to be

301

calm. And if he'd spoken to Archer it would have been man to man, which, even in this day and age seemed to count for a lot.

As time ticked on, Mumtaz began to replay what she knew about John Saunders over in her head. When all of this was over, it would probably shake out that he was just some deranged man who didn't have any sort of agenda. After all, the man had been sold like a piece of meat when he was only ten and God only knew what he'd been through in his gilded American cage. Brenda reckoned he'd been abused, but Mumtaz wasn't so sure. How he was, to her way of thinking, was much more due to a disconnection that he'd always had, an undiagnosed position on the autistic spectrum. His US parents were probably just well meaning, even if their method of obtaining their child seemed so very wrong.

'I'm going to tell you a story,' Vi said to Rifat.

'You what?'

'A story,' she said. 'And I don't want you to interrupt or comment until I've finished, OK?'

He shrugged. Clearly confused, but then who could blame him? Coppers didn't usually tell stories to people in custody. She slid her gaze over towards Tony who looked, to say the least, dubious.

Looking back at Rifat, she said, 'It goes like this. Once upon a time there was a king whose family had some jewels and gold. They didn't have a shitload because they weren't greedy and anyway all kings had the same and they didn't feel hard done by. But then that changed when one of the other kings bought loads more. The first king said to him, "What you got all that for? It might get nicked if people find out about it?" And the second king said, "Oh yes." So he took the extra gold and jewels out of his palace and hid them in his old palace what was derelict and where no one would find it. But the first king was way ahead of him and knew exactly what he'd do. And so, when it came to hiding the extra gold and jewels he'd just bought, he put them under the ground where no one would find them.'

She looked across at Tony again, who'd been watching the young man as she spoke, and then she said to Rifat, 'Wondering whether that rings any bells? Not with you and your situation, of course. I mean Mr West and his boys never found no jewels when they went down that sewer. But I think that for a king in the position of the first king, an underground option does make sense, don't it?'

'What is this about?' Rifat said. 'Why you telling me stories? I'm not a kid!'

'I'm doing it, love,' Vi said. 'Because stories ain't real. I'm doing it because, unlike real life, stories can't be used against people, even if they are true. No one, as you can see, is recording either my story or your response to it. So there's not anything serious going on here, just a bit of banter. Know what I mean?'

West hadn't understood why she'd wanted him out of the way – she'd been obliged to promise him something, which she had. Of course, she'd have to break that promise if this didn't work but she didn't care. She had no doubt that Rifat was an evil little scrote who had been dealing drugs to Ruby Henderson, who'd been off the gear for years. But she also felt pretty sure he'd never had any designs on killing the President of the USA – even if he just might have killed Henry Dubray.

Rifat said, 'What do you want me to say?'

'Something that will make me believe in the idea that you was down that sewer with Henry Dubray for reasons other than scoping it out to make a hit on Donald Trump,' she said.

Then she sat back in her chair and added, 'You can tell me a story about that too, if you want to. I mean, if the first king had actually gone underground with his gold and his jewels . . .'

'I didn't,' Rifat interrupted. 'I wouldn't, not with someone else . . .'

'There's no one called Gustavsson on the guest list or the staff,' Archer said as he sat down opposite Mumtaz. 'Every guest, every member of staff has been security checked. No one's getting into Winfield House without being thoroughly vetted – and that includes cops.'

Mumtaz breathed out. She felt stupid but also, in a way relieved.

Her phone rang. She looked at the screen and saw that it was Lee.

'Do you mind if I take this?' she asked Archer.

'Go ahead.'

But he didn't leave the room to give her any privacy, which, as it turned out, was an intimation of things to come.

Lee asked where she was and so she told him and vaguely outlined why. She asked Archer whether he could or should join her and the DI said that was fine.

While they waited for Lee, Mumtaz filled Archer in on some more details about the John Saunders case. He was too young to remember it, but he quickly declared himself intrigued.

When Lee arrived, Mumtaz was a little shocked at his appearance. He looked grey and drawn and she thought it was probably because he'd had a very busy day. She resolved to cook a nice meal for him and for Shazia when they all got back to her place. Then a quiet night in in front of the telly.

But Lee was drawn and grey not because he'd been busy all

day but, in view of the fact Mumtaz had come to the police with details about a possible hit on Trump, their protocols required they were not allowed to let her go until they were entirely satisfied she posed no threat.

Lee knew it was going to, potentially, be a very long night for both of them.

She hadn't been drunk, no. Just a bit tipsy. And when he'd first said that he'd take her home, she had refused, but then he'd just done it anyway and she was glad.

When they arrived at Liverpool Street, Krishnan looked up at the destination boards and said, 'There, Gidea Park train. Platform ten.'

They had to run to catch it, Shazia giggling all the way. She'd had tequila before but never that other, stronger Mexican spirit mezcal. Krishnan liked it and so she'd joined him. However, while he'd stopped at two shots, she'd had four and it showed. Laughing was only the half of it, there was the wobbling around too. When they jumped onto the train, she flung herself down in the nearest seat and said, 'I've not felt this relaxed for years!'

Her companion, smiling, sat beside her.

'Maybe a little too relaxed . . .'

She prodded him with her finger. 'You encouraged me!'

'Oh, I did not!' he said. 'I told you it was two shots for a good time, three for double vision and four for bladdered!'

'Which is what I wanted to do!' she said. She let her head flop on his shoulder. 'Because bladdered, sometimes, is a good idea.'

By the time they got to Stratford she was asleep and snoring. Krishnan thought she looked sweet. She was a bit of a mad girl and had some really weird ideas, but he liked her. They'd had fun in the pub, even though she'd got arse'oled in very short order, but he really fancied her and he thought that she probably fancied him too.

He woke her up just before they got to Forest Gate and offered to walk her home. But she wouldn't have it and so they parted at the ticket barrier.

'You sure you can get home all right?' he asked her again as they stood to one side to let other passengers get out.

'Course,' she said. 'I'm a big girl now. My amma calls me a force of nature . . .'

'Yes, I think you are,' he said.

She smiled.

'Well,' he said. 'It's been very nice spending time with you, Shazia Hakim, and if you keep hold of my card, then maybe we can do it again sometime.'

'What, with me up in Manchester?' she said.

He shrugged. 'That's not far.'

'It is!'

He leant towards her. 'Not when you've done the advanced driving course it isn't . . .'

She gasped. 'You . . .'

He pulled her towards him and kissed her on the lips. When he'd finished, he said to her, 'Keep my card safe, Shazia Hakim. You and me, we have a date at whatever Manchester pub you recommend.'

And then he ran down onto the westbound platform.

DI West had fallen asleep in his chair. Vi had to shake him awake.

'Oi!'

'What?' He sat up and held his head. 'Ow!'

Vi sat down beside him. 'You know,' she said, 'back in the day when me and my old DI used to pull all-nighters, he used to avail himself of a bit of Wizz to keep going. They all did back then, the top brass. Not me, though. But I gave it some thought. I knew a couple of tasty dealers back then . . .'

'DI Collins . . .'

'Oh, Rifat Peja, yes,' she said. 'I'd search that sewer underneath Regent's Park again, if I were you.'

He shot up in his seat. 'You mean . . .'

'Oh, he's admitted to nothing,' she said. 'And I doubt whether you'll find anything. Belt and braces operators like him. But he was scoping it out and I'm pretty sure our mate Henry knew that. A growing revenue stream for urban explorers, drug dealers.'

'But he killed him? He admitted that?'

'Oh no,' she said. 'But then that's up to you to prove, not me. No, you underestimate kids like Rifat at your cost, DI West. He's far too involved in things you don't understand to be bothered by Trump. And FYI I'd do what my DS done a long time ago and read up about Albanian blood feuds before you pull one of them in again. It's not religion as pushes their buttons so much as tribal allegiances. Just because he's a Muslim . . .'

'But how did you do it?' West asked. 'How did you . . .'

Vi tapped the side of her nose and said, 'Stories, mate. Everyone loves a fairy tale. Fun, exciting, not about them . . . Tell a story and you've caught their attention. Much better than stopping them from using the bog. And, as I say, he might've killed Henry. And that's wrong. But then Henry weren't such a good boy, even if he did talk like you.'

She got up.

'Well,' she said, 'seeing as I can't do no more here . . . I was due to knock off a couple of hours ago and so I think I'll go back to the nick for a bit and then sod off home.'

He shook his head. 'You'll write . . .'

'Oh, I'll write a report for you, yes,' she said. Then she gave him one of her business cards. 'I'll email it to you.'

'Thank you.'

'Oh, and if you fancy a jar when all this is over, drop me an email and we'll go out,' she said. 'I've got a bit of a vacancy in the male escort section of me diary, at the moment.'

'Oh . . .'

She laughed. 'Oh, don't look so frightened,' she said. 'It'll just be sex. You don't have to actually fancy me or nothing.'

He got a taxi. He could've walked and under normal circumstances he would have done so, but arrival in a car would be expected. It only took ten minutes, which was just as well because he could feel himself begin to hyperventilate.

When he got out, after he'd paid the driver, he looked at his watch. It was five forty-five. So he was early. But they were already looking at him. One of them was walking towards him. Of course, he was still a long way from the actual house . . .

'Sir?'

John looked at him. American, sharp-suited, built like a tank. A G-man.

'Yes?'

'This is a restricted area, sir.'

'I've an appointment,' John said. 'I have a letter . . .'

He knew better than to simply take his letter and his passport out of his inside pocket. That was a sure-fire way to get yourself killed.

'Top inside left pocket,' he said as he held his arms up.

The G-man took his documents, looked at them, then

photographed them and gave them back. Then he patted him down. When he came to the bulge in his outside left jacket pocket he said, 'What's that?'

'A gift. Look at it.'

His face unmoving, the man took out the small box John had been carrying.

'What is it?'

'Open it,' John said.

The man called over one of his colleagues. Then he put the small box on the ground.

'Who's your gift for?' he asked John before he opened it.

'Mr President,' John said.

Then the G-man and his colleague opened the box and they both smiled.

'Do you wanna cup of something?' Lee asked Mumtaz, pointing to the drinks machine in the corner of the room.

She shook her head. 'I've had coffee from here before,' she said, 'With Vi. It's awful.'

'Could try the hot chocolate?'

'No . . .' She looked down at her hands. 'How long are we likely to be kept here?'

'Dunno. You gave them some intel about Trump and so until he's locked down tight, this is it, baby.'

'Oh God!'

He put an arm around her and whispered in her ear. 'Pity they've got CCTV . . .'

In spite of herself she laughed. Then she said, 'If you can think of anywhere less romantic . . .'

'Our office?'

She nudged him in the ribs.

He said, 'Just saying. Don't think romantic locations are everything, do you?'

She shook her head.

He moved in close again and whispered, 'I could do it with you anywhere.'

'Well, that's because you're . . .'

'Besotted with you,' he said.

They kissed. Not for long but they both felt better for it. Lee for one knew that the door behind them could only be opened with a key card and DI Archer was unlikely to do that for some long while. In the meantime, they had access to drinks and a toilet and chairs that were not too uncomfortable.

After a short silence, Mumtaz said, 'So if John Saunders or Gustavsson isn't on the president's guest list, then my idea was clearly rubbish.'

'But not without some substance,' Lee said. 'If plod had thought you were a screaming nutter we wouldn't be here.'

'I s'pose so. So what is John playing at?'

'From what you've told me he's just a confused man, damaged by his fucked-up childhood. Maybe he just wanted to hurt his sister, after all.'

'Yes, but that book . . .'

'He was educated in America,' Lee said. 'Political assassinations are part of their history.'

'So I shouldn't have come here?'

'Yes, you should, because you had a legitimate concern,' he said.

'You just said I didn't!'

'Mumtaz, it was unlikely to be anything—'

'So I was an idiot!'

'No! No, you weren't, it's just that . . . I don't know much

310

about it, but I do know that President Lincoln was shot in full view of everyone in a theatre,' he said. 'And if John Saunders can get a gun past all the FBI, CIA, Special Branch, bloody spooks around that house in Regent's Park, then good luck to him. It's just not possible.'

'But what if he plans to do something else?' Mumtaz said.

'Like what?' Lee asked.

'I don't know!'

The current Winfield House had been built by the heiress to the Woolworth fortune, Barbara Hutton, back in the 1930s. He didn't know why or how it had then become the American Embassy. But he did know a bit about Hutton, who'd had a rather tragic life. Back in the States she was known as the 'poor little rich girl'.

John could only partly empathise. Poor old Barbara had never been without money but he had, so he knew it as a no-win situation. Besides, none of these rich folk who complained about being trapped by their money ever gave any of it away. Himself included.

The main barrier between Winfield House and the rest of the city was a fifteen-foot-high metal wall. This was the main entrance where yet more security checks would happen. Conducted by a joint US/British contingent, John wondered whether it would be any different from the security he'd already been through, but it wasn't, except for added metal detectors. But that didn't bother him.

Even before he'd arrived at the first gate, he'd been photographed on the approach, he'd undergone US and British security clearance for weeks in advance and now they were letting him move forward to the pathway leading up to the house. Soon he'd be at the front door where he'd have to sign in, have another metal detector session, this time probably handheld, and turn his pockets out yet again.

He was nearly there . . .

Did Britain have its own version of G-men? If they did there was one standing to the left-hand side of the front door now. This was yet another level of security after the final tranche of metal detectors, and physical searches he'd already endured in front of the main entrance.

This huge individual said to him, in a distinctly Liverpudlian accent, 'Name?'

John told him. The great brute looked for it on a list and then said, 'Purpose?'

'I've a ten-minute private meeting with Mr President,' John said. 'At six o'clock.'

The man appeared to consider it for a moment and then said, 'Proceed.'

And so John Gustavsson stepped over the threshold of the US Ambassador's residence in London for his prearranged meeting with Donald Trump. The president had been keen to meet a representative from one of America's richest and most venerable families for years. Unfortunately, John's father Michael would never countenance such a meeting because as a sincere, good-living Christian he could not buy into the fact that someone as overtly sexualised and anti-philanthropic like the president could be of any possible interest to him. His son, so the president had been led to believe, was a rather different proposition and John had no doubt that the Commander-in-Chief was looking forward to their meeting. After all, John was the future . . .

John took a second step, which proved excruciating. He screamed and fell to the floor where he was set upon by what looked like a pack of wolves.

It wasn't even seven o'clock when DI Archer let them out of the interview room. Lee for one, had expected them to have been detained at least until the president's banquet began at eight.

'No, it's all right now,' Archer said as he checked them out at the front desk.

'So what . . .'

'Nothing happened,' he said.

'I know Mr Gustavsson wasn't on your list . . .' Mumtaz said.

'Apparently not,' he said.

Lee and Mumtaz walked towards the front door of the station. Then Archer said, 'Thank you.'

Mumtaz frowned, 'For what?'

But by then he had disappeared back into the bowels of the building.

He was detained in what they called 'American style' – that was with his wrists cuffed to his ankles, which were held together with shackles. It was the worst stress position imaginable. Even sitting made him gasp.

But then it wasn't as if they wanted him to talk. Not yet. They didn't know that he never would but that wasn't his problem.

One of them, a thin, dark Brit with a face like a walnut, held the president's present down so that he could see it. He opened the box. There was the platinum crucifix surrounded by the thin glass globe containing shining white dust.

'Like a pious snow globe,' the man said to John. 'How

thoughtful. Although isn't the glass supposed to be broken upon gifting?'

John said nothing.

'Shall I break it, then?' the man asked.

Was he expecting him to scream and pray and plead for him not to do that? If he was, then he either didn't know him at all or he underestimated him. Probably both.

'Shall I?' he repeated.

John didn't even blink.

The man took the box and its contents away and John could hear him speaking to another man who said, 'Are you sure? He seems unaffected by it.'

And then the walnut-faced man said, 'Oh, he'd probably have ended up killing himself as well as the president. I've no doubt his own life is of little use to him, given what he was about to do. Baffling, I grant you. Billionaires usually want to live.'

'And what did you say the substance in that snow globe is?' the second man asked.

'Ricin,' the first one said. 'Causes a really lingering messy death. Mr Gustavsson must have a lot of hatred in his soul for some reason . . .'

'Seems he was always a bit of an oddball, according to our East End constabulary.'

'Oh?'

'Good bit of intel, that,' the second man said. 'If we hadn't been looking for this chap's name on the guest list for that mob, we would never have looked at Trump's private meeting schedule . . .'

TWENTY-TWO

Three Weeks Later

Brenda went into the kitchen to make them both tea, leaving Mumtaz alone with the letter she'd received from John. No one had heard a word from him ever since his outburst at her in the Woolwich Foot Tunnel on the night of the 3rd June.

Word-processed rather than handwritten, it was a nice note thanking Brenda and her family for their hospitality. He was sorry he'd rushed off without telling them, but a relative back in the States had fallen ill and so he'd had to go home. He doubted he'd be able to come back to the UK in the near future, but assured Brenda that his decision to leave all his fortune to her and the kids in the event of his death still held. Included was the name and contact details of his attorney. It was strange.

And then he'd signed the letter in what looked like an extremely shaky hand. Perhaps he was ill?

When she came back into the living room, Brenda said, 'Weird, innit?'

'Not the kind of letter you get every day,' Mumtaz said.

Brenda sat down and lit a fag. 'Strange bugger, my brother,' she said. 'Damaged. But probably better he went back to the States. He belongs there now, certainly don't belong here.'

'How do you feel about it all now?'

'I dunno, really,' she said. 'I s'pose I wish I could've got to know John better, if such a thing was ever possible.' Then she laughed. 'Mind you, at least the kids'll be provided for when he pops his clogs!'

Mumtaz laughed. 'God, you must think why didn't he give you a lump sum now!'

'Ah!' Brenda waved a hand in front of her face. 'What we've never had we'll never miss! What would me and Des do if we didn't go to work?'

Mumtaz drank some tea. 'How's Ruby?' she asked.

'Oh. That. Well, she was right shook up when the police took her in that night about that Albanian. I think she thought they were gonna search her place for drugs.'

'Did they?'

'No. Dunno why. She says she never had none, anyway but . . . Seems to have made her think, and we ain't seen hide nor hair of that Rifat since. Maybe she'll find someone nice like that Henry again . . .'

Except that as Vi had told Mumtaz when they'd met, 'that Henry' probably hadn't been as nice as everyone thought. According to Rifat, Henry made money taking drug dealers to remote places where they could stash their goods. If Rifat had been telling the truth. It had been established, however, that Henry had met with an accident rather than been

316

murdered – although a question still remained about why Rifat hadn't called for help.

Brenda brought out some biscuits. 'So how's your girl, then?' she asked. 'You was a bit worried about her when all the demonstrations was going on.'

Mumtaz smiled. 'Oh, she's fine, thank you,' she said. 'Actually she's down from uni now for the summer holidays. Not that I think I'll see that much of her.'

'Why's that?'

'She's got a new boyfriend,' Mumtaz said. 'An absolutely lovely young man. Got a good job, they're besotted with each other. Oh, what it is to be young, eh?'

But she knew she didn't have much to complain about either. If they weren't around at Lee's place they were round at her flat. It was a bit awkward working together too, sometimes, and they probably argued more than they had ever done in the past. But she was happy. The world may be in a parlous state, but at least she had her man and her daughter by her side.

However, when she did finally leave Brenda's place and began to drive back to the office, she was hit by a sudden fit of melancholy. At Brenda's, they'd briefly talked about the Woolwich Foot Tunnel and how, in a sense, John really had disappeared that day back in 1976. Although DNA evidence had proved that John Gustavsson was indeed that boy all grown up, John Saunders had gone. Whatever had happened to him in that forty-two-year interim had changed that boy forever in ways Mumtaz still didn't understand.

Why had he really come to the UK? And why had he disappeared on the night of the 4th June? Unless he came back to the UK one day, they'd probably never know. Lee had suggested that maybe John had gone back to sort his head out, maybe get some treatment. Maybe he was even detained somewhere?

Mumtaz drove to North Woolwich almost without thinking. It was a warm if grey day and she spent a few moments looking at the river and the foot tunnel's northern rotunda. She didn't believe for a second that the thoroughfare was some sort of portal to another dimension. But as she stood and looked at it, she did feel a strange shudder run down her spine.

In a way the Woolwich Foot Tunnel had captured John Saunders and never let him go. He was, she felt, still held hostage by it now, wherever he was.

While John – whoever he was – lived, the tunnel could never truly be empty . . .

Mumtaz got back into her car and drove back to her office.

BARBARA NADEL was born and brought up in the East End of London. She has a degree in psychology and, prior to becoming a full-time author, she worked in psychiatric institutions and in the community with people experiencing mental health problems. She is also the author of the award-winning Inspector Ikmen series. She lives in Essex.

@BarbaraNadel